I0666340

Ghosts of Lock Tower

An Abby Renshaw Supernatural Mystery

Jack Massa

Published by
Triskelion Books
www.triskelionbooks.com

Ghosts of Lock Tower

ISBN: 978-0-9976461-6-0

Print Edition published August, 2019

Cover design by Ida Jansson, http://amygdaladesign.net/

For she who inspired it,

And She who inspired it.

1. No Entry Sign

Lock Tower might be the weirdest place in Florida.

I know that's saying a lot.

But picture this: a pink marble bell tower, 23 stories high, set inside a moat full of goldfish. The tower stands on a hill in the middle of the state, surrounded by acres of flowery grounds with ponds, trails, and a visitor center. They say Emanuel Lock had tons of black soil trucked to the top of this sandy hill so they could plant the gardens. These days the place gets its share of tourists—those willing to drive the back roads to discover "old Florida." Of course, the inside of the tower is closed to the public.

But that's not stopping us today.

"I really believe you need to rethink this," Ray-Ray warns, as Molly and I approach the gate that leads to a little footbridge over the moat.

From here we have a good view of the stained glass windows and carvings on the tower walls—images of birds, alligators, people in robes, and symbols that I recognize as occult. The front entrance is on the other side, huge bronze doors sculpted with scenes from the Book of Genesis. But the back door is small and narrow, just across the bridge from this gate. Molly spotted two maintenance men going through a few minutes ago. If they left the door unlocked, we'll walk in. If not, we'll knock until they open it.

Either way, this seems to be our only chance to get inside.

Which I have to do—for magical reasons.

"It will be fine," Molly insists. Although to be fair, the *No Entry* sign on the gate doesn't exactly boost her case. "We've got a story ready. We're a couple of students doing research. We're harmless and charming. What are they going to do, *arrest* us?"

"Uh, maybe," Ray-Ray says. "More likely they'll call security and have you escorted off the premises—which, I have to say, would be what you deserve."

Why is he even here? He's not my boyfriend anymore, if he ever was. That thought makes my heart cringe as I look up at him, all tall and hunky in his sleeveless T-shirt and Claremont State cap. But I have to sweep those feelings aside. I've got more pressing issues than my lack of a love life.

Like trying to awaken an ancient goddess to protect myself from an evil ghost and his monster. And maybe protect the rest of the world while I'm at it.

"Don't be a *doomsdayer*, Ray-Ray," Molly tells her brother. "We're not being frivolous here. Abby has work to do—*magical* work. I explained that to you, and you promised that if you came along you'd be supportive."

"Yeah. I didn't know that meant breaking and entering."

"*Supportive*, Ray-Ray," Molly says. "And it's not breaking and entering. At most, it's criminal trespass."

"Okay. Okay." He shows his palms in surrender. "I'll stand here and do my best to block the view. When they escort you off the grounds, I'll meet you in the parking lot."

He steps aside, and Molly opens the gate.

One thing I learned growing up in New Jersey: if you're not supposed to be somewhere, don't let it show. Act like you own the place. As we cross the bridge, I put that intention into my stride.

Molly's a step ahead of me, walking like she really *does* own the place. She didn't grow up in New Jersey. For her, it just comes naturally.

She reaches the door and tries the handle. With a click and a creak of hinges, it swings open. Cool, sweet air drifts from the dim interior.

I suck in a breath as we cross the threshold.

2. I am so looking forward to a relaxing summer

42 days before

I'm sitting with my mom in a café on the concourse of the Orlando Airport. Mom is flying back to London, and I'm ready to begin my new life in Harmony Springs. I look forward to a relaxing summer in Florida, helping my grandmother in her antique shop, taking one class at Claremont State—and of course, catching up on my magical studies. No matter how good my intentions, my training as a true magician always got pushed to the back of the line while I lived in New Jersey.

Mom's plane's been delayed, so we're waiting outside the security gates till they post the new departure time. Mom sits across from me stiff and erect, staring and typing furiously on her laptop. She has a high-pressure job with an investment bank in London, and she's a bit of a workaholic. Well, more than a bit. The past two days at Grandma's house, the lack of internet clearly put her on edge. To her credit, she tried not to show it.

In fact, she's been wonderful this whole trip. When I graduated from high school at the end of May, mom took two weeks' vacation. We turned my move to Florida into a road trip, packing my little Mazda3 and taking our time driving down the coast—Washington, North Carolina, Charleston, St. Augustine. I had a really fun time, and for once even Mom seemed pretty relaxed—only checking in with her office for an hour or so before breakfast.

I notice her typing has stopped, and I look up from my phone. She's staring at me with a weird, startled look on her face.

"I'm sorry, Abby. Our last few minutes together, and I'm wasting it on work."

"That's okay, Mom. We've had lots of quality time lately."

"That's true, but ... I don't know. Suddenly I'm worried about you. Maybe it's seeing Harmony Springs again, and that moldy old house you'll be living in—I know! You feel at home there. You love your grandmother, and I get that. You even love the town, though for the life of me I can't see why ..."

"Mom. Don't start."

"I'm sorry. I drive you nuts with my nagging mother routine. It's not like you haven't been on your own a lot this past year."

"That's right." Mom was in London three weeks out of four my whole senior year. Since my step-dad Jim also travels for work, they hired a live-in housekeeper. And really, I managed fine.

"But this feels different," Mom says. "Like I'm abandoning you ..." She stares out at the hustling crowd, a glint of panic lighting in her eyes. "The world just isn't as safe as it used to be."

Well, *this* is not like her at all, and it's creeping me out.

But then I see where it's coming from. I've noticed before that Mom sometimes relies on me for emotional support. I suspect that, deep inside, she feels like *she* is being abandoned.

"It's okay, Mom. We'll stay in touch. And like you've been telling me this whole trip, I *am* pretty grown-up now."

Her eyes get shiny. "You are wonderfully grown-up, Abby, and definitely your own person. And I am *so* proud of you. I suppose I'm being a ridiculous, clinging mother. But I just have this feeling ... Abby, do you ever have intuitions?"

That question almost makes me laugh. Mom doesn't know that I am a true magician, a member of a magical order begun by the founders of Harmony Springs, including my ancestor, Thomas Renshaw. I was initiated last summer when I was having terrible nightmares and hallucinations—except they turned out not to be hallucinations, but actual visions. Seems I am excessively prone to arbitrary supernatural communications.

Intuitions? I have them by the boatload.

I try to answer with a straight face. "Sure. And I think they can be accurate. What's your intuition telling you?"

She answers reluctantly: "Well, I usually don't credit this stuff, but I don't know ... I suddenly feel like you're in danger."

Well, *that* freaks me out even more. But I try to be adult about it, acknowledging to Mom that yes, the world can be dangerous, but that I'm a very responsible person, and that Harmony Springs is as safe a place as any—probably safer than most.

A little later, they post her flight's departure time. We leave the café, and Mom hugs me goodbye. I promise again to text and call her often. She resumes her usual square-shouldered, businesswoman look and heads toward the security line.

Walking back through the terminal, I ponder our conversation. I have to admit it caused some prickles of worry in my gut. But examining that with *my* intuition, I don't feel any danger—at least not at present. By the time I get out to the parking deck, I've convinced myself that Mom and I both were just suffering separation anxiety.

Catching sight of Veronica immediately boosts my mood. Veronica is the car mom bought for my 17th birthday. She's a Mazda3 and everything I wanted: smooth, fast, stylish. I even got to pick the color, *eternal blue water*—a shade that reminds me of the crystal clear waters in Harmony Springs.

After revving the engine, I scan myself in the mirror: steady brown eyes, straight nose, strong (if narrow) chin—Abby the confident grown-up.

Well, semi-confident.

I grin at myself. Abby Fighting Eagle, True Magician. Even better. In her eternal blue water Mazda3.

~~~

I turn off County Road 245 onto an unpaved trail lined with ferns and cabbage palms. Veronica's tires slip and bump in the ruts until I slow down.

Easy does it. Don't let the excitement turn to anxiety.

The woods along the road grow thicker, spidery live oaks and towering ash trees draped with Spanish moss. As a child, I thought of them as old men and women. I called this place the enchanted forest—the place where my grandma lived. I follow the trail around the top of Bliss Spring and past two big houses built in Victorian times. Grandma's is the third house; it's been in the Renshaw family since it was built in the 1890s.

When I pull into the front yard, I see a battered electric bike leaning against a tree. The bike's owner jumps up from her seat on the front steps and waves at me.

"Abby! I thought you'd never get here."

I climb out of the seat and am immediately wrapped in Molly's arms. She feels all soft and loving. And sweaty from waiting in the Florida heat.

"Mom's plane was delayed," I explain. "I texted you."

"Of course," she laughs. "No signal out here."

Molly's one of my closest friends. She knows me in ways almost no one else does. We shared lots of fun and our deepest secrets last summer—along with some spooky adventures. We've stayed in close touch over the winter while I was up in Jersey. But, although I've been in Harmony Springs two days already, we haven't gotten together till now. Molly said she didn't want to intrude on my mom and Grandma having me all to themselves.

But I wondered if there wasn't more to it.

"Love the car!" Molly runs a finger over Veronica's paint. "The pictures don't do it justice."

"I'll take you for a ride later. Let's go inside. I promised to fix dinner."
~~~

"Oh, speaking of dinner," Molly says as we climb the porch steps. "My family would love to have you over. Mom told me to ask you."

"Ah." I pause, looking down at the key in my hand. Collecting myself, I stick it in the lock. I guess my hesitation says it all.

"Abby, you'll have to see him sometime."

"I know ... I guess."

We're talking about Ray-Ray, of course.

I hooked up with Molly's brother at the end of last summer. My final week in Harmony Springs we saw each other every day—running together in the mornings, driving around town in his old truck, parking at night in the woods overlooking the river. I thought it was love and would last forever.

But I had fallen more in love than he had. We parted agreeing it would be sensible if we were both free to see other people. Then we didn't talk or text much over the winter. I assumed he was just not comfortable communicating long distance. But in March he called me. The conversation went something like this:

"Ray-Ray! How are you?"

"Fine. You?"

"Okay. Glad to hear from you. What's going on?"

"Abby, there's something I need to tell you."

(With my stomach disappearing through the floor): "You're with someone else."

"Yeah, I'm sorry. I felt I owed it to you to let you know."

"Sure. No problem, Ray-Ray. We said there were no strings."

"Right ..."

"What's she like?" *Stupid! Why did I ask that?*

"Oh, she's nice. Her name is Jen. She's in a couple of my classes. She wants to be a lawyer."

Well, I'm planning on law school too. Stupid again. Luckily I didn't say *that* out loud. "So how are things otherwise? How's your family?"

It went on for another excruciating half-minute. After we hung up, I fell into bed and cried.

Standing on the porch, Molly says to me: "Abby, I'm so sorry for how it turned out. I was so mad, I wanted to kick him."

I open the door. "He didn't do anything wrong. It just happens."

"I know." Molly follows me inside. "But you two were so perfect together. I don't know why he couldn't see that. He's such an idiot."

"No, he's not. People change." *If there's an idiot in this scenario, it is surely me.*

We walk down the hallway to the kitchen.

"So will you come to dinner? We could pick a night when he's not home, maybe."

"That's okay. I'll come. Any night that works for you guys will be fine."

♒

Molly sits at the kitchen table drinking iced coffee while I fix dinner. To change the subject from Ray-Ray, I ask her about her own love life.

"Oh, nothing happening there." Her tone indicates the subject is a bore.

"Really? What about that guy you went to junior prom with?"

"He's okay, and the prom was fun. But I spent most of the time talking with the other kids and chaperones. Lately, the whole physical thing with guys just doesn't seem worth the trouble ... You think I might be asexual?"

"Whoa. I don't know." Last summer Molly definitely seemed interested in the male sex. "I wouldn't have thought so. But then, people do change."

"Yeah. Well, don't mention that around my parents, okay? Not sure how they would feel about it."

"Of course not."

"Anyway, unless somebody really interesting comes along, I might put the whole thing on hold until I've finished college and established my career."

Molly's an aspiring reporter. She writes a news blog about Harmony Springs called *The Quick Report*. After senior year, she plans to go to Florida State and major in Journalism. Now she tells me she's also just started a job at our favorite coffee shop, Springs of Coffee, and is learning to be a barista.

"I can save money for college," she explains. "Besides, it's a great place to talk with people about what's going on around town."

I laugh at that. As if Molly needs any help finding out what's going on in Harmony Springs.

Grandma arrives a little after six, and Molly stays for dinner. We have baked chicken with pineapples and salad. Grandma seems tired, so Molly and I handle the cleanup.

After Molly leaves for home, I sit with Grandma on the back porch swing. The day is cooling off, birds chirping in the high branches. Glimpses of Bliss Spring are visible through the trees and undergrowth, crystal blue water sparkling in the late afternoon light.

Grandma and I sigh in unison, then laugh about it.

"I'm so happy to have you here, Abby."

"I'm happy too. But you seem tired, Grandma. Is the foot bothering you much?"

I've noticed her limping. She broke her foot last summer in a fall down the stairs. Except she didn't fall exactly: an evil entity pushed her. That same evil being who caused all the trouble in town, and who I vanquished, with some magical help, at the source of Bliss Spring.

She sighs again, not so happily. "It hurts a bit from time to time. Mostly it's just old age, I'm afraid. I don't have the stamina I used to."

Grandma is in her mid-sixties, with blond hair going white, green eyes and a wide, generous mouth. She's slim, shorter than me, and generally healthy. She seems a little frailer than last year, but I try not to think about that.

"Well, Mom and I kept you pretty busy the past couple of days." I know she worked hard, cooking and baking and cleaning the house for our visit. Then she drove us all over.

"That's true." Grandma smiles. "Your mother is one intense lady, I have to say."

"Oh, I know. I love my mom. But I guess you can see why I find you a refreshing change of pace."

Grandma chuckles and pats my wrist. We're quiet for a while.

"Now that I'm living here, Grandma, you know I can help you with stuff. Not just in the shop, but anything you need. Hopefully, I can make your life a little easier."

"Oh, listen, Abby. Please don't worry about that. I mean, I love having your help, but only as much as you feel like. You've got school to prepare for, and you've got your own life to live. The last thing I want is to be a burden."

"You're not, really."

"Well, let's keep it that way. I really want you to be happy here."

I take in a deep breath and stare out at the darkening woods. The familiar peace of Harmony Springs flows over my skin like a breeze.

"Don't worry about that, Grandma. This is my place."

♒

That night, the terror begins.

I am in some kind of virtual reality space—muted colors and huge shapes looming all around. My body is an avatar, a robot or two-legged bug, and I'm running. Running frantically.

Something is chasing me.

The dream is charged with much more emotion than you would expect from an online game. Besides, I've hardly done any gaming since I was thirteen and had my breakdown. That was when I started hallucinating, seeing goblins and alligator men from the games appearing in my waking life. Terrifying me.

Terror like this dream. Except, this feels different—less about me and more about the whole world.

The world isn't as safe as it used to be.

I dash into a long building that looks like an office or school. But when I get inside, I see it's a dungeon. I flee through stone-paved rooms with low ceilings. There are kids everywhere, mostly guys, but some girls. Some are running, like me. Some are just milling around, or standing in front of monitors hung on the walls, hypnotized by VR displays. I watch one boy get sucked into a monitor and changed into a wriggling reptile.

I run up a long corridor, climb a flight of steps. I pass a girl collapsed on the landing, sobbing. Her hands are gone, her arms bloody stumps. I want to stop and help her, but I'm too afraid.

I enter an upper chamber, like a temple or throne room. Suits of glittering armor stand along the walls. More kids are lined up in a queue, approaching a throne. On the throne sits a huge white frog, with mad angry eyes in its head—and dozens more eyes in its stomach. A girl approaches the throne, and the frog monster opens its mouth. She shrieks as he sucks her in, like sipping cola through a straw.

I wake up, horrified, shaking, I stare into the corners of my bedroom, looking for monsters or floating eyes. It takes me a long time to catch my breath.

Climbing out of bed, I sit down on the rug. I do the Ablution exercise, the basic meditation designed to calm and center the spirit. Taking long, slow breaths, I visualize the five Springs of Harmony as fountains at the nerve centers of my body.

Love, at the root of my spine, pure water, clear and cleansing.

Endurance, at the solar plexus, filling me with strength.

Balance, at the heart, centering my energies.

Amity, at the throat, filling me with serenity and love.

Bliss, at the crown of my head, the water pouring out and down over my body, washing away all fear.

Bliss is a long time in coming.

3. These two things are somehow connected

41 days before

"You look tired this morning, sweetie," Grandma says as she sits down to breakfast.

I gaze into the bowl of oatmeal. *Really not hungry*. "I had trouble sleeping. Probably just over-excited."

Grandma stares at me, appraising. She's a true magician herself and pretty psychic. Besides, with our deep connection, she reads me really well. "Are you sure that's all it is?"

I take a long sip of coffee, then tell her about my dream. She listens quietly, with little winces of sympathy when I describe the ugly parts.

After I finish, she considers for a moment, then smiles. "You're probably right. Just anxiety over all the changes in your life."

"Yeah. I'm sure that's all it is." But I really don't think so, and again Grandma senses it.

"I have an idea," she says. "Why don't you stop in and see Violet today? Have her do a reading? I know she'd love to see you."

♒

Violet's my magical mentor. Back in the day, when Grandma first hooked up with George Renshaw, my grandfather, they both joined Violet's study group—the last remnant of the Circle of Harmony, the magical order that was created when the town was founded. Last summer, when I was haunted by the evil entity linked to my family curse, it was Violet who initiated me into the Circle and taught me magic to protect myself.

I feel strangely in need of protection this morning, so I'm glad when Violet answers her phone (which she tends to do about 50% of the time). She's excited to hear from me and invites me to come right over.

Violet lives in wood frame "cracker" house on the outskirts of Harmony Springs. The road is lined with small houses and a few old trailers, with backyards shaded by huge live oaks. I pull Veronica into the driveway around 10:30 a.m.

As I march up the creaking steps to the front porch, Violet throws open the door.

"Abby! Welcome home, dear." She knows me well, including that I consider Harmony Springs my true home.

Violet's a stout, sparkling lady in her seventies with lovely, pale blue eyes. She wears her white hair long and brightly dyed. This morning it's orange, with white streaks around her wrinkled face. She gives me a powerful hug, then leans back to peer at me.

"Oh, you look fine! Strong and beautiful as ever."

"Thanks. You're looking good too." Just being in her presence gives me a boost. "Is Kevin not here?"

Kevin is Violet's boyfriend, a retired Anthropology professor. He owns a bookstore adjacent to Grandma's antique shop. It being Sunday, the shops wouldn't open till noon, so I expected to find him at home. I noticed his car missing from the driveway.

"No. He's on a mission today." Violet's laugh sounds brittle. She leads me back to the kitchen.

"Mission? What do you mean?"

"He's gone up to the University, to a protest rally." She waves me to a chair and busies herself with the tea kettle.

"Really? What's that about?"

"Oh, some group on campus invited this terrible person to give a talk. Kevin feels he's a racist, and that his message is hate speech. As a former professor at the school, he felt a duty to take a stand."

Anxiety tingles at the pit of my stomach. I haven't followed the news much lately. To be honest, it too often scares me and freaks me out. I mean, I keep track of the big events and do what I can, which is little enough. I won't be 18 for another couple of months, so I can't even vote. But I do send emails, sign petitions, try to convince Mom to donate to some causes I believe in. Up in New Jersey, I even marched a couple of times, once to protest cuts in school funding, once with my friend Franklin for LGBT rights. Beyond that, my coping mechanism is to try not to dwell on it. I am aware that protests are becoming more frequent, and sometimes turning violent. People are fearful and angry in lots of places, in lots of ways. The last few years, it all seems much worse.

The world is becoming more dangerous.

"Well, I hope Kevin will be okay."

"Yes, me too." Violet sits down. "But I'm sure he will. And I'm proud of him. If I was a few years younger, I'd be right there beside him. As true magicians, we have to oppose evil where we find it."

I nod. That is a lesson I learned last summer—and still have a few scars on my arms to prove it.

"But tell me about you." Violet pushes a plate of muffins at me. "These are cinnamon chocolate chip. They're delicious."

In an attempt to shrug off the troubles of the world, I grab a muffin. Violet is right, delicious. I tell her about my senior year and my trip down the coast with Mom. I admit, a little shamefully, that I haven't done more than the minimum to keep up with my magical studies.

The kettle whistles, and Violet gets up to fix the tea.

"But now that I'm here, I'm going to buckle down," I assure her. "I have my dagger, and next I need to circle back and make the wand."

As a true magician advances to each Spring, they create a magical tool. It's like a merit badge to show that you've completed that grade, but it's also a tool that you actually use. Over the winter, while visiting England, I had a bit of an emergency and needed to make my dagger on the fly. The dagger's supposed to be the second tool, made in connection with the Spring of Endurance. As usual, I am following my own loopy path.

"That's wonderful, dear." Violet beams as she sets down my teacup. "I'll give you the wand instructions before you leave. We're planning a group ritual in a couple of weeks for Midsummer. I hope you'll join us."

"Wouldn't miss it."

Violet settles into her seat. "So tell me about this dream."

I take a deep breath and let it out. Between sips of chamomile, I recount my weird nightmare. As I talk, the feelings rear up again, like angry snapping reptiles. Sometimes my dreams turn out to be true, forecasts of things that might happen, or visions into other realms of being. The longer I talk about this dream, the more real it seems.

When I finish, Violet looks solemn. She stands up without a word, goes into her study, and returns with a deck of Tarot cards. Sitting down, she unwraps the silk handkerchief, then hands me the deck to shuffle. After I cut the cards, she holds them close to her heart.

She lays out a standard Celtic Cross spread. It looks serious: lots of *Major Arcana,* the heavy-duty picture cards.

The Moon is in the immediate future, a shadow of dangerous journeys.

Strength is at the crown, a woman taming a red lion, the power of Spirit overcoming the lower nature.

The outcome card is *The Tower Struck by Lightning*, the world blasted apart, the tearing down of present structures, violent change.

Violet rests her chin in her hands and stares at the cards. I wait.

The phone rings—the loud, unnerving jangle of the landline. Violet looks startled, and a shade of fear passes over her face. She gets up to answer.

Shuffling out to the hallway, she picks up the receiver. "Hello? ... Yes, I can hear you, Kevie. Is something wrong? ... Oh, no ... Oh, no!"

I jump up with a gush of adrenaline, hurry into the hall to stand beside her. She glances at me, anguished.

"Well, you certainly can't drive with a concussion. Is there someplace you can stay up there?"

"What is it, Violet?"

"Hold on. Abby's here." She turns to me. "It's Kevin. The protest turned into a riot, and his head got bashed. Seven stitches in the scalp and they think he has a concussion. I don't know how we're going to get him home."

♒

Within an hour we're on the road—Violet, Grandma, and I—driving Grandma's Honda Odyssey up County Road 245 toward Ocala. Grandma had to close her shop, but she insisted on coming along so we'd have someone to drive Kevin's car home. Because Violet, of course, doesn't drive. And because that's what friends do for each other.

We take the Interstate from Ocala to Gainesville, then bumble around until finding the Medical Center on the edge of the UF campus. Kevin was brought here in an ambulance from the site of the protests—which, according to a news report I picked up on my phone, are still going on. In fact, they've spread all over campus, rival crowds clashing and running, University police and state troopers trying to keep order.

We find Kevin in the ER waiting room. He's in his early sixties, a slender black man with a narrow face and large, sensitive eyes—the picture of a quiet intellectual. Except that today he looks awful, head bandaged, forehead swollen so the left eye is almost shut. When he sees us he produces a weak, ironic smile.

"You brought the whole Circle of Harmony to my rescue."

Violet grips his hand. "I'm sorry that was necessary, Kevie—Easy!"

He's stood up, a little shaky. "It's okay. Just a bad headache now."

"What did the doctors say?" Violet asks.

Kevin sighs. "Sorry to worry you, Vi. Definite concussion symptoms. Lots of rest for that. And I need to see a doc in about five days to get the stitches out." He looks at Grandma and me with a lopsided grin. "Thanks for driving up here, Kat. Abby, nice to see you, despite the circumstances."

"I'm glad you're going to be okay," I tell him.

Standing up made him slightly dizzy, so Grandma and I walk beside him, ready to brace his elbows, as we head out to the parking deck. He sits in the front seat and directs Grandma to the other side of campus, where he left his car. On the way, we pass straggling lines of marchers, watched by police with plastic shields and riot gear.

Kevin shakes his head sadly. "I might be getting too old for this sort of thing."

As we turn a corner, my whole body goes tight. One of the marchers is carrying a banner, the image of a fat gray frog dressed in a tuxedo and top hat. A silly cartoon image, and yet I feel *evil* flowing from it. It's not the same image as the frog monster in my nightmare, but I sense the same power, and for an instant I'm certain it's the same creature.

"Abby, are you okay?" Grandma asks.

"Yes. Sure." I'm just freaked out, between my bad dreams and Kevin's injury. *At least that's what I tell myself.*

Kevin's battered RAV is parked on a side street near the Anthropology building. The group consensus is for me to drive with Kevin, while Violet rides with Grandma. Violet looks a little stricken to be separated from him but doesn't object. She fusses over settling him into the passenger seat while I get behind the wheel and adjust the mirrors.

The RAV rides heavy and clunky compared to Veronica. It takes me a while to adapt. I hit the brakes too hard at first, and have to sheepishly apologize for jolting Kevin around. *He already has a concussion.*

Kevin just laughs and says not to worry. He guides me on the campus roads and through downtown. I keep an eye on the rearview mirror to make sure Grandma is keeping up. Once we're back on the Interstate, I relax a little.

"Still doing okay, Kevin?"

He winces. "Splitting headache, as you would expect. Thank you, Abby. I really appreciate you and Kat going to all this trouble. Vi would have been terribly worried if I'd had to stay up here, or tried to drive myself."

"No trouble at all. Like Grandma said, it's what friends do. Besides, after everything you and Violet did for me last summer, I owe you big time."

"Nah. You really don't," Kevin says. "It was a pleasure. I can't tell you how much it meant to us to have a young person in the Circle again. For a while there, we thought your friend Molly might initiate too. But that hasn't worked out."

"Yeah. What happened with that?" Over the winter, Molly had gotten interested in studying magic and talked about joining the Circle. But after trying the introductory exercises, she suddenly shut it down. "When I ask her, she gets all close-lipped. Says she's still undecided."

Kevin nods. "It takes a lot of self-examination. I think maybe she found the inner work too challenging. It's not for everyone."

I thought as much. Magical work involves a lot of sitting still and looking inward. Molly's not exactly an introvert. "I just wish she wouldn't be so defensive when I ask her about it."

Kevin's quiet for a time, staring out the window as we cruise past the nature preserve south of Gainesville. I keep two hands on the wheel, staying in the slow lane, making sure to keep Grandma's minivan in sight behind us.

"Young people today have a lot to contend with," Kevin says. "I think it's even harder than when I was a kid."

He grew up in the Sixties, which I know were pretty chaotic. I flash back to what Mom said at the airport. "Do you think the world's even crazier now?"

"Oh, it's always been crazy. But now ... Well, when I was young it was scary, but at least our choices seemed clearer. We protested the war; we marched for civil rights. Many of us believed in non-violence. Today, we're constantly bombarded with uncertainty. So everyone gets defensive and angry and unreasonable. I understand the rage. A lot of it is justified. But I didn't march this morning to stop that man from speaking. My idea was to let him speak, and to stand up on the other side and say that his views are wrong—historically, morally wrong. But most of the marchers just wanted to shut him down and kick him off-campus. Folks around me were full of rage, and the counter-protesters were even worse. That's how the violence started. That's why I got my head bashed in."

Mention of the protesters brings back my memory of the frog banner. I ask Kevin if he knows anything about it.

"Oh, yeah. *Ranae Virum*, the Gentleman Frog."

The name causes me tingling, irrational fright. "What is it?"

"Just some cartoon image from the internet. It's become a kind of emblem for certain extremist groups—white supremacists, neo-Nazis. Angry disaffected white boys. Pitiful, really."

"Well, it gives me the creeps."

≈

Late in the afternoon, I ease the RAV into Kevin's driveway, with Grandma following close behind. Violet unlocks the front door, and

Grandma and I help Kevin up the steps and into the bedroom. While Violet puts him to bed, we wait in the living room. Grandma suggests we leave them both to rest, but when Violet comes out she invites us to stay for a bit.

In the kitchen, our teacups from the morning are still on the table, along with the Tarot cards.

"Oh, Abby. I never finished your reading," Violet says.

"Don't worry about that," I tell her. "We'll do it another time."

But Violet is staring down at the cards, her hands gripping the back of a kitchen chair, knuckles turning white.

"No. We'd better do it now. These two things are somehow connected."

4. You better go ahead and make your wand

"What do you mean by 'connected'?" Grandma asks.

Violet pulls in her lips, looking worried. "This reading, Abby's dream, what happened to Kevin. I don't know how, but they're all connected."

Agitation wriggles in my stomach. I remember the crushing dread in my dream. It *did* feel a lot like the fear I experienced driving around the riots at the college. *And seeing the frog banner ...*

"Stay and we'll talk." Violet's complexion is pale. "I'll, uh, get you something to drink."

"You sit down, Violet," I tell her. "I'll get some water."

I put ice cubes in three glasses and fill them from the tap. I set the drinks down in front of Grandma and Violet, and take a seat at the table. We all stare at the Celtic Cross spread. My eyes fix on the *Tower* card at the outcome position—a lightning bolt cracking open a stone tower, two people falling from the top. The agitation crawls out of my stomach and into my chest.

Suddenly Violet sweeps up the cards. "I'll do another reading and ask *how* they are connected."

She shuffles and cuts the deck herself. This time she lays out a different spread—21 cards in three rows of seven. It's an arrangement I've seen her use before. The middle row shows the physical world, the top row influences from *spirit planes* above, and the bottom row forces on the *inner planes* of the subconscious.

This spread includes Major Arcana again, plus lots of swords and a sprinkling of wands and cups. Looking it over, I sense conflict, violent change. *The Tower* is there again, smack in the center of the middle row. As I stare at it my eyesight flutters, and the world dissolves into vapors and mist.

Sometimes when I do magic, or when I'm really stressed, the veils of the physical world disappear and I *see* into other realms. I used to believe these episodes were hallucinations. But last summer, I came to know them as *visions*, manifestations of a talent I have—whether I like it or not. Sometimes it's scary as hell, but I've learned I have to go with it.

I stare at a card in the middle row, the *Eight of Cups*. A man in a red cloak marches into a dark landscape under the moon. I am starting a long and perilous journey.

My eyes shift to another card, the *Knight of Wands*. He rides a rearing orange horse, wears golden armor. A red plume dances above his helmet. He is riding into battle—something about him frightens me.

On the top row, I see the card called *Strength*, the image of a woman with a wreath of flowers, taming a red lion. As I watch, the woman changes, sprouting wings and a horned crown of gold. She holds a wand and points it at the lion, causing him to lie down.

Violet must have sensed that I've gone into a trance. I hear her voice like from the far end of a tunnel. "What do you see, Abby?"

The winged woman's mouth opens. I hear her voice coming from my own throat. "Times are shifting. Thunder rolls. Barriers between the realms are opening, ghosts and demons breaking through."

I don't want to do this anymore. But I know it's important, so I force myself to keep looking. My eyes find the *Tower* card. The lightning bolt hardens into a frozen snake. The people falling from the tower plunge into a swamp of slimy gray water. A giant white frog creeps out of the depths—the monster from my nightmare. A blood-red tongue slithers out of its mouth. The people scream as they're were sucked in and swallowed. Then the glaring eyes turn on me. The tongue whips out, wraps around my body, pulls me to toward the open mouth.

"No!" I come awake in Violet's kitchen, arms on the table, head down, staring at the floor.

"It's all right, sweetie. You're safe."

Grandma stands by my chair, stroking the back of my head. I lurch over and hug her. Slowly, the terror fades, my grandma's love driving it away. Just like she used to do when I was a little girl. I reach for my glass and gulp down some water.

"As soon as you feel ready," Violet says gently, "tell us everything you saw."

After calming myself, I stare at the cards and relate the vision. Violet presses me for details, especially to describe the giant frog, and repeat what the winged woman said.

"The barriers between the realms," she mutters. "That's interesting."

"What do you make of it?" Grandma asks.

Violet lifts a shoulder. "Well, we're in a time of major transition. You only need to keep an eye on the news to know that. Such times correspond to shifts in the flows of energy between the worlds. The movements of the planets supposedly correspond to the movements of those energies. If I were a better astrologer, I could probably explain it from that angle ..."

I know from my studies that occult philosophers believed in multitudes of worlds surrounding this one. You can think of them as different planes or dimensions, or simply spirit realms. If the barriers between them are tearing open—well, that sounds like a problem.

Grandma still has her hand on my shoulder. "I think we're all pretty tired, Vi. Maybe we should pick this up tomorrow?"

Violet raises her eyes from the cards, looking distracted. "What? Oh, of course. You're right, Kat. I'll do another reading later. You two go home and get some rest. It's been a tough day."

Before we go, we cast a circle of protection. The three of us stand in the center of the tiny living room and join hands. We envision the blue waters of the Springs rising up from around our feet, bubbling like a fountain, surrounding our bodies, then the whole house, then the whole town. When we finish, I feel steady and peaceful.

As we're headed for the door Violet thinks of something else.

"Oh, Abby, I was going to give you the instructions for consecrating your wand."

"It can wait."

"No, no." Violet shuffles over to the antique cabinet where she stores Circle of Harmony papers. Sorting through the stacks of pages, she says: "That woman in your vision used a wand to control the lion, right? There's meaningful synchronicity there, don't you think?"

She finds the instructions and brings them to me: three pages with black lettering from an old typewriter. *Consecrating the Wand at the Fountain of the Love of Truth*.

"I think you'd better go ahead and make your wand."

♒

40 days before

Oddly enough, I sleep great that night, no nightmares. I guess I'm pretty exhausted.

In the morning I go for a long run. Because of the road trip, I haven't been getting my usual workouts. I started running for fitness, but I soon found that it helps Abby the high-strung Jersey girl stay calm and centered. I ran on the track team the last three years, both middle-distance and cross-country. Senior year I was one of the better track athletes at Hudson Heights High.

I follow a route I used a lot last summer, along sandy roads through the forest, around the sources of the Springs. Despite the heat and humidity, it feels great.

After my shower, I have breakfast with Grandma, then ride with her into town. Her shop, Glenda's Antiques, is in the middle of two other shops that share an old warehouse space on Main Street. Wide openings in the walls lead between the shops. The Harmony Gallery on the left sells arts and crafts—weaving, pottery, jewelry, and stained glass. It's run by a blonde lady named Jenny Nesheim. When I see her, she gives me a hug and welcomes me back to town.

The shop on the other side is Palmer's Books, owned by Kevin. He phoned earlier and left a message on Grandma's machine, saying he wouldn't be in and asking her to cover the shop if she could, or else hang the "Closed" sign on the front door. The three shop owners often cover for one another, sort of like a co-op.

So this morning I get to play bookseller. Kevin's shop is larger than Grandma's, crowded with shelves arranged in narrow aisles, stuffed with hardbacks and paperbacks of every description. The air is kept dry by good ventilation and holds a slight old-paper smell.

Customers are scarce today, leaving me plenty of free time. I start looking through the papers Violet gave me for making the wand. But then I have another idea. Here in town, I have phone service, so I can use the internet. I do a search on "Renee Virum" and—after figuring out that it's spelled R-A-N-A-E Virum—I find plenty of hits.

The "Gentleman Frog" started as a character in a game. But the image went viral after it got picked by some online forums. First, it was only on gaming sites, then it spread to other groups. As Kevin said, the character became a kind of folk hero, appearing in flash fiction and online comics full of racism, misogyny, white extremism. Some of the content I read makes my skin crawl. But it's like some horrible car wreck—I have trouble looking away.

While I'm reading, someone walks in from the antique shop. I glance up to see Molly grinning at me.

"Hey, girlfriend. What's happening?"

"You ever hear of *Ranae Virum*?"

"Uh, yeah. Some meme right? Creepy gamers? Why do you ask."

I lift up the phone. "I've been reading about him.'

"Well don't read too much." Molly snorts. "That stuff will give you nightmares."

Well, she's got that right.

"What put you on to that?"

I tell her about seeing the frog banner during my fun trip to Gainesville.

Half her mouth twists up. "Yeah, your grandmother told me what happened to Kevin. Concussion and stitches. Did he look awful?"

"Awful. Scary stuff."

Molly walks around the counter and sits down in an old office chair beside me. "I saw the protests in the news. I didn't realize he'd gone up there to march."

"Did Grandma also tell you about the Tarot reading at Violet's?"

"No." Her eyes widen. "Fill me in."

First, I describe my nightmare, then my visions over the reading—the Knight of Wands, the Lion-Tamer Lady, the blasted tower, and the monstrous white frog. Molly's eyes get bigger and bigger.

"Wow. So 'creatures from other realms are leaking through the barriers.' That sounds like a dumb superhero movie."

"Story of my life, right?"

"Well." Molly laughs. "Sometimes it's a dumb superhero movie. Sometimes more of a creepy horror movie. You think this frog monster is like the shadow monster we enjoyed meeting last summer?"

Thinking about that makes me shiver. "I don't know. Shadow Man was slimy and creepy, but he was *local*—tied to Bliss Bayou and the people here who created him. This guy feels bigger. *Way* bigger. Like world-wide big."

Molly frowns. Is there a shade of disbelief on her face? "I don't even know how to get my head around that. I mean, how do you begin?"

"Well, Violet's going to do more readings. I guess we'll get together at some point and compare notes." I gesture at the papers lying on the counter. "Meantime, she's told me I need to make a wand—You know, one of the magical tools."

I can feel Molly's energy withdrawing. Lately, when I start talking about the Circle of Harmony, she goes quiet. I know she feels left out. But that was her choice. I don't know what I can do about it. Still, it makes me feel bad.

She stands up. "I need to get over to work. I just stopped in to check with you about dinner. Mom said to invite you for Wednesday. Will that work—around six?"

"Oh, yeah. Thanks." I had forgotten all about agreeing to go to the Quick's house for dinner. Which means I will be seeing Ray-Ray again. For the first time since his phone call made me cry.

Molly reads my apprehension. "He'll be there. You sure that's okay?"

"Yeah. Of course."

She flashes her smile. "You can show him your car. I bet he'll be jealous."

Good, is my instant thought. I push it aside. *Unworthy, Abby*.

"Stop by Springs of Coffee later if you can. I get my break at 2:30." Molly heads for the door of the shop. "And go easy on that frog monster research. Studies have shown that reading a lot of depressing stuff on the internet leads to paranoia."

Hmm. Just what I need, more paranoia. Glancing at my phone, I decide maybe she's right. I've read enough about Ranae Virum for now. Before shutting down the browser, I set up an alert. When new content about the frog is posted, I'll get notifications, which I can scan for anything that might be worth knowing.

♒

No word from Violet that day about new readings. Given that she is probably nursing Kevin, I don't want to disturb them by calling their house.

Still, I feel the need to do *something*.

So, after dinner, I walk up the road toward the mouth of Bliss Spring. There's still an hour or two of daylight, but I bring a flashlight just in case. I also have a small saw from Grandma's tool drawer, stuck in my backpack. I'm determined to begin making my wand.

I've read and reread the papers Violet gave me. In the lore of the Circle of Harmony, each of the magic tools corresponds to one of the first four Fountains on the path, which in turn correspond to the first four of the actual Springs: Love, Endurance, Balance, Amity. The magician is supposed to make the tool in preparation for an Advancement Rite, where you absorb the energy of that Spring, assimilate it into your body. I went through the advancement ceremonies in sort of emergency fashion last summer. At the time, Violet told me not to worry about making the physical tools, that they could wait until I had more time.

Now I have the time, and making the wand is suddenly urgent. The instructions tell me I need to go into the woods around the Springs and find, or cut, a branch that "speaks to me." Once I have the right piece of wood, there are detailed instructions for scraping off the bark, soaking it in a mixture of salt and spring water, anointing it with oily resins—all these steps accompanied by chants and visualizations.

The air is hot and breezy, the sky flowing with gigantic Florida clouds, gray and gold in the late afternoon sun. Thunder rumbles now and then in the distance. I leave the road and tramp through the slash pines and cypress trees. The woods thicken, but I wore long sleeves for wrangling my way through the low branches. Overhead, crows are cawing, flying from tree to tree.

I keep an eye out for any length of branch that seems to call to me, to want to become my wand. In a little while, I step into a circular clearing.

Two magic circles were laid out by the founders of Harmony Springs—this one, near the mouth of Bliss Spring, and a larger one at the top of the main channel west of here, where the other four springs have their source. Covenants require that the town clear-cut the areas every few years, so the circles are always here—for anyone who knows about them.

I stand in a space 60-feet across, completely hidden from the road. In the center, three slabs of gray stone are set up as an altar. This is the place where I glimpsed the ghost of my great-great-aunt, Annie Renshaw, when she and two of her friends created the entity I called Shadow Man. And this is the place, at the end of July, where I finally banished Shadow Man, with help from Annie and a whole troop of other deceased magicians.

I figure it's a good place to look for my wand.

A fallen tree lies along one edge of the circle. I remember it from last year and walk over to give it a look. Saplings have pushed up from the soft ground around the dead trunk. A few look like cypress, with piney needles. One has black bark and thorny branches—some sort of wild fruit tree. I don't want my wand to be thorny, and I don't want to cut down a living tree. But despite my wishes, I'm compelled to kneel down and touch the stalk.

Ouch! I draw back my hand and suck the spot on my palm between my thumb and forefinger. As I taste the blood, I glance up.

A woman stands on the other side of the dead trunk: tall and beautiful, with a wreath of flowers in her brown hair. The air around her gleams and pulses. For a second, I'm not sure if she exists in the physical world. Then a red lion sidles up and rubs against her thigh. She looks down at me with dark, shining eyes.

I must have fallen over. Now I'm lying on my back, dizzy, staring up at the sky. And now it's night, the sky black with a wheeling spiral of stars. My brain is swimming in the stars. Enormous power flows into my body.

Next thing I know, I'm kneeling again, my hand clutching the thorny black stalk. But my eyes are on the lady. I recognize her now, the figure of *Strength* from the Tarot. Her voice is deep and rolls like the faraway thunder.

"Go ahead and cut the wand. You are going to be needed."

She's gone. The clearing is golden pink again, and my hand is still on the thorn bush.

I don't know if this sapling has spoken to me. But now I'm sure it's my wand. I take the saw out of my backpack and start cutting. The pulse is pumping in my ears, my whole body humming. I cut the sapling off at the base and pull it free. Sweating and breathing hard, I saw off the thorny branches, then the top—leaving a length a little longer than my forearm.

I'm still charged with the raw energy of the Lion Tamer Lady as I carry my wand home.

I guess that's why they call her Strength.

5. Can this get *any* more awkward? Yes. Yes, it can.

39 days before

Next morning, Violet calls Grandma's house just as we're cleaning up breakfast. Kevin is improving, but still not able to drive. Violet asks if we wouldn't mind picking up some groceries for her. I want to check in with Violet anyway, so I volunteer.

I drive Veronica up Route 245 to the nearest supermarket, at a little crossroads called Feaster's Grove. I buy the items on Violet's list and make it back to her house around eleven.

"Abby, I'm so grateful to you," Violet whispers as she lets me in. "Kevin is resting, so let's try to not disturb him."

As quietly as we can, we carry the bags to the kitchen and unpack them.

"How is he doing?" I ask her.

"Still having headaches. He wanted to drive, but I convinced him to wait a couple more days." Violet looks frazzled. This has taken a heavy toll on her. "He has to have his stitches out on Friday."

"If he needs a ride, Grandma or I would be glad to help."

"Thank you, Abby."

When the groceries are put away, we go out to the back porch, where we sit on rusty metal chairs with vinyl cushions. Even with the shade of the wide oak trees, the air is steamy.

Violet sips a glass of iced tea. "I don't mind telling you, Abby. This thing with Kevie has worn me out. He's usually the one that takes care of all the chores around here."

"I know it must be hard. If there's anything you need—"

"No, dear. But I did want to talk with you. Have you had a chance to start on your wand?"

"Yes. I cut it yesterday, and now I need to start the scraping and soaking bits." I tell her all about my adventure last night at the top of Bliss Spring.

"The same woman you saw in your vision from the Tarot reading?" Violet says. "And she said, you are going to be needed ..."

"That's right. Have you done any more readings about this?"

Violet clenches her lips and gives a slow nod. "I have. But I haven't been able to tell much. You remember last summer, how we could feel bad energy building, but it took a while for it to grow strong enough to really see it clearly on this plane?"

"Boy, do I ever." It took weeks before Violet and I, working together, were able to piece together an idea of the forces that were driving events, and more weeks before it all came to a head.

In my time as a true magician, I've learned that the spirit realms can be awfully confusing. Some things you perceive turn out to be delusions, created by your own mind—like the hallucinations I had when I was twelve. Other things can be real but vague, rising like phantoms, then disappearing without ever manifesting in the physical world. Still others can be powerful forces or entities, but with their true natures deliberately hidden.

I wish psychic vision was clear-cut, but it just doesn't work that way.

"It's all rather murky," Violet's voice echoes my thoughts. "The riot at the college, the things in your nightmares—they feel like the first shoots pushing out of the ground, all rooted in the same evil—something big, but hard to get clarity about, either because it's still far below the surface, or it's being deliberately concealed ..." Her face is sweating, and she sighs. "Or, maybe I'm just off my game. When you're emotionally unsettled as I've been the past few days, it's hard to get reliable psychic perceptions."

"So what can we do then?"

She rises stiffly out of her chair. "What we always do. Keep on with our best. You finish making your wand. I'll keep reading and meditating. Next week, we'll have our Midsummer Ritual and raise energy. That might bring us a clearer picture."

♒

38 days before

Wednesday at 5:30, I drive over to Molly's for dinner. The Quick family lives in a brick ranch house a few blocks from downtown Harmony Springs. Molly's dad is the chief of police.

I'm wearing a sleeveless yellow sundress and sandals. I've pinned up my hair and even applied a little eye makeup and lip gloss. I know it's silly, but it makes me look more grown-up—and feel more confident.

And less anxious.

Why am I so nervous about a simple dinner invitation? Seeing Ray-Ray, of course. This will be the first time I've seen him since that wonderful week last August when we were together. I remember it so clearly, lying in the back of his pickup truck under the stars, talking quietly, cuddling, kissing. Sometimes, I fell asleep in his arms. In all my life, I've never felt so happy, so safe, so filled with love.

Because Ray-Ray was my first love.

And my first broken heart.

That reminds me of something Violet advised me once, something that stayed in my mind because I found it so surprising: "Love recklessly," she said. "It's good for your health and good for your magic. If you get your heart broken, that's all right. Cry, patch it up, and do it all over again."

I stop in front of the Quick House. Ray-Ray's pickup is parked in the driveway.

All righty then. Let the patching up begin.

After a glance in the vanity mirror, I gather up the leather shoulder bag Mom bought me in London and the plate of homemade cookies that Grandma baked. I climb out of the driver seat, lock Veronica, slip the keys in the bag. I don't usually carry a purse, but my backpack didn't go well with the sundress and, like I said, I'm wanting to look grown-up.

I march up the sidewalk, determined to have a good time. When I get to the porch, Molly opens the door. She looks me up and down, grinning.

"Wow, you look nice."

As I step inside, Molly's mom toddles in from the kitchen. Beatrice Quick is a heavyset woman with curly brown hair and a big, friendly face. She simultaneously gives me a hug and takes the plate of cookies.

"Thank you for bringing these. You really didn't have to. My, you look lovely, so grown-up!"

Now I'm afraid I'm overdressed. The Quicks are a casual group. Molly's dad, Arthur, sits in a recliner with his shoes off. He waves a hand without getting up."Welcome, Abby."

"Thanks. It's great to see you all." My eyes are darting around, looking for you-know-who.

"Have a seat." Molly points me to the living room. "I'll get you some water."

She and her Mom head back to the kitchen. With an awkward smile plastered on my face, I shuffle over to the sofa. Chief Quick smiles at me and takes a sip of his beer.

A door opens, and Ray-Ray walks in, wearing shorts, a tank-top, flip-flops. He's six-foot-three and moves with the easy, loping grace of a basketball player—which he was in high school. Now he's just finished his first year of college at Claremont State. His sandy hair is longer, and his shoulders look bigger, all of which only makes him more gut-wrenchingly attractive—and seeing him more painful.

He gives me a shy, low-key smile. Maybe he's a little nervous about seeing me too? It's bound to be awkward for him. "Hey, Abby. Welcome back to Florida."

"Thanks. Nice to see you." Jeez, I hope that didn't sound *too* forced.

He takes a seat on the other side of the room. We avoid looking at each other, both of us trying to come up with something to say. Molly trots in with my ice-water.

"Hey, you have to see Abby's car," she tells Ray-Ray. "It is *fabulous*."

"Sure," he says. "Maybe you can take us for a ride later."

"Of course. Glad to." Oh, this is going *so* well. I wonder if I'm thin enough to crawl under the couch.

Molly perches on the arm of the sofa. No one seems to know what to say next.

Finally, Chief Quick breaks the painful awkwardness. "Abby, I understand you're going to be starting at Claremont State this month."

I sip my water. "Yeah. I start next week. There's an orientation on Tuesday, and then I'll be taking one class over the summer. I'll drive down there two days a week."

"No loafing around and enjoying the quiet of Harmony Springs this year," Molly says.

"I wish. Not with my mom. She wanted me to get started to see how I liked the school. She's never one for wasting time."

"Well," Chief Quick says. "If you're going there two days a week, maybe you and Ray-Ray can share a ride sometimes."

I glance at Ray-Ray, who stares at the floor.

"Yeah," I answer. "That might work out."

Can this get *any more* awkward?

Turns out, the answer is *Yes*.

We're eating in the dining room, Molly beside me, Ray-Ray on the other side, their parents at the heads of the table. We serve ourselves from plates of salad, fried chicken, green beans, and rice. Chief Quick hands around a basket of rolls.

I'm anxious and sweaty. My cheeks are flushed, and I'm worried my eye-makeup will smear or my deodorant stop working. They ask me about my road trip with Mom and the different sightseeing excursions. I try to make fascinating conversation. But I hear the nervous edge in my voice, and I keep losing track of what I'm saying.

I feel more and more frightened.

I glance down at my plate. *The food has turned to liquid and is oozing around.*

I blink and look up. *Tiny white frogs are crawling over the table.*

"Abby, are you okay?" Molly asks.

"Yeah. Sure."

But more and more frogs appear, leaping out of some spirit dimension into the Quick's dining room. Looking up, I see bulging yellow eyes floating disembodied in the air. My terror must be obvious. The whole family is staring at me.

"Are you sure you're all right?" Mrs. Quick says.

"You know what? I'm feeling a little dizzy. I'm sorry, but I think I better go home." I jump up and flee from the room.

"Abby, wait!" Molly calls.

I hear the whole family getting up, but I don't stop. I grab my shoulder bag from the living room and rush for the door.

"No. I'll go," I hear Molly tell everyone.

The eyes have followed me outside, hovering over the lawn and in the sky above the other houses. Molly catches up to me as I reach Veronica's door.

"Abby, it's okay. Tell me what's going on."

"I'm freaking out."

"Come on. Sit down."

She opens the car door and I climb in behind the wheel. I shut my eyes and wait while she circles around and gets into the passenger seat.

When I look again, the apparitions are gone. The neighborhood looks normal in the shadows and slanted sunlight.

"Tell me what's going on," Molly says gently.

"I'm sorry. I lost it for a minute there. I started seeing things."

"What kind of things?"

"Frogs, eyeballs—apparitions. I'm okay now. I'm going home."

I put the key in the ignition. Molly's hand grips my wrist. "If you're having visions, you probably shouldn't try to drive."

As I'm pondering the wisdom of that, I see Ray-Ray tramping down the sidewalk.

Great.

Molly pops open the car door, and he leans in and looks at me.

"You okay, Abby?"

"Yes. I'm fine. Just a dizzy spell. It's over now."

"You coming back inside?"

I wipe sweat from my forehead. "No. I better go home. Tell your parents I'm sorry for ruining dinner."

"I don't think she should drive," Molly says.

"Why don't you come inside till you're feeling better?" Ray-Ray says softly. "You don't have to eat."

"No! Really." My tone is sharp, frustrated.

"I can drive you home," Ray-Ray offers. "You can come back for your car tomorrow."

That just makes me explode. My hands fly off the wheel, fingers spread out straight and tight. "Look. I'm okay. I appreciate your concern, but I'm grown-up now. You don't have to take care of me."

They look at each other, startled by my outburst.

"Listen, Abby," Molly says.

"No!" I turn the key in the ignition. "Both of you, please just leave me alone!" I'm furious now—angry at myself, *humiliated.* So naturally, I'm taking it out on the people who are trying to help me. *Good job, Abby.*

Molly looks wounded. I know how sensitive she is beneath her bravado. Without another word, she scoots out of the car. She slams the door and stands next to her brother, who just stares at me, grim and worried.

I put the car in gear. "I'm sorry! Please apologize to your parents." I step on the gas.

"Drive carefully," Ray-Ray warns as I roll away.

♒

"You're home early." Grandma's sitting on the sofa with a book and her feet up. "Is everything okay?"

"Well ... Not really." I stomp into the living room and collapse into an armchair. I'm breathing hard, trying not to cry.

Grandma straightens up. "What is it, sweetie?"

I stare at her, trying to collect my thoughts. Then I give up on that and let it all pour out. I hear myself babbling the story in a torrent of frustration and misery: my nervousness, how much it hurt seeing Ray-Ray, the food turning liquid on my plate, the hopping frogs and floating eyes, my freaking out and leaving, screaming at Molly and Ray-Ray when they tried to help me. Somewhere in the middle of spewing all this, I move over beside Grandma. When I finish, her arms are around me, and I'm sobbing.

"Oh, my poor baby." She strokes my hair. "I am so sorry. What an awful time you're having."

"I feel so out of control. When visions happen like tonight, I'm afraid I'm going insane, that I'll end up in a mental hospital."

"Don't say that, Abby." She leans back, peers hard into my eyes. "Listen: I can't pretend to understand everything about your talent, and what it brings you. Even Violet is baffled by it sometimes. But I do know that you are *not* insane. And I also know that you have a wonderful life ahead of you, full of accomplishments and adventures and much love. I know that because I've seen it in *my* visions."

I hug her tight. "I'd be lost without you, Grandma. It helps so much that you believe in me."

"Well, I do. Absolutely. Would you like a cup of tea?"

♒

Back in the kitchen, I sit at the table while Grandma puts on the kettle. She asks if I want something to eat and I realize, having skipped out on dinner, I'm hungry. So she puts bread in the toaster and brings out butter and blueberry preserves.

As the kettle starts to rattle, I'm staring out the window at the darkness. "Maybe it's partly my own fault."

"What do you mean, sweetie?"

All the introspection you do as a true magician is supposed to lead to self-knowledge. Sometimes, I do pick up insights. "Well, I'm more prone to episodes like this when I'm anxious or unsettled. And tonight my emotions were running wild."

"Because of seeing Ray-Ray," Grandma says.

"Yeah ..." I think again about how I felt with him, that one wonderful week last summer. Wanting it to last forever. "It hurts to love somebody so much, and then one day it's all over."

Grandma's mouth turns down, and I realize what I've just done. She lost my grandfather to leukemia after they'd been together only a few years. "Oh, Grandma, I'm so sorry. You're the last person I need to say *that* to."

She smiles sadly. "It's okay. I do know how much it hurts. But I also know something else. After your grandfather died, I shut down my heart. I only left room for your father, and then later for you when you were a little girl. But after he died and you moved away, I closed myself off completely. That was a mistake. My life became very lonely. It's only when you came back here last summer that I allowed myself to open up again. Don't make that mistake, Abby. Don't ever let the hurt make you stop loving."

I go around the table and hug her. "I won't, Grandma. I promise"

♒

After taking a shower and putting on my night-clothes, I light a candle and sit cross-legged on the woven rug in the middle of my bedroom floor. Spine straight, I close my eyes and take slow, deep breaths. Eventually, I start the Ablution exercise, moving my consciousness to the base of my spine, visualizing the first Spring as a pure fountain. I stare into the waters, allowing my emotions to wash away.

When I reach the third Spring, at my heart-center, I envision two basins, blue and silver. The crystal water spills back and forth between them—the image of Balance. A slender young woman stands beside the fountain, in a long skirt and white blouse. Ringlets of black hair spill below her straw bonnet. She smiles at me lovingly, her dark eyes luminous.

"Oh, Annie," I whisper. "I am so glad to see you."

"Hello, Abigail."

In life, Annie Renshaw was my great-great-aunt. She's helped me more than once from the spirit world. Tonight I can really use her advice.

"I'm such a mess." My voice cracks, the painful emotion surging back. "All these scary monsters are haunting me. And I made a fool of myself with my friends. Molly's going to hate me now. And Ray-Ray will be more convinced than ever that I am a silly freak—not that that matters anymore."

"It matters to you, Abigail. Our friends are precious to us. And you still have love for Ray-Ray."

"Well, I need to get over that. But these visions—these creepy frogs. It reminds me of when I was twelve and had hallucinations. I was hoping for a nice, peaceful summer. But now everything's spiraling out of control. I feel sick. Like I'm losing my mind."

Annie leans her head. "Look into the Fountain of Balance, Fighting Eagle."

She uses my Circle of Harmony name, I guess to remind me that I am a true magician. I follow her gaze and watch the waters pouring back and forth, frothing and bubbling. My fears quiet down.

"What do you see?" Annie prompts.

Beyond the veils of water, I see a stone hall. It reminds me of the castle in my nightmare. A man appears, in gold armor, reminiscent of the Knight of Wands. But he wears no helmet. Instead, I see white-blond hair and piercing blue eyes. He gestures with a long, crystal-tipped wand, raising tiny white frogs from the floor. They swarm and crawl and jump, their bodies feeding into a giant fat form—the frog monster with the yellow eyes and blood-red tongue.

Annie's voice comes to me, soft and hollow. "The frogs are thought-forms, manifestations of the collective human mind. They may appear in your visions as many or one. At this time, in your world, forces are tearing at the fabric of reality, allowing such beings to spill through. But I also perceive there is another, a magician, using their power. His goals are obscure, but the creatures he directs are definitely evil—as you have rightly perceived. You are gifted with psychic vision, Fighting Eagle. The sickness you feel is not yours. It is the sickness of your world."

"What can I do, Annie?"

"You are a true magician. It is at times like this that we are needed most, to oppose evil and support harmony in the world. That is the essence of the Springs and of their spirit, Lebab. I advise you to finish your wand, then seek the counsel of Lebab."

After the meditation, I walk into the bathroom. My wand, minus thorns and bark, is soaking in a bucket of water from Bliss Spring. I bend over and touch it, wondering how this small length of wood can possibly help me cure the sickness of the world.

6. Guess I'll do until someone better comes along

37 days before

As I'm driving to town the next day, my phone chirps with an incoming text. When I park Veronica in front of Grandma's shop, I pull out the phone and check it.

Molly Quick: "If you don't want to be my friend anymore, please just say so."

I stare at the message, my stomach twisting, remembering how I acted last night, how hurt Molly looked. I don't know how well I can explain, but I have to try. I send a message back:

"Can you meet me at Founders' Park?"

Molly: "When?"

Me: "Now?"

Twenty minutes later, I'm sitting on a bench in front of empty tennis courts. The morning is hot and muggy and the sky deep blue with white, puffy clouds. The park slopes away, green lawns and treetops, down to the Harmony River. The peaceful scene is a zillion miles from my nightmare visions. How can I hope to make Molly understand?

An electric motor buzzes behind me. I turn to find Molly climbing off her bike, eyeing me warily. The hurt on her face is painful and clear. She pushes the bike up to my bench and chains it.

"So, here we are," she says.

I swallow. "Yeah. Let's walk, okay?"

She falls into step beside me, and we stroll down the path. I've had twenty minutes to think but I'm still not sure how to begin. So I just begin.

"Listen, Molly. I love you. You are my best friend in the world. I am so sorry about last night. I know I acted like an ass. I couldn't help myself."

Molly looks at me sidewise. "You really hurt my feelings. I can't stand it when you shut me out like that."

"I know." I understood this about Molly, but I see it now more clearly than ever. All of her relentless investigations—her need to find out things about people, about what's going on—all come from this deep-seated fear of being left out.

"I need you to be my friend, Molly. Can you forgive me?"

"Well, I can forgive almost anything. But you say you want to be my friend. Friends don't act the way you did last night. If you're having terrible visions, and I can't see them or know about them, then even if I want to help you, I can't. Not if you won't talk to me."

We're walking down a winding path of faded black asphalt. Tall oaks stand around us, their bent branches draped in Spanish moss. What comes out of my mouth next surprises me. "Sometimes when I try to let you in, you back away. I felt it the other day when I told you about my vision and making the wand. I feel you don't really want to hear about it."

"That's not true."

I glance at her and keep walking. I'm pretty sure it is true.

Finally, she says: "You really think *I'm* the one closing *you* out?"

"Not all the time. But when the conversation comes around to the Circle of Harmony, I sense you clamming up. Think about it, Molly. How does it make you feel?"

I perceive her clamming up right now, and she realizes it too. "I guess I don't want to know about that stuff because it scares me."

"It is scary. I can testify to that."

"No. Not like that. It scares me because I can't do it—any of it. I tried the exercises Violet gave me: Quiet your thoughts, visualize the Springs. My mind keeps jumping around. It all just makes me restless. I suppose I don't want to admit it, but I can't do it. I'm not wired that way."

"Believe me. Sometimes I wish I wasn't wired this way."

She stops on the path, stares at me with sympathy. "I know, Abby. I know it's tough for you. Still, what you did last night hurt my feelings. Really bad. I admit I've closed myself out of the magic circle, if you want to look at it that way. But to have you closing me out of what you were going through. That made it all worse."

Now I'm the one feeling sympathy. I take her hands and stare into her eyes. "I know. I acted terribly. I am really, really sorry. Can you forgive me?"

Suddenly, Molly laughs and hugs me. "Of course, I can. You're my bestie."

I hug her back, my eyes filling. "Thank you. I can't believe how I acted last night. I know I left an awful impression on everyone."

She nods. "They were pretty worried about you. Especially Ray-Ray. They'll be relieved to hear you're okay."

"Especially Ray-Ray?"

"Yes ..."

We've come to the bluff overlooking the river. I stare down at the rushing blue waters. I'm sure now that my anxiety about seeing Ray-Ray last night is what triggered my freak-out. I've decided to avoid seeing him for a while.

Still ... It's nice to know he cares that much.

♒

34 days before

Late in the day on Sunday, I leave Grandma's house and walk up the road to the top of Bliss Spring. I'm wearing Thomas Renshaw's ring on a chain around my neck and carrying my backpack. The wand is in there, wrapped in a black silk scarf. Scraped of bark and thorns, it has soaked for five days in the water of the springs.

The past few days have been edgy. No big scary episodes, just nagging anxiety—sensing things around me, glimpses at the edge of my vision. I've been keeping it under control with deep breathing and the Ablution exercise. Maybe some of it is just energy I've been accumulating, drawing in for this ceremony.

I walk into the clearing, open the backpack, place the contents on the stone altar: the wand, my dagger, a candle, matches, a stick of rose incense. Crickets are chirping, and the air ripples with a little breeze. I sense power in the ground beneath my feet—power I'm about to awaken.

Standing with shoulders back, I take long slow breaths to clear my mind.

I pick up the dagger. Holding it at arm's length, I pace around in a circle with the altar at the center. I imagine blue fire trailing from the dagger's tip, and I stop at the four points of the compass to trace flaming pentagrams.

With the circle closed, I walk back to the altar. The sunlight is fading, and the woods seem alive with energy. With the dagger in my right hand and the wand in my left, I lift up my arms. Mentally, I extend the circle of blue fire into a sphere of protection that surrounds me. Then I face the mouth of Bliss Spring and speak out in my strongest voice.

"I call upon the true magic of the Springs. I am Fighting Eagle, initiate of the Circle of Harmony. I call upon our Friends of the Element Fire, that you might aid me in this work. My purpose is to consecrate this wand as my tool and weapon, that it may become an instrument of my will and a channel for my magic."

By the Power of the Springs
By the Truth that Loves all Things
I call ye Fires of the night
Into this wood, cast your might
Grant me power to command
By this wand and by my hand

As I repeat the chant over and over, sparks appear in the woods outside the clearing. They quiver and grow into floating balls, drifting through the ferns and under the trees. I know them as Elementals of Fire.

But something feels wrong. A vague sense of evil slips around my heart.

The balls of light drift closer, dozens of them, then hundreds. As they move into the clearing, they fall to the ground, bounce, and change into slimy white frogs.

I tell myself I'm safe in the circle. But the frogs leap and scramble over each other, moving toward me. Terrified, I stumble over the chant, forgetting the words. Hundreds of frogs are slithering and jumping all around me. They reach the barrier of blue fire.

And they keep coming.

My knees buckle and I collapse backward, my head bumping the altar stone.

I've fallen into a vision. I'm back in the Virtual Reality world from my dream. I'm running through a curving corridor in a castle, fleeing in terror from the frogs. I hear them on my heels, slithering, croaking.

Crazy with fear, I wheel around a corner and almost crash into someone. Staggering back, I find myself staring at a tall man in gold armor. White blond hair and piercing eyes—the figure I saw in my vision a few nights back. He lifts his wand and shouts in a language I do not know. The frogs chasing me freeze, scuttle backward. The man with the wand stares down at me.

"Who are you?"

I straighten, try to sound powerful. "I am Fighting Eagle, initiate of the Circle of Harmony. What is your true name, spirit?"

His blue eyes glimmer with amusement. After a second, he nods. "We shall meet again, I think."

With these words, he fades away, and the rest of the vision with him.

I'm back in the circle above Bliss Spring, sitting on the ground, slumped against one of the stones that supports the altar. The clearing is gray with twilight. I stand up, touch the back of my head, grimace as I feel a painful lump.

Now what? The frog monsters invaded my circle, chased me on the astral plane. I was rescued by the Knight of Wands—or whoever he is. When I tried to find out his identity, he vanished ...

Get a grip, Abby. Finish the ritual.

Instinctively, I know that's what I must do. Having started the ritual, it feels unwise not to finish. Maybe even dangerous.

And I'm going to need this wand.

I pick up the dagger and retrace the circle, redrawing the pentagrams. I stand again in the center and repeat the opening invocation and chant. This time, I see the Fire Elementals as wisps and sparks in the trees. They hover but don't come closer.

Holding the wand and dagger, arms raised overhead, I summon the power of the Springs into my body. I speak into the night.

"By the forces of Elemental Fire, by the waters of Love Spring, in the name of the greatly honored Founders of our Circle, I call upon Lebab, who is the true spirit of the Springs. I ask that you charge this wand with your power, that it may aid me in my workings, that it may focus my will and strengthen my magic, which I vow to use only in service to Harmony and the Love of Truth."

I lower the dagger and hold the wand out in the direction of the spring.

What happens next surprises me. I've heard the voice of Lebab in my visions. But never before have I seen him.

A rumble moves under my feet and shudders through the clearing. In the fading twilight, the spirit rises, streaming up from the ground. His body is like a waterfall, translucent and flowing. Long arms, long hair and beard, long and ancient face—all of silvery blue water. The face has no eyes, just holes where the waters part. *But I feel him looking at me.*

His voice is deep and seething. "Greetings to you, Fighting Eagle, true daughter of the path."

While I'm pretty sure I know him, it's not wise to take chances. "What is your name, spirit?"

"I am Lebab, whom you have summoned."

His hand of water reaches out, and fingers flow around the wand. I feel his energy pouring into the wand and into my body. It's like diving into a cold pool, chilling and exhilarating. I'm surprised my skin and clothes are not drenched.

"Your wand is blessed with all the power I can bestow," Lebab tells me. "But this alone is far from enough. You stand in a dangerous time, Fighting Eagle. Forces of malice and hate are spreading in your world. You have been called to fight this evil. Will you accept the charge?"

A tremor moves inside me. Lebab's words feel undeniable. I *have* been called to this fight. I have no idea where it might lead me. But it feels like my job—because there's no one else.

"I guess I will," I answer. "At least until someone better comes along."

The Spirit of the Springs nods. Is he laughing at me behind those missing eyes? "That is a cautious and virtuous answer, Fighting Eagle. You have the talent for this role, I assure you. As a true magician, you also have the duty. I charge you then to learn the sigils that were developed by your Founders and those who came after. They can summon power beyond mine, power you can use to banish evil spirits from your world."

In the *Book of Lebab*, and other papers from the Circle of Harmony, there are diagrams and drawings. I've seen some of them labeled *sigils*, but I'm not sure what that word means exactly.

"Umm, sorry. I don't even know what a sigil is."

"Seek in the Founders' books, and learn."

With those words, the vision of Lebab disappears. I'm standing alone in the circle, dusk fading, the air of night drifting through the forest. The wand in my hand tingles with energy. In the east, the moon peeks through the trees.

7. A shaman doesn't *choose* to be a shaman

33 days before

Next morning, I drive into town, thinking about sigils all the way. As soon as I park outside Grandma's shop, I take out my phone and check messages. I have an email from Claremont State with details about orientation—which is tomorrow and which (I must confess) has not been foremost in my mind.

But it's the second email that really turns my morning sour. It's from the alert I set up for stories about Ranae Virum. There's a whole slew of new posts. Sighing, I tap the first link and start reading a bizarre fanfic on the subject of chasing and assaulting women. The other posts are reactions, mostly enthusiastic support. After following three more links, I can't take anymore and shut down the browser in disgust.

The frog meme is expressing and encouraging all kinds of hatred and rage—in this case, targeted at women just for being women. Like all ideas, no matter how crazy, it's amplified by the power of the internet.

An infection, a sickness of our world. And now I've been called to fight this evil.

Abby the clueless true magician.

♒

Kevin is back at work in the bookshop. Since business is slow, I take the opportunity to pay him a visit. He looks up at me from behind the counter, where he's sitting on a tall stool and reading a book. His face looks much better than the last time I saw him—just a pink scar and bruises on the forehead and around the eye.

"How are you feeling, Kevin?"

He waves fingers past his head. "Not bad. Doc took out the stitches on Friday. I still need to take it easy for a while, but no long-term effects."

"That's great. I was hoping we could talk. I could use your scholarly advice."

"Of course." He waves at the chair beside his stool. As I walk around the counter, he says. "Violet told me about your visions over the Tarot reading."

'Yeah. There's more—a lot more."

I summarize my horrible dinner at the Quick house, then seeing the frogs and the wand wizard in my vision at the Fountain of Balance, then my experience last night, with the frogs invading my wand ceremony. Kevin listens with mouth turned down and an occasional grimace of sympathy.

"So my spirit guide, Annie Renshaw, told me the frogs are *thought-forms*, manifestations of the collective mind. But I'm sure they're connected to this Ranae Virum character. Does that make sense, or am I totally crazy?"

"It makes sense," Kevin assures me. "You know from your studies that all thoughts have power and, to some degree, consciousness. What is a meme except a thought that's picked up and amplified by a lot of minds? The more minds and emotion behind it, the more power. Given enough power, thought-forms can certainly manifest in the real world."

"Okay. But if it's manifesting in our world, how come I'm the only one whose reality is being ripped apart by frog monsters?"

"Well, the only one we happen to know. Most of the manifestations are more subtle—posts and images online, banners at demonstrations. But as to why you're so deeply affected ..." Kevin pauses, contemplating what to say. "We've talked before about you having the natural abilities of a shaman."

"Yeah ..."

"You know that's a gift, a talent that sets you apart. It's what lets you see so easily into other realms and communicate with spirits."

"Right. Be nice if I had a little more control over that."

"And that's exactly what you're working on, as a true magician. But the point I was going to make is that, in traditional societies, a shaman doesn't only serve as an interface to the spirit world. He or she also carries the consciousness of the community, embodies the soul of the tribe."

That reminds me of something else Annie said: that the scary visions weren't a symptom of my sickness, but the sickness of the world. I mention that to Kevin.

"That sounds exactly right. A shaman is visited with the psychic ills of the community and is charged with healing them."

Lucky me.

Kevin reads the self-pity on my face. "It's not easy, Abby. In those societies, a person doesn't usually choose to become a shaman. The choice is made for them—by the spirits, the ancestors, Fate—whatever you want to believe."

Well, this explanation at least makes me feel a little less crazy and alone.

"What about this other character—the gold armor guy with the wand? Annie seemed to think he was some sort of magician, summoning the frogs and directing their power."

"Could be ..." Kevin puts the fingertips of both hands in front of his chin, thinking it over. "One magician, or a group, or many occult groups, could be tapping into the thought-form, drawing on its power, *or* using magic to amplify its power ... Scary possibilities."

"Yeah." *And I'm charged with fighting this evil ...*

"Did you manage to finish consecrating the wand?" Kevin asks.

"I did. Lebab came into the circle and charged it up."

"Lebab himself? Wow." Kevin shakes his head, smiling. "You know, Abby, the Circle of Harmony may have found only one magician in your generation, but at least we got an ace."

"Thanks. I don't feel very *acey* this morning ... What do you know about sigil magic?"

The question makes him frown. "Not a lot. That's a pretty advanced subject in magical lore. Why do you ask?"

"Well, Lebab told me that I should learn about the sigils that were developed by the Founders and those who came after."

"Oh." Kevin's eyes widen. "Well, I did say you're an ace. And far be it from me to second-guess Lebab. Still, I have to warn you, Abby. Sigil magic is really powerful. I haven't worked with it much, and neither has Violet. So we won't be able to give you much guidance."

I throw up my hands. "I have no idea what I'm even looking for."

"Well," Kevin says, "I expect, if you're meant to look into this, you'll get guidance along the way. Just go slowly. And be careful. Don't go invoking any powers unless you're sure it's right."

"Right ..."

"You know what I mean. Like Violet taught you." He points to his chest. "Ask your inner self first and listen to your heart." Next, he touches his brow. "Then analyze here, to make sure the action is in accord with the Five Principles of Harmony."

"Yes. I remember."

"Come on, I'll show you the books."

He climbs down from the stool and leads me to the back of the shop. Taking a key from his pocket, he opens the door of the climate-controlled reading room. This is where he stores original documents from the Founders—some on shelves, some in locked glass cases. There are old books in regular bindings, but also big heavy volumes bound in brass and leather, and portfolios of loose papers. The room feels like the library in a Harry Potter movie—on a very tiny scale. A dehumidifier hums in the corner.

Kevin unlocks one of the glass cases and pulls out a large book bound in maroon leather. He opens it on the reading table in the middle of the room. We both lean over and read the title page, written in calligraphy with burgundy ink.

Sigils of the Order
Volume III
Being a compendium of the true names of spirits and the formulae of magical workings, extracted to visual symbology by true magicians of the Circle of Harmony.
Published at Harmony Springs, Florida. Anno Domini 1923

The Circle was founded in the 1890s, and I know that by the 1930s it had dwindled to just a few practicing members. Violet was trained by the last of those in the early 1960s.

I ask Kevin about the date. "So this work was probably done a generation or two after the Founders?"

"Probably. Some of it may have been done earlier and just not published till '23. Starting in the early 1900s, things went in several directions. Sigil magic was one of them. Violet and I have preserved all the writings that were handed down from those days, but not all of it would be considered validated by the Circle of Harmony. I'll get you the other volumes."

Turns out there are five volumes altogether, with dates from 1907 through 1936. I'm thinking I've got over two thousand pages to go through, and again no idea what I'm looking for. After stacking the volumes on the table, Kevin goes and hunts up another book—a small one with a worn binding.

"This should help you get started."

This book is called *Fundamentals of Sigil Magic*. The title page says it was published in 1873 and translated from the German. Kevin pages through the opening chapter. "This illustrates how it works. The magician composes a formula or writes out the true name of a spirit they have contacted. Then they gradually reduce the written script, extracting the lines that contain the most power, until it's boiled it down to a single diagram."

The pages show the steps in the process, each ending with a diagram—lines shooting off in all directions, sometimes forming triangles or other shapes, sometimes curving or looping. Some are intricate, almost like flowers or butterflies, others just jagged abstractions, like stick figures.

"But how did they know which lines to keep and which to throw away?"

Kevin shrugs. "Intuition, psychic guidance. That's where the magic comes in. That's about all I can tell you, Abby. Look these over and see what you get. Then, if you have questions, Violet and I will of course do our best to help."

"Thanks, Kevin. Uh, would you tell my grandma I'm back here, in case she needs me?"

≈

I start with Volume 1, reading some of the pages in detail, skimming others. Each section has an introduction explaining when and where the work began, or how and when the particular spirit was first contacted. They're written in a formal Victorian style and tagged with the name of a true magician. In the early days, the Founders mostly used Latin for their magical names. I take out my phone and search up the translations: *Seeker After Wisdom*, *Radiant Brow*, *Owl of Minerva*.

Quaint.

Some of the sigils seem to vibrate on the page. Others are so complex I just stare at them in confusion. But none of them seem remotely related to my problem—the Gentleman Frog and whatever mystery occultists may be summoning him. After a while, I realize I'm scanning the pages and understanding nothing, my brain in a fog.

I check my phone. Two hours have passed, and I've only gone through about a third of the first volume. If I'm supposed to get some guidance here, it hasn't shown up.

I stand and put the books away, thinking again about those hateful posts I read this morning, and feeling utterly discouraged.

8. Welcome to the Home of the Bobcats

32 days before

Of course, along with my quest for magical knowledge and my battle against demon frogs, I have other problems. Eight o'clock the next day, I'm driving Veronica down Highway 7 toward Claremont State. Today is orientation for the summer session, my first day of college.

I actually don't feel too bad. To be honest, it's a relief to set aside all the mystical conundrums and focus on normal life. Of course, I'm also anxious. But that's reasonable, right? Who wouldn't be anxious on their first day of college? Anxiety over something so normal almost feels like a comfort.

On the seat beside me is my backpack, containing my tablet, paper and pens, and some printed information they sent when I enrolled. I've got the orientation schedule and campus map on my phone. I've gone over it carefully and know where and when I'm supposed to show up.

I struggled over what to wear, finally deciding on blue jeans and a green T-shirt. Now I'm thinking it's going to be over 90 degrees, and I'm likely to be too hot. *Oh, well.* At least my feet will be cool, since I opted for sandals. In fact, I spent over an hour last night painting my toenails. I've never done this before, but I'll be wearing sandals a lot, and most women down here paint their toenails. Normal college student Abby doesn't want to look out of place. In high school, things were simple. My style identity was "jock," and that answered all the questions.

Claremont State sits on the edge of a town called Murdock, about a forty-minute drive from Harmony Springs. As I approach the town, the open ranch country and patches of wetlands give way to civilization—roadside businesses, gated communities with golf courses, the eastern edge of Orlando's urban sprawl. Nearing the "historic downtown," I pass a mixture of new housing developments and older buildings—garages, a shopping center, small businesses in ancient, wood-frame houses.

The campus is just past downtown, marked by a tall marquee sign: "Claremont State," and under that in smaller letters: "Welcome to the Home of the Bobcats."

I make the turn and drive up a long curving road, past parking lots, athletic fields, and wide green lawns. There's a quadrangle of red brick buildings with tiled roofs, built I guess to resemble some Ivy League school. But most of the campus buildings are plain concrete block, linked by tile walkways. And a lot of parking lots, already half-filled with cars.

Claremont State started as a community college. But, with the expanding population around Orlando, it grew and grew. Six years ago, it became a four-year institution. For a mid-sized commuter college, it has really nice facilities, many of them new. Now they're talking about maybe building dorms.

I've been here once before. Ray-Ray drove me down for a tour last summer after I told him I was planning to apply here. That was my last week in Florida, the week we were together. I decided to come to school here mostly because I wanted to live in Harmony Springs with my grandma. But also, I have to admit, because Ray-Ray was studying here. *Well, Abby, we know how well that turned out.* I believe he said he's here for classes on Tuesdays, so I hope I don't run into him.

One more thing to be anxious about.

I would have expected orientation to take place in an auditorium. But it turns out less than twenty new students are starting in the summer session, so we'll meet in a classroom. Leaving Veronica in the parking lot, I follow the "Welcome New Bobcats" signs to the second floor of Harper Hall. I sign in and introduce myself to the administrative assistant, Gail, and the college provost, Dr. Patricia McKay. The room is set up with a buffet breakfast in the back—coffee, juice, donuts, and bagels—and rows of tables and folding chairs. I grab a coffee and sit in the back. A few other students are already here. I smile at them, and they smile back.

When everyone's arrived, Dr. McKay gives a welcome speech. Since there are only seventeen of us, she asks each of us to stand up and introduce ourselves. A couple of the new students are older, but the rest look around my age. My turn comes, and I tell them my name, that I graduated high school last month in New Jersey, and that I live now in Harmony Springs. I'm planning on a BA with a dual major in Business and English, with the plan of eventually going to law school. It all feels a little surreal, but also exciting.

Abby the enterprising young adult.

Members of the college staff take turns addressing us, aided by PowerPoint slides. They talk about registration, course requirements, codes of behavior, counseling services, security, student resources. I type notes on my tablet. It feels really different from high school but pretty interesting, and nothing I can't cope with.

Abby Renshaw, capable college student.

The meeting ends and we're conducted down to the Registrar's office to get set up with our classes. The Registrar lady goes over everything with me very carefully. Because of my test scores and high school honors classes, I'm exempt from some of the core requirements. For the summer, I'll start with just one class, *Business and Law I.*

Next, we go back to the classroom and meet with our two student mentors. They're responsible for showing us around campus today and helping us as needed during our first term. One is a tall girl named Mirna Hinds, and the other is a good-looking guy named Ariel Henriquez. Mirna has the build of a basketball or volleyball player. Ariel definitely looks like a runner. They joke about how we're now "Bobcat cubs" and explain the plan for the rest of the day.

We follow them on a walking tour of the campus. It's late morning now and very hot. I'm kind of regretting the blue jeans choice. But mostly I am enjoying myself. We walk through some of the classroom and office buildings, the health center, the library. We circle the big pond and end up at the student center. We get lunch in the cafeteria, which is designed in a curve with tall glass walls facing the pond. We sit together at a long table.

As we eat, the mentors answer questions—online resources, social events on campus, local restaurants and shops. The talk breaks into separate conversations, and after a while, Ariel turns to me.

"So, Abby, I saw in your records that you ran track in high school. Middle distance, right?"

"Right. Also cross-country. I really loved it." There is something about him I find fascinating.

"Well, I'm sure you know we don't have a track team. But we do have a running club. It's very informal. We meet at the health center and run on the trails around campus. You're welcome to join us any time, if you're interested."

"That sounds like fun. Thanks. I'll be here Tuesdays and Fridays starting next week." From his name and appearance, I know he's Hispanic, maybe Cuban. He doesn't have much of an accent, but his voice has this deep, soft tone that I find soothing. And attractive.

Easy, Abby.

He smiles. "Great. In the summer we start at 6 p.m. In the winter, when it's cooler, more like 4:30."

"Nice. I'll be sure to bring my running clothes next week. Thanks, Ariel."

"My pleasure."

♒

After lunch, we adjourn to the lobby of the student center. Many of the organizations on campus have tables set up, and we newbies are invited to roam around and get acquainted with any we're interested in. My high school had a lot of extracurricular activities, but nothing like this. Every possible interest has a group: yoga, flag football, Young Marketers Association, Black Student Union, a Caribbean dance troupe, Chemistry and Biology clubs, cybersecurity, intramural volleyball. The tables circle the round lobby and stretch down a couple of hallways.

I stop in at the running club table and introduce myself to a girl named Alicia. I tell her I've already been invited by Ariel to join them.

Her face lights up. "Oh, yeah, Ariel is a honey."

I just smile.

"You look fit," she says. "Have you been running long?"

I explain about my track team experience up in New Jersey. When she presses me for details, I brag a little, mentioning that I made quarter-finals in the NJ State Championships in the 3,200 meters, and finished in the top 50 in the 5,000.

Alicia is impressed. "With those creds, you could have gotten a scholarship at a college with a real track team. How did you end up here?"

"Well, I kind of fell in love with Harmony Springs when I visited last summer. I'm living there with my grandmother." *Also fell in love with a guy named Ray-Ray, but never mind about that.*

"Well, we're glad to have you," Alicia says. We exchange phone numbers, and she encourages me to get in touch if she can help me with anything, which is really sweet of her.

I visit a couple of other tables, the Pre-Law Study Group and the Bobcat Business Forum. I meet the reps, snap pictures of flyers showing their meeting rooms and times. Wanting to make sure I don't miss anything interesting, I look around the corner into a hallway. There are only a few tables there, but the one at the end grabs my attention: The Realm of Valor.

Cold fingertips tab on the back of my neck. The name reminds me of my nightmare: the suits of armor in the hall of the giant frog.

I'm sure my imagination is getting the better of me. But an insistent urge makes me walk into the hallway. The table has posters set up of guys in medieval costume fighting with swords and shields. A banner on the wall shows a coat of arms with a gold lion. A little red-haired dude sits behind the table, tapping on a big-screen phone. He looks up at me, startled like I've caught him doing something he shouldn't.

I smile to reassure him. "Hi, I'm a new student. I was just curious about your group."

"Oh." He gives a nervous laugh and puts down the phone. "Sure, sure. We're the Realm of Valor. We're a LARPing group. Do you know about LARPing?"

"Live Action Role Playing, right?"

He grins, surprised. "That's right. We're actually the Claremont State chapter of a national group. We have weekly meetings where we get together and talk and stuff. And once a month we do games: knights and orcs, some combat, some treasure hunts. It's a lot of fun."

"Sounds pretty cool."

"It's not just the college," he says. "We have some local high school kids and some older guys too. And it's not *all* guys. There are a few girls. Have you done any role-playing?"

"Not the LARPing kind. I've done online gaming."

"Sure, sure. Most of us do a lot of that. We get together for tournaments sometimes. My name is Wendell, by the way."

He extends his hand, and I shake it. "Abby."

"Nice to meet you, Abby." Nervously, he scans the table and picks up a printed sheet. "This has our meeting times and more information. Get in touch if you'd like to learn more or just hang out with us."

I take the paper and slip it into my pack. "Thanks a lot. Nice to meet you, Wendell."

I wander away thinking it highly unlikely this LARPing group could have anything to do with my nightmares. It must be just a coincidence.

At the end of the hallway, I meet Mirna, one of my student mentors. She eyes me suspiciously.

"I saw you talking with the Realm of Valor guy. What did you think?"

I lift my shoulders. "Oh. He seemed nice. LARPing isn't really my thing. I was just curious."

She frowns down at me, like she's weighing whether or not to say more. Then she decides. "Well, I wouldn't presume to tell you what groups to associate with, but just so you're aware, there were some rumors about them during spring term."

The anxious tingling in my gut comes back. "What kind of rumors?"

Mirna sighs. "Well, for one thing, you'll notice there are no people of color in the group and almost no women. There hasn't been any trouble on this campus, but there's talk online that some of the people in the Realm of Valor are affiliated with political extremists—mainly white supremacy and anti-feminist groups."

That leaves me confused. Nervous and nerdy little Wendell seems not at all like the raging counter-protestors I saw up in Gainesville, the ones who bashed in Kevin's head. On the other hand, the pictures on the table did remind me of the suits of armor in my nightmare, and the gold-armored wizard who commanded the frogs ...

Scratching my head over all this, I conclude that I've had enough excitement for one day. The Student Org Bazaar was the last planned activity for orientation, so I'm free to leave. Only a few people are still in the lobby. As I wander toward the door, I run into Ariel again.

"Heading out, Abby?" he asks.

"Yeah. I think I've absorbed all I can for one day. Listen, thank you for all your help, Ariel."

"My pleasure. Come on, I'll walk out with you."

He falls into step beside me, and I feel an odd little glow. Attraction, I suppose.

"I saw you at the running club table," he says. "So you met Alicia."

I have to grin. "Yeah. She says you're a honey."

He laughs quietly, glances at me sidewise. "We have fun. It's a nice group. I know you'll enjoy it."

"Yes. I'm sure I will." The glow feels brighter. My first day at college and I'm actually making friends.

"Abby! Hi, how are you?"

I stop, startled, just in front of the outside doors. Ray-Ray is walking in from the bright sunshine. I haven't seen him since I humiliated myself in front of his family, so his sudden appearance makes me cringe. He looks me up and down, then glances at Ariel.

"I thought you might be here for orientation," Ray-Ray says. "How did it go?"

"Oh, it went great. Um, this is one of my mentors, Ariel Henriquez. This is a friend of mine from Harmony Springs, Ray-Ray Quick."

They flick smiles at each other. *Is there tension between them, or is it all mine?*

"Ray-Ray Quick?" Ariel says. "I've seen you around campus, I think. Pickup basketball, right? But I didn't know you were a superhero."

Ray-Ray scowls. "What?"

"Ray-Ray Quick. Sounds like a superhero." Ariel grins.

"Oh. Ha-ha. You know, I've never heard any jokes about my name before."

Ariel holds up his hands. "Whoa. Sorry, man. No offense meant."

"Forget it." Ray-Ray turns to me. "Good to see you, Abby. Glad it's going okay."

He nods with a smirk at Ariel and walks on into the lobby.

"Wow," Ariel says. "Something between you two?"

"Nope." *Just a lot of continuing awkwardness.*

"Doesn't have much of a sense of humor, huh?'

"No. He's pretty much a straight arrow."

9. Abby's Midsummer Night's Dream

31 days before

Text from Molly: "Hey, how did orientation go yesterday?"

Me: "Fine."

Molly: "???"

She wants details. I haven't seen her since our big talk in the park last week. Between the wand ceremony and prepping for orientation day, I've been swamped. I meant to update her about what happened in the circle—my weird visions and then researching the sigils—but I hesitated, not sure how she'd take it.

Anyway, I *can* tell her about school. "It was good. I think I'll like college. Met some nice people."

Molly: "Cool. I asked Ray-Ray if he'd seen you."

Me: "And..."

"Got all frowny-face. Said he saw you but only for a second. Wouldn't tell me more."

Hmm. "Yeah, we didn't really get a chance to talk."

Molly: "Tomorrow's my day off. Wanna get together? Maybe go for a ride in Veronica?"

"I'd like to, but I can't." We're having the Midsummer Ritual tomorrow. I feel awkward mentioning it to Molly, but then again I don't want to *not* mention it.

"I'm doing a ritual tomorrow. For Midsummer."

"Oh."

"Meet you the next day at Springs of Coffee? We can talk on your break."

"OK."

Have I hurt her feelings? I hope not. I click off the phone with a sigh.

♒

30 days before

"The circle is duly scribed, the perimeter is magically guarded, only initiates stand within. Therefore, in the name of the great spirit Lebab and the names of our greatly-honored Founders, I declare that the Circle of Harmony is established in this place, in this time."

Violet's voice comes out a bit shaky. All the stress around Kevin's injury has left her worn out. But she insisted on performing the ritual, and she stands straight and still, holding her wand and dagger high. Her wrinkled face is tilted up, eyes wide and shining. Her robe is royal blue, sewn with gold and silver emblems of the sun and moon.

Grandma and Kevin stand beside her, also in ceremonial robes. I haven't made a robe yet, so I'm wearing a white gown that Violet gave me—the same one I wore last summer for my initiation into the Circle. Just as on that day, we're assembled in Grandma's living room. Grandma and I left the shop early to come home and set up. We pushed some of the furniture to the center of the room and set up five stations along the walls. Each station has a table or stand, with a cup and candle and a picture hung above it—portraits of the Five Fountains. Afternoon sunlight slants through the tall bay windows. The air smells sweet with incense.

So, here I am, standing under a high ceiling in a Victorian house in central Florida, with two elderly ladies and one elderly man, performing a magic ritual. If my high school friends could see me now, they would think for sure I had finally gone around the bend and arrived in Insanity Land. But this is a big reason I came back to

Harmony Springs. I learned last summer that magic is real, and no more crazy than the rest of the world.

Maybe a lot *less* crazy.

"All within this sacred space are true magicians," Violet is saying. "We walk the ways of wisdom and love, seeking illumination. Always, our steps are guided by the Five Principles: Love, Endurance, Balance, Amity, and Bliss. Dear companions on the quest, let us now walk to the springs, the springs that are fountains and the fountains that are way-markers on the path of true magic. Let us review their lessons, that we may be nourished and renewed."

She turns and leads us slowly around the edges of the room. I walk behind her, waving an incense burner on a gold chain. Kevin beats a drum in time with our footsteps. Grandma shakes a tambourine, the little bells singing in the air.

I came back to Harmony Springs to be part of this circle, to fill myself with its magic. Yet with all the weird stuff that's happened recently, I feel separated from the energy now, walled off by this goopy barrier of defensiveness and dread.

We stop at the station of the first Spring. The painting shows a white marble fountain with a single spout of water. A white candle and a goblet of clear glass are set on the table. Violet lifts her wand.

"Before us flows the Fountain of Love—love of knowledge and of truth, which first inspires the magical quest." She picks up the goblet and holds it out to me. "We drink from this spring to dispel confusion of spirit and see past the illusions of surface appearance."

I set the incense burner down on the table, take the cup in both hands. It shakes a little as I bring it to my lips. Violet is staring into my eyes—with compassion, concern, worry?—I'm not sure. I pass the cup to Kevin.

Violet drinks last of all, and then we resume our march. We move past the fireplace and come to the second station. The portrait shows water gushing over gray boulders. The embossed letters on the picture frame say "Endurance."

Violet lifts her dagger. "We stand before the second Fountain, the Spring of Endurance. From these waters, we grow in courage, strength, and purpose, so that we may overcome our fears."

She hands me a goblet of pewter, set with a turquoise stone. I drink, mentally calling on all the magic I can to dispel my fear. The water seems to stir a current of peace and strength in me. I smile as I pass the cup.

The next station is Balance. The painting shows two fountains, equally high, one silver and one blue, the waters flowing into each other. Violet holds up a round stone, like a crystal ball, but with rough facets, and blue in color. This is her *seeing stone*, one of the tools I will make in the future.

"Behold the Spring of Balance," she says. "Here we may learn to reconcile contending forces, by seeing clearly and weighing their many roots and extensions, until at last we perceive the Unity of all things."

This time the cup is silver. As I pass it on, my brain quivers and tingles. I glimpse hundreds of contending energies, all flashing at me, pulling in different directions–like bees swarming over each other in a hive. But I sense no *hive mind*, no unity.

I'm still unsettled when we reach the next station. The painting shows a fountain of gold, and a gold cup holds the water. Violet takes a smaller cup from her robe. The cup is the fourth magical tool, corresponding to the Spring of Amity. Hers is of glass, blood red and shiny.

"Now we have reached the fourth Spring. As you grow in magical power, temptations and deceptions increase. We desire control, power, to bend others to our will. Only by Amity can these temptations be overcome. That is, selfless love, extended to all beings in all the worlds."

She hands me the gold cup. "Drink, dear friend, that you may grow strong in Amity."

As I drink, I consciously summon the spirit of love. It calms me some, the thrumming fear subsiding.

The procession resumes, and we come at last to the Fountain of Bliss. The portrait shows it just as I have seen in visions, a curtain of crystal blue water that seems to flow out of nowhere and disappear again—no basin, no edges, no source.

Below the portrait is a smaller picture. An image of a woman with a crown of gold stars. She sits on a throne between two pillars, black and white. A stream of water flows beneath her feet. The image is like a combination of two Tarot Cards I know very well, the *High Priestess* and the *Empress*. According to the teachings of the Circle, it is a portrait of a goddess. She sits at the point of creation, where the material universe flows into manifestation. We call her the Goddess Who Shapes All Things.

Violet holds up no magical tool this time, only her empty hands.

"Now we have arrived at the final Spring, the goal of our questing. It is Bliss. It is union with the soul's Higher Nature, that which is a fragment of the One Eternal Mind, the Spirit of the Universe."

The goblet she hands me is cut blue glass, which spreads a shimmering blue color over the water. I drink, and the feeling of calm deepens. Under the white gown, I am wearing the ring I inherited from Thomas Renshaw. It has a cameo image of the Goddess Who Shapes All Things. As I pass the cup to Kevin, the ring touches my skin and a current flutters around my heart. I look at the portrait, and the Goddess seems to smile.

♒

We sit on cushions arranged in the middle of the floor. Violet leads us in a centering exercise, timed breathing in and out, with Kevin tapping beats on the drum. When we open our eyes, I see that Violet has placed her seeing stone in the center of our little circle.

"On this day of greatest light," she says, "we celebrate the sun. We call its energy into our spirits, that we may be illuminated in the year ahead and guided in our magical quest."

Her voice is faltering again. She instructs us to visualize the sun inside the seeing stone. We repeat the rhythmic breathing, this time with eyes open. Staring into the blue glass, I see a ball of white light, pulsing and gleaming.

Violet's voice comes from far away. "A current of sunlight flows from the center into our bodies. Now the current moves around our circle from heart to heart, growing brighter and stronger. The light unifies us in harmony and strength."

I envision the current, brilliant like blue starlight, flowing through us. As it grows stronger, I'm lifted out of myself, becoming aware that I am not only Abby but part of a larger being, the magic spirit of the Circle.

"Now," Violet says, "as the magical current grows stronger and stronger, let us form our intention. We are aware of forces flowing into our world, disruptive beings that would harm us and others. But as yet the source of these beings is hidden from our sight. By the magic of the Circle and the sacred sun, we summon clarity to see and know these forces. And we call for guidance, to know how we may best oppose them. Let each of us seek clarity and guidance in the current of light."

I stare at the spinning blue light, trying to summon clear vision.

Violet's voice trembles, pitched high. "The current of light moves faster and faster. With all of our power, we cast our intention out into the world!"

The blue light explodes, a silent burst rushing out in all directions. As I look around, the room appears normal—fading daylight at the windows, candle flames, wafts of incense smoke.

Violet coughs. Kevin looks at her with a frown.

"Now," she murmurs, "let us gaze into the seeing stone."

All of us stare at the blue globe. I open my mind to impressions. Again, I sense the larger being that is our circle. I feel it settled now, into each of our minds. I feel it reaching, straining to pierce barriers of darkness, to find answers ...

And getting nowhere. I sense disappointment and frustration in all of us.

Violet starts coughing again. This time it goes on for a while, and she struggles to clear her throat.

"I think we'd better stop now," Kevin says.

Violet gasps, patting her chest. "Yes. I'm afraid you're right."

With Violet resting in an armchair, Kevin and I clean up the circle. Grandma heads into the kitchen to put on the kettle and set out some dishes.

When the magical accoutrements are packed away and the living room furniture back in place, we adjourn to the kitchen for a post-ritual feast. We share toast and jam, cheese and crackers, fresh blueberries, ice cream, pound cake.

After some tea and honey, Violet seems better. "Sorry about my coughing fit," she tells us. "That can happen sometimes when the atmosphere is jagged."

"It's all right, Vi," Grandma says. "It was a beautiful ceremony."

Violet beams. "You're a dear, Kat ... Did any of you perceive new insights?"

We look at one another around the table: frowns and little headshakes.

"Oh, well. Not to worry." Violet sighs. "Oftentimes, with this kind of work, the insights come later. Be sure to take note of your dreams tonight."

♒

Violet and Kevin leave a little later. I can tell Kevin and Grandma are both concerned about Violet's condition, and I am too. Wielding magical energy takes stamina, and Violet is in her mid-seventies.

As I help Grandma wash and dry the dishes, I'm feeling more and more discouraged.

I haven't experienced any frog monster visitations since my wand ceremony four days ago. But I sense the creatures are out there, at the periphery, and will burst through again sooner or later. I was hoping the ritual today would help us figure out their source and give us some plan for dealing with them.

Nada.

Worse, now I'm wondering if Violet is going to be any help at all. Last summer, she trained me in Circle of Harmony magic and gave me lots of support. She grappled with the Shadow Man, and it nearly cost her life. I'm beginning to appreciate that she is frail, and this frog monster problem might be too much for her.

And I've still gotten nowhere with trying to learn sigil magic.

What am I even doing in Harmony Springs?

First Ray-Ray abandons me for another girl. Then I have to tiptoe around Molly because my magical self makes her feel uncomfortable and shut out. Now Violet and Kevin seem unable to help me or even guide me. Of course, Grandma is still on my side. But except for being supportive, there's just not much she can do.

By the time I crawl into bed, I am feeling pretty sorry for myself.

♒

I wander the woods on the shore of Bliss Spring. It's a pitch-black night, but the rushing water shines with a light of its own.

The sky is full of eyeballs—yellow, floating, detached from any face. All of them stare down at me. In the real world, the shores of Bliss Spring are swampy and covered in trees and sawgrass. But in the dream, there is a path, muddy and slippery. My running shoes get slimy.

Frogs creep out onto the path, tiny white ones, hopping and croaking. I see more and more of the little devils, but I have my wand, and I'm not afraid. Overhead, the eyes watch me.

Around a curve, I see a figure. A tall man in gold armor—the Knight of Wands again. Just like in the Tarot card, the yellow vest over his armor is embroidered with red salamanders biting their tails, symbols of Elemental Fire. But unlike the Tarot image, he wears no helmet. Instead, he has the wild, white-blond hair and ice-blue eyes I recall from my earlier vision. He smiles as I approach.

"So young lady, we meet again."

I hold up my wand. "What is your name, spirit?"

He laughs. "I am not so easy to compel."

The frogs have followed me. They rush and slither around our feet. I look down at them, then back at the knight.

"You do not fear them," he says.

"I guess that depends. But at the moment, no."

"That is good. You know, they are just a source of power, power that you can tap and use as you will."

I glance down at the frogs, pondering that. When I look up, Gold Armor Guy is gone. Suddenly the frogs feel creepy, and I don't want them near me. I march up the slope, away from the water.

I come to the clearing, the place where I found the wand. The air is damp, warm, sweet-smelling. Above the altar stone floats a rectangle of light. As I draw near, I see it is a portal, a window into another realm. Inside sits a lady, on a throne between two black pillars. She wears blue robes and yellow slippers. At her feet is a waterfall and a crescent moon. I know her from the Tarot deck, the *High Priestess.*

I believe she is an image of the Goddess Who Shapes All Things, but I have been taught always to ask. Lifting my wand, I announce: "I am Fighting Eagle, initiate of the Circle of Harmony. What is your name, spirit?"

She smiles, that same smile I remember in the ritual today when we stood at the Fountain of Bliss. She fades, and the image changes. Now I see a stony path, winding through mountains, and in the distance, a tower standing against a dark sky. It reminds me of the *Tower Struck by Lighting*, but at the moment the sky is still.

"I see that you have a journey before you."

The goddess is back, but now she's the woman in the *Strength* card. The red lion lies at her feet, bound by a leash made of flowers. He stares at me solemnly.

"A journey where?" I ask. "What for?"

"To free my power," she answers. "My power would bless your world. But I have been driven far away, my power thwarted and contained."

"How can I free your power?"

She gazes at me, frowning. Because she's been driven far from our world, I sense she cannot see the answer.

"The sigils?"

Her face lights up. "Yes!"

She changes again, becoming a figure of gold, with a brilliant crown and wings. Rays of sunlight shoot from behind her back. They surge and fly above her, changing direction, crisscrossing in the air. They trace figures that *look* like sigils.

The tendrils of light reach out to me. They surround my body like a web, piercing my spine. Enormous energy surges through my nervous system. I shudder all over. With this power, I can do anything. If I want to, I can fly.

Next moment, I *am* flying, rising into the air. The clearing is far below my feet.

I panic. *Stop flying, Abby. Get back on the ground.*

Instantly, I'm standing before the altar again.

The golden lady smiles at me. "One of my names is Inanna."

♒

My eyes flutter open. I stare at my bedroom ceiling, dim in the twilight before dawn.

The incredible power lingers in my body.

I imagine I could fly if I wanted to. With that thought, I rise from the bed, float up to the ceiling. Twisting in the air, I gaze down at myself, resting peacefully under the covers.

I've read that people who first experience astral travel like this typically panic. But I'm not afraid. Not with all this power. Floating out of my body does not feel scary. But after a moment it *does* feel frivolous. This power is not for my amusement. With that thought, I drop back into myself.

I take a deep breath, relaxing in a warm current.

I know instinctively that it won't always feel this way: the sensations will fade over time. But I'm also thinking that her power lives in me now. I can learn to invoke it again. Gradually, it can grow in me.

One of her names is Inanna.

Something new has been born in me, and my life will never be the same.

10. We really need to sort through this stuff

29 days before

"So, Abby. What's new with you?"

Molly sits across from me, behind a bagel and cream cheese and an iced double mocha. Her frizzy red hair is pulled back by a kerchief. She's a little flushed, having worked the past few hours serving customers and bussing tables. Despite our recent bumpiness, she smiles like she's happy to see me.

I'm glad. I've decided to tell her everything and let the chips fall where they fall.

I put down my iced tea. We're at our favorite table, in the corner of Springs of Coffee. The room is fragrant with delicious baking smells and the tang of espresso. Dark paneled walls are hung with photos, portraits of the springs and their crystal-blue water. The shop owners, Lewis and Benjamin, are working behind the counter. Otherwise, the place is empty, the mid-afternoon lull.

"Well, Molly, I've got a lot to tell you."

"I am all ears, girlfriend."

I begin with the night I consecrated my wand—Was that *only last Sunday*?—when the frogs invaded my circle, and I met the wizard in gold armor who wouldn't tell me his name, and then met Lebab who charged me to learn sigil magic. I skip over the details about the Midsummer Ritual, except to mention the goddess smiling at me. But I narrate all the gory details of my dream last night—the slippery path, the frogs, Gold Armor Guy again, and the goddess in the portal with her different shapes.

All the while, Molly chews her bagel and sips her coffee, listening intently, eyes bright.

"Wow. Just wow," she says. "So the frog monsters are still around, and now Lebab is giving you orders. You've got a mystery wizard controlling the frogs, and a Tarot card lion-tamer lady goddess sending you power."

"Inanna."

"Huh?"

"Inanna. That's the Tarot card lion-tamer lady's name."

"Oh."

"Well, one of her names."

Molly peers, searching my face. "But with all this, you don't seem scared or upset."

"I know. Weird, isn't it? I think that must be Inanna's energy. Anyway, there's more."

"Tell me!"

"This morning I asked my grandmother, but she never heard the name Inanna. So I went into the bookstore and asked Kevin. He remembered that Inanna was the name of an ancient goddess from Mesopotamia. We looked through an encyclopedia of Mythology and found this."

I show her a picture on my phone. A page from the encyclopedia, showing a gold image of Inanna, with a seven-pointed star in the sky and a lion at her feet.

Molly's mouth gapes. "Wow. Lion Tamer Lady!"

"*Exactly*."

"This is so exciting."

"Wait. There's more. So then I went back to Kevin's locked room and looked in the sigil books—the ones I'm supposed to be researching? Inside one of them, I found this."

I swipe to the next picture on my phone and show her.

She stares at it, then touches the screen to expand so she can read the caption." 'Sigil of Inanna. One of Eight by Frater Statera.' What does that mean? Who or what is *Frater Statera*?"

"It's Latin for 'Brother of Balance.' It's the magical name of the guy who made the sigil. I was actually hoping you might help me out here."

Molly looks puzzled. "Me? How?"

"Well, I'm still clueless about what I'm supposed to do with these sigils. But this one feels extremely important, like the Universe has dropped me a clue. This is only one of eight, and I suspect I'm going to need them all. I searched through the other books, but this is the only one I could find that refers to Inanna *or* Frater Statera."

Molly's done a lot of research into the families that founded the town and the Circle of Harmony. She sees where I'm heading. "So you're thinking, if you're going to find the other sigils, it would help to know who Frater Statera was, in case he left other writings behind."

"Exactly. I asked Kevin, but he never heard of him. He promised to look through the materials he has at home. But the magical names were secret outside of the Circle. He only knows a few places that mention both someone's real name and their magical name."

"Right." Molly's eyes light up. "But there *are* old diaries in the library, and I've seen a few that mention real names and magical names together. And there might also be cases where we can find out which people were interested in drawing sigils and infer their magical names by clues they left behind. It's a long shot, but I'll find out all I can, I promise."

She's almost bouncing with excitement. Molly the investigator is back.

"Thank you," I tell her. "I would be so grateful."

"No problem. This is *really* interesting." Molly reaches over and grabs my wrist. "I am so glad you're not shutting me out."

I put my hand on hers. "I'm glad *you're* not shutting *me* out."

"Let's make a vow." She picks up her mocha. "No more shutting each other out."

I raise my glass. "I'll drink to that.

♒

After Molly goes back to work, I spend another two hours in the coffee shop using their wifi. I divide my time between researching sigil magic and doing prep work for my Business and Law class, which starts next Tuesday.

On my way home, I stop to see Violet. I want to check on how's she's feeling after the ritual yesterday, and if she's gotten any new insights. Also to fill her in on my dream and everything I've learned.

I haven't called ahead, and Violet looks bleary-eyed and rumpled when I open the door.

"Oh, I hope I didn't wake you!"

"No. I was just resting. Come in, dear. Come in."

She shuffles back to the kitchen and waves me to a chair. "Can I get you some tea or ice water?"

"No, I'm fine. I would like to talk with you, if you've got a few minutes."

"Of course. " She sits down, eyeing me expectantly. "Kevie called earlier. He told me about your dream and communication from the Mesopotamian goddess. That is very exciting."

"Yeah. She really charged me up with power."

Violet's blue eyes twinkle. "I can feel it. You are radiating. That must feel good."

"It does. But it's left me a lot to think about. Did Kevin tell you about my finding the sigil."

"Yes." Violet looks solemn. "I have to tell you, Abby. Of course, I'll help you any way I can, but I know almost nothing about sigil magic. It's not something I've worked on."

"That's okay." The last thing I want is to put her under any new strain. "Kevin's explained how sigils are created—starting with the name or symbol of a spirit, then reducing it to a diagram. And I've found some information online about how sigils are used in magic. Basically, they help you summon the power of the spirit or entity, and then cast the power to manifest your intention. Is that right?"

"Yes. Sometimes a number of sigils were used in a ritual, either to raise multiple spirits or different images to amplify the power of a single spirit. That's all based on what my teachers told me. They didn't use that kind of magic themselves. They adhered strictly to Circle of Harmony principles. They viewed sigil magic with disfavor because it can easily lead to focusing on power for its own ends, rather than spiritual harmony, you see?"

"I guess that makes sense. But it was Lebab himself who told me to learn about the sigils."

"I know. When Kevin told me that, I have to say I was surprised. If it were anyone else, Abby, I would be suspicious, and reluctant to help you. But I know you, Fighting Eagle." She speaks my magical name and points to her heart and then her head. "I know you are a true magician and are walking the path of harmony. I also know your talent. So I believe Lebab really did contact you. Therefore, it's my duty to help you as best I can."

I clear my throat, a little choked up. "Thank you for that, Violet. So, the sigil of Inanna I found is only one of eight. My intuition is telling me I'm going to need the other seven. Any idea how I can find them?"

Violet's lips turn down. "No, I'm sorry to say. We can look through our old papers. I know there's nothing here in the house. But we have boxes and boxes of stuff in the garage. I don't think there's much on sigil magic, but you never know."

She pushes away from the table and stands.

"Are you sure you're up to this? It's hot out there today." I hadn't intended to drag her outside.

But Violet's already heading for the door. "It's fine. I know this is important, Abby. I need to help you if I can."

We go out to the back porch, the screen door slamming behind us. The air outside is like a sauna.

"Looking at the papers may help," I admit, as we head down the steps. "Even if I can just find out who Frater Statera was, it might lead to something. Kevin didn't recognize the name."

"I don't either," Violet tells me. "Many of the magical names from the Founders' generation were preserved. I'm almost sure he wasn't one of them."

The garage is a separate wood building, small and badly in need of fresh paint. Violet opens a side door, the hinges creaking and the wood groaning as it scrapes the concrete.

"We don't come out here very often." She laughs and flips on the light.

The space is cluttered with rusty tools, old furniture and car parts, a lawnmower in one corner. The air is like an oven and smells badly of mildew. Violet coughs.

"Just my allergies," she says.

Crates and cardboard boxes are stacked along the walls. Some have labels etched in magic marker: "Palmer's Books biz records" "Taxes", and many older, crumbling boxes with markings like "C of H 1910s." Violet pulls down one of these and sets it on the cement.

"We really need to sort through this stuff. Kevin's done a lot of work on preserving and documenting it, but there's just so much."

She lifts the lid and gets blasted by a cloud of dust. She starts coughing again.

"Listen, Violet. I think it's too hot to do this right now. I'll come back when it's cooler if that's okay."

When the coughing fit subsides, she reluctantly agrees. "You're probably right. Come back whenever you want. I'm sure Kevin will help you when he's here."

We go back inside. Violet seems relieved to be back in the air conditioning, She settles onto a kitchen chair, grunting and clearing her throat.

"I'm afraid I haven't been any help to you, Abby. To be honest, I'm beginning to feel like a useless old woman."

Well, I'm not going to stand still for that. I kneel beside her chair and look her firmly in the eye. "Listen to me, Violet. You are certainly not useless. I can't begin to tell you how much you and Kevin have helped me. Without you, I would never have survived last summer, and I certainly wouldn't have become a true magician. As much as your teachers meant to you, you mean that much to me. And don't forget it."

Her eyes light up with tears. "You're a good girl, Abby. I always thought that when Kevie and I passed on, the Circle of Harmony would die too, and the magic of the Springs would be over. But seeing you charged with energy like this, and knowing all you've gone through and *are* going through, and how well you've handled it ... you've given me hope for the future."

♒

27 days before

Sunday morning, Molly and I go back to Violet's garage. Hearing about the boxes of old documents, she insisted on coming along to help me look. I arranged it last night with Kevin, so at 9 a.m. he lets us in. His shop won't open till noon today, and he promises to come back and help us after he's had some coffee.

It's cooler than the other day, but the garage still smells like a mildew bakery. At Grandma's suggestion, I've brought dust masks. I pass one to Molly, and she grins.

"I feel like we need plastic gloves and hazmat suits too."

With our masks in place, we pull down the first box. Inside we find yellowing typewritten pages. Some are journals of astral travels, others magical rituals. Officially, Molly's not supposed to see this stuff, because she is not an initiate. She's agreed not to read the magical texts, and only glances at the pages before handing them to me. I can feel her discomfort with the magic of the Circle straining against her curiosity to know everything.

As we rummage through more cartons, she finds plenty to hold her interest: attendance lists for public rituals, membership roles by year, and records of different initiates and their advancement ceremonies. These list lots of magical names, but Frater Statera is not among them.

Kevin comes and goes, bringing us coffee, collecting the papers we've sorted, and taking some of them back to the house. In all, we search through 19 boxes. We find a few references to sigil study groups, but no actual sigils. By the time we're done I'm grimy, sweaty, and disappointed.

Molly, on the other hand, is intrigued. "There is so much fascinating stuff here," she says as we close up the cartons and rearrange the stacks. "And most of it has never been recorded. I'm tempted to write a book ... I know I'd need to avoid the actual magic information, but the history itself. Do you think Kevin and Violet would let me do that?"

"I don't know. We can certainly ask them."

"Great! Let's ask before we leave."

Great. I'm happy Molly's found something interesting in all this. I am.

But I'm absolutely zero inches closer to solving my problems.

♒

So that night, alone in my room, I try a more direct approach. I've summoned ghosts before, so why not the ghost of Frater Statera?

I gather the implements and tools—my wand and dagger, candle, incense, a cup of water, and an empty bowl. On my phone, I page back to an old picture, a page from *The Book of Lebab*. Violet showed it to me last winter, during an online chat session, and I saved it.

The Formula for Calling and Binding Spirits.

I used it on my holiday in England, to summon and troubleshoot some difficult ghosts.

Holding the dagger, I trace a circle of blue fire, pausing at each of the four directions to draw a pentagram. When the circle is closed, I envision it extending into a sphere, a blue translucent globe of protection. Sitting down again, I light the candle and incense, then pour water from the cup into the bowl—a libation to attract the ghost.

Stretching my spine, I lift the wand and dagger high. "I call on the true magic. I am Fighting Eagle, initiate of the Circle of Harmony. I call upon our Friends of the Elements, of Fire, Water, and Earth. I ask your aid and blessing on my purpose: to summon the spirit of the initiate named Frater Statera, that he may speak with me."

I leave out the part about binding him to my will. Violet's stressed that it's dangerous to compel a spirit—also unethical unless you have a really good reason. At this point, I just want to chat.

Lowering my arms, I see bands of energy rippling outside the circle—the presence of the elementals I have summoned.

"To this protected circle, I call you, spirit of Frater Statera, I call you here that you may talk with me and help me."

Staring into the ring of blue fire, I chant in a low and solemn tone.

By the waters, bright and deep,
I call thee spirit, from thy sleep.
By this fire, clear and bright,
I call thee forth into the light.

I repeat the verse over and over. The blue energy beyond the circle condenses, brightens. The ghost is trying to come through.

But something prevents it, some force I cannot fathom.

Even as I realize that, the blue light blinks out.

I stare for a long time, wondering if I should try again. Intuition tells me, no. Wherever in eternity Frater Statera's ghost has gone to, he's beyond my reach.

Discouraged, I close the circle and go to bed.

11. Something terrible is going to happen

25 days before

I'm flying down Route 7, music from my phone blasting on Veronica's Bluetooth, the sunroof open, my hair loose and flying in the wind.

Call me a Jersey girl, but I love my car.

I feel excited, almost elated.

True. I'm not any closer to solving the frog monster mystery. And when I check my intuition, I still sense evil forces out there, hovering, gathering. But I haven't seen or dreamed anything weird and frightening since last week. I'm grateful to be able to push all that out of my mind for now. Today is my first college class, and I've resolved to focus on that.

I turn at the "Home of the Bobcats" marquee and cruise up the driveway. It's 9:45 and the campus is busy, parking lots half-full, students hustling on the sidewalks. I pull into the lot for the business school and park Veronica in an empty row. I don't want *any* scratches on her beautiful, eternal blue water paint.

After checking my face in the mirror, I pick up my backpack and head for class. I'm wearing shorts, a lightweight tee, and sandals. I have my running clothes and towel in a gym bag in the trunk. I'm going to hang out on campus all day, have a late lunch, and then work out with Ariel and the running club.

Feeling only mildly nervous, I march into the business school and across the lobby. The babble of conversation is a lot like high school, kids walking to class or standing in small groups talking. I climb the stairs and find my classroom on the second floor.

Class starts promptly at ten. The teacher, who at first I took to be another student, introduces himself as Marty Ramirez. He's actually in law school at the University of Miami and is working here this summer as a teaching assistant. There are twenty-five students, mostly around my age, a few older. We go around the room and introduce ourselves, state our preferred pronouns and why we're taking this course.

"Hi. I'm Abby Renshaw, she/her. I'm a freshman, and this is actually my first class. I'm planning on a dual major in English and Business and hope to go on to law school."

I sit down, relieved to have that over with. As the introductions continue I feel more relaxed.

Marty hands out a three-page printout of the course syllabus. He walks back and forth as he lectures, occasionally writing on the whiteboard. For the next 90 minutes, he goes over the course outline. We'll be covering the concept of law, its sources and uses as an instrument of social order. We'll study dispute settlement and legal ethics; examine torts, crimes, business organizations, and contract law. I type notes on my tablet, listen to the questions and answers, try to absorb as much as I can. It's all pretty conceptual. I see I'm going to have to work hard at this (unlike many of my high school classes).

Abby Renshaw, diligent young college student.

After class, I go to the library and get online. I have access to an online textbook for the class, and I do the assigned readings, take notes, and write down questions. I then answer three essay questions based on the reading. By 3 p.m. I've finished the homework. I head to the student center for lunch.

I'm famished, and I'm going to be running in three hours, so I load up my tray at the snack bar: chicken fingers, fries, salad, corn muffin, a slice of key lime pie. I truck it all over to a corner table and settle in with my tablet and phone.

I have a text from Alicia, who I met on orientation day, reminding me about running club. That she thought to invite me again makes me smile. I boot up the tablet and sign in to my Claremont State email account. Nothing new there except a welcome email to the Business and Law class. So I check out the student forum and scan through the posts. Living as I do in the Bliss Spring dead zone, access to the campus wifi is a luxury.

Halfway through the meal, I sense someone approaching my table. I look up and my shoulders rise with tension. Ray-Ray is standing over me.

"Hi. I saw you sitting here. Just wanted to say hello."

"Well, hello. Have a seat?"

"No, thanks. I'm on my way to class. How's everything going?"

A little tense at the moment. "Good. Fine. You?"

"Oh, fine. I hear you got Molly researching about the Founders."

"Yeah. She's helping me with some stuff ... How are your parents?"

"Oh, they're fine. Well, I gotta go. Good seeing you."

"Yeah. You too."

As he walks away I'm wondering: *When* is seeing him going to stop feeling so uncomfortable?

Maybe never?

♒

For a mid-sized commuter college, Claremont State has excellent facilities. The fitness center is amazing: there's a gym with three courts for basketball and volleyball, a huge exercise room with glass walls overlooking the campus pond, whirlpools for those aching muscles, even an indoor swimming pool. I check in at the desk and pick up a locker key, then wander around admiring the place. A little before six, I change into my running clothes.

The running club gathers outside the back entrance. I say hello to Ariel, and he introduces me to his friends. There are two guys, Pete and Ricky, a girl named Kaliah, and two other folks with buzz cuts who present as non-binary, Jayden and Mackenzie. While we're doing our stretches, Alicia arrives with another girl, Madison.

Alicia asks everyone to welcome the new members (myself and Madison) and then explains our route. We'll follow a path around the pond and through the woods at the back of the campus property, then out to the highway, then back around the north end of campus. The whole run is just over a mile.

"Most of us do between three and five laps," she says. "But don't do any more than you're comfortable with. Remember, this is Florida."

We set off at an easy pace—I'm guessing around ten minutes to the mile. I've haven't run much in the past few weeks, so my conditioning has lapsed. Between that and the heat, I have to push myself at first to keep up.

The path around the pond and through the woods is pleasant. It's still a couple of hours until sunset, but the deep blue sky is already turning pale. I fall into the easy mindfulness of running, focused on my breathing and the pounding of my feet. After the first lap, the pack spreads out, Pete and Jayden and Kaliah pacing ahead. I'm toward the back, keeping an easy, regular stride. Ariel is running ahead of me and Alicia is in front of him. From time to time she checks on me and Madison to make sure we're doing okay.

As we're passing the fitness center again, I hear wheezing in my ears. It is not my breathing. It's not anyone else's breathing either. I blink and look at the sky. The pale blue patch over the forest is wavering, rippling with some weird force. I shake it off and keep running.

When we get to the pond I see him: the giant white frog. He sits on a big rock at the waterside. Just like in my first nightmare, he is huge and fat with bulging yellow eyes on his head and dozens more eyes on his belly.

He appears and vanishes, blinking in and out of my sight. I know he doesn't exist on the material plane, but I keep seeing him: there and gone again. No one else sees him, of course, and I figure if I just keep going the vision will stop.

I keep running.

Only now it feels like I'm moving in slow motion, my legs slogging through molasses. Still, I'm keeping up with Ariel and Alicia.

As we near him, Frog Monster flickers faster and faster in strobe-light rhythm. Then he stops flickering and just sits there, as real as everything else. I stop, terrified.

Alicia runs past him. Just like in my nightmare, his tongue darts out. Next instant his mouth opens and sucks her in.

"No!"

"Abby! Abby, you okay?"

I've fallen in the dirt. The ground is spinning, and my skull is splitting open.

"Abby?"

I'm on my knees, gripping my head. My knee hurts where I scraped it on the ground. Ariel and the others are leaning over me. Alicia is with them.

Frog Monster is gone.

"Stay down," Ariel warns. "Catch your breath."

I look around at the running club members, terror fading—embarrassment taking its place.

"I'm okay." I climb to my feet. "Are you okay, Alicia?"

She smiles. "Of course. You're the one who fell."

Ariel offers to walk me up to the infirmary, but my knee's not bleeding and I tell him I'm fine. I don't want anyone around me right now. The club continues their run while I head up to the locker room.

My knee stings in the shower, but it's the psychic wound that's bothering me. I don't know what that vision was supposed to be telling me, but I know it can't be good.

Something terrible is going to happen.

After getting dressed, I head out to my car—skipping the after-run social hour. It's night by the time I get back to Harmony Springs.

♒

Terror.

I'm running through the woods near Bliss Spring. At times I catch glimpses of the blue water, shining in the dark. Otherwise, the night is pitch-black. I scrape my arms, pushing through low hanging branches.

Something is chasing me.

Vaguely, this reminds me of my nightmares from last year, when a creature pursued me through these woods and I ended up jumping into the bayou and drowning. But this time it's not some shadow creature from the astral plane after me. It's a crazy man with a knife.

I'm trying to reach the clearing, the circle with the altar. I know I'll be safe there. But I can't find it in the dark. I'm not sure I'm running in the right direction.

Footsteps slither behind me. He's getting closer. I'm losing my breath and can't run anymore.

In blind panic I slam into a tree, cracking my forehead. Turning, dazed, I slump against the rough bark. Through glazed eyes I see him, stalking toward me—slowly now because he knows I'm caught. He's a tall gawky young man wearing jeans and a T-shirt. His hair is pale blond and his pupils are shining gold. He smiles with delight as he raises the knife and plunges it into my chest.

I wake up, flat on my back in bed, shuddering.

I don't sleep much the rest of the night.

12. You cannot carry all the sorrows of the world

24 days before

I finally get back to sleep around dawn. If Grandma ever knocks on my door, I don't hear it, and she lets me sleep in. By the time I stagger downstairs, she's already gone to the shop. She's left me a note saying there's cooked oatmeal in the fridge. I just gulp down a cup of coffee, get dressed, and drive into town.

I can't shake the nightmare. Yesterday, I sensed something terrible was going to happen.

Now I know it *has* happened. I just don't know what or where.

That is until I park Veronica in front of the antique shop and pull out my phone. There's a text from Molly asking if I've heard the news. Then another, saying she's here for me if I want to talk. A feeling of doom squeezes the back of my throat.

I start to text Molly, but instead open my email. There's a message on my Claremont student account, from the college president. The phone shakes in my hand as I read it.

Last night, a student was murdered on campus, stabbed to death. Her body was found in the woods near the Bioscience building. Her name was Alicia Morrison.

Alicia from the running club.

Who I saw devoured by the frog monster.

I drop the phone in my lap and stare into space.

I don't know how long I've been sitting there when someone taps on the car window. Grandma talking in a loud, worried voice, asking if I'm all right.

I realize I haven't shut off the motor. I do it now, pull the key from the ignition, then gaze at the key in my hand.

I'm frozen.

"Abby!" Grandma is tapping again. "What's wrong, honey?"

≈

Later.

I'm sitting behind the counter in the antique shop. Grandma's with me, and so is Kevin. They're talking to me in slow, calm voices, staring at me with deep concern.

I've been away, my mind withdrawn to some alternate plane, trying to escape the pain.

And the guilt.

"It's my fault," I whisper. "I should have been able to stop this."

Grandma and Kevin exchange a look.

Kevin says, "Abby, there is no way this is your fault."

"Of course not, sweetie." Grandma hugs me.

I lean on her and sob uncontrollably.

When all the tears are gone, I feel numb inside. No longer terrified. The worst has already happened. I tell Grandma and Kevin about the vision I had yesterday, seeing Alicia devoured by the giant frog.

They exchange that look again.

"You had a premonition," Grandma tells me. "It's horrible, and it's horrible what happened to your friend. I don't know what I can say to comfort you at a time like this. But you mustn't feel it's your fault."

"Maybe I should have warned her. But of what? It would have sounded crazy."

Kevin puts his hand on my wrist. "You had a vision, Abby. But you didn't have enough information to act on it. Or the power to stop what happened. I understand how you feel. But there's a lesson in the Circle of Harmony that says 'you cannot carry all the sorrows of the world.' A true magician is prone to see many things. Sometimes that can include terrible evil. You cannot let yourself be crushed by it—not if you want to keep any hope of doing good."

As he speaks, a current of energy moves from his palm up my arm. "We haven't been able to figure this out yet. But Violet and Kat and I will do all we can to help you, I swear it."

I stare at him and then at Grandma. Their warmth is starting to thaw the ice inside me. I realize Kevin is right, I failed to save Alicia, but the evil is still out there.

I might be able to save someone else.

If I can keep my head in the game.

♒

Satisfied that I've calmed down, Grandma reopens the shop—which I now realize she closed—and Kevin goes back to the bookstore.

My phone is lying on the glass counter. I pick it up and finish reading the president's email. Extra security is being instituted on campus. Extra guards will be patrolling at night. Students are asked to carry their IDs at all times. Plans for a memorial service will be announced later. The message ends with the president's plea that all students, faculty, and staff be careful and watch out for each other.

I wish I'd done a better job of watching out for Alicia.

I search the news and find two reports of the murder, which I force myself to read. Alicia was working late in the Biology lab and was last seen leaving the building around 10 p.m. The police believe she was attacked either in the parking lot or on the path that runs along the woods. She died of multiple stab wounds to the chest and abdomen. Police sources say no suspects have been identified at this early stage of the investigation.

The second report is basically the same. As I'm hunting for more information, I hear the shop door open. Molly comes in. Grandma's at the front, sorting some merchandise, and they share a few whispered words, both of them casting their eyes back at me. Molly walks toward me, her expression grim.

"Abby, I am so sorry. You knew the girl?"

"It's worse than that."

I gesture for her to follow me to the back room. The place is cluttered with dusty boxes, shelves, filing cabinets. We sit on a couch near the back door. I tell Molly about the running club and the vision I had of Alicia being devoured.

Her jaw falls open. "Oh my god. That is so horrible ... But it fits with what I found out this morning."

"What do you mean?"

"The picture that was found beside the body."

"What?"

"It didn't make it into the news stories. You know, police don't release a lot of details in an investigation like this. So I asked my dad if he had received any bulletins on the case. He let me read what they'd gotten—with the understanding that I won't post it, of course. Anyway, there was a printout found next to the body, a picture downloaded from the internet, a cartoon of a man with the head of a frog."

"Ranae Virum."

"Yeah." Molly has plucked out her phone and is tapping on the screen. She enlarges a photo and shows it to me—an image of the page found beside the body, a drawing of a frog-faced man with bulging eyes. Beside the figure is his name, printed in a red font like dripping blood.

"Ranae Virum."

I hand back the phone, feeling sick to my stomach.

"Abby, you okay?"

"No. Not okay."

"Oh, Abby. I am so sorry. I shouldn't have shown you this."

Next thing I know I'm in Molly's arms, crying on her shoulder, trembling uncontrollably.

The frog monster is not just a meme expressing hate on the internet, not just an evil spirit haunting me. He's slithered into the minds of people, preyed on their fears, loneliness, hate, eaten up their humanity. Now he's turned at least one of them into a murderer.

And Alicia is dead.

It's the duty of all true magicians to oppose evil. And I have a special charge from Lebab to fight this thing. But I'm just a kid. I've had *one day* of college! Violet and Kevin keep saying how talented I am, how gifted. But they're as clueless about this as I am.

It's strong and growing stronger.

What am I going to do?

♒

As soon as I feel able to drive, I tell Grandma I'm heading back home. She looks worried, reluctant to let me go. But I manage to convince her I've calmed down enough, and just need time alone.

As I drive through town, I think about Harmony Springs and everything it has meant to me—my childhood home, the place where I discovered magic, the place I became a grownup. And I realize something for the first time: I wanted to come back here not only because of Grandma and Molly and Ray-Ray, but because this place felt *safe*. The sleepy little town with its Victorian buildings and hopelessly beautiful springs. Despite all the terrors I faced here last summer, or maybe because of them, at some unconscious level I believed that living here would keep me safe from the huge and terrible world.

But that was just a fantasy, after all.

Because now the huge, terrible world has come looking for me.

Back at the house, I go immediately up to my room. I light a candle, take out my wand, and trace a circle of protection. I'm intending to summon Annie Renshaw, or Inanna, or maybe even Lebab. I need some heavy help here.

The summoning turns out to be unnecessary. I start with the Daily Ablution, growing calmer as I rise from spring to spring. When I reach the center of Bliss, I fall into a deep trance.

What I see is not the Fountain of Bliss I usually envision. Instead, I'm standing on water—a fast-flowing stream of the same crystal-clear water that flows through the springs. There are no shores, only boulders and rapids and waterfalls everywhere, tumbling in all directions.

Lebab stands before me, formed of that same water. "Open your spirit to accept the strength of harmony," he tells me.

I shut my eyes and let the waters flow into me and through me. They feel wonderful, cleansing. For a while, I forget everything except the sensation of calm and peace.

When I open my eyes, we're still standing on the rushing water. But even in this impossibly wonderful place, the pain and despair come rising back.

The evil is real. Something I cannot escape. Something I have to deal with.

"What can I do?" I stare at Lebab, his watery face without eyes.

"What a true magician must always do—the best you can."

"But this thing is too big. Bigger than me or even you, bigger than Harmony Springs. It is infecting the whole world."

"Courage, Fighting Eagle. You are not called to cure the evils of the whole world, only your small portion of it. Look at the waters. What do you see?"

Following his gesture, I gaze down at the stream gushing under my feet. The current flows violently, spilling from all directions, crashing in waves and spinning in whirlpools.

"Now watch." Lebab points and a single drop falls from his fingertip. It splashes below and sends out a ripple. The surface around us grows calm with the spreading wave.

"You see? One tiny action can have untold effects."

That all sounds nice, but ... "What if I fail?"

"Do you not remember the lesson of Bliss?"

Yes. I learned that one last summer at my moment of crisis. *Do your best and let go of the results.* By releasing all hope and fear about the results, you can potentially place yourself between the pillars of light and dark, where the Universe flows into manifestation—the seat of the highest magic.

"Go, Fighting Eagle," Lebab says, "and do what your spirit calls you to do."

13. I would be careful if I were you

Coming out of the trance, I feel centered and full of energy. I fix some lunch, then decide to drive back into town. I sit in the back of Grandma's shop and spend the rest of the day online.

Even though I've been getting alerts about Ranae Virum, I haven't been diligent about following them up. And there's plenty of older content about him that I never looked into—because I was so disgusted I couldn't face it.

Now, I have to face it.

So I wade through the muck, stories, posts, comics, the products of creepy and disturbed minds. Ranae Virum champions their viewpoints, which (depending on which splinter group we're talking about) is anti-minorities, anti-immigration, anti-government, anti-LGBT people, anti-Feminism. Often some crazy combination of all of the above. The authors tell outrageous stories and make up facts that are clearly untrue. When called out on their distortions and lies, they shirk off responsibility by claiming that it's satire. No one's supposed to take it seriously.

Tell that to my friend who was murdered.

I find out something else interesting. In several places, the frog is referred to as an 'egregore.' Researching the term leads me to some occult sites. I learn that an *egregore* is a 'thought-form' created by two or more people. This fits with what Annie Renshaw told me and Kevin confirmed. Egregores can become conscious entities, especially if enough minds are engaged or if the people holding the thoughts are powerful enough. Annie perceived that a magician was behind Ranae Virum, raising and directing his power—the Gold Armor Guy from my dreams and visions.

Of course, whether he's directed by magic or not, here in the digital age Ranae Virum the cartoon frog, the *egregore*, has a vast number of minds feeding him energy—which must make his power enormous.

How can I find the power to stop him?

♒

23 days before

Next day I have lunch with Molly, and we compare notes. She's been spending her free time in the library, hunting through old journals and newspaper articles on microfiche, trying to track down the identity of Frater Statera.

So far, she's found nothing. Also, she's seen no new police bulletins on the murder investigation. She does tell me that Ray-Ray was asking about how I was doing. He's offered to drive to campus with me tomorrow if I like and to stay as late as necessary so he can drive me home.

"That's really sweet of him," I tell her. "But it's not necessary. I'll be okay."

I'm touched by the offer, but don't feel right about accepting. Too many other feelings would come up.

Anyway, it kind of becomes a moot point.

Because, later that day, I learn they've arrested a suspect in Alicia's murder. I scroll through the news story on my phone. The guy's name is Lester Tobias, 23-years-old, a resident of the town of Murdock, but not a student at the college. His only connection with Claremont State is his participation in one of the student groups—the Realm of Valor.

The skin on the back of my neck tingles. I remember someone telling me on orientation day that the LARPing society, the Realm of Valor, supposedly had associations with extremist groups.

I look at the suspect's picture. Thankfully, I don't know the guy. Because his creepy, vacant stare makes me cringe.

♒

Searching for a way to combat the frog egregore, my mind circles back to the sigils. Lebab told me they could summon power to banish evil spirits from the world. The sigil of Inanna that I found is "one of eight." All along, I've assumed I needed to find the other seven.

But maybe the one I have can unlock *some* of the power. It might even point me to the rest of the set. Okay, I admit I don't know what I'm doing here, and it could be dangerous. But if there's even a remote chance, I decide I have to try.

So that night, after performing the Ablution exercise, I light a candle and set it down on the woven rug. I take the image of the sigil that I photographed and trace it on a sheet of drawing paper. Eight tiny stars are arranged in a circle. If you drew lines along the outer edges, the figure would form an octagon. But the lines of the sigil crisscross, making triangles. When I finish the sketch, I have a pretty good approximation of the image drawn by Frater Statera a century ago.

I set the paper before the candle and stare at it, letting my thoughts relax. Focusing on the little stars, I recall the image of Inanna from the mythology book. Above her shoulder shines an eight-pointed star, said to depict the planet Venus—the morning star and evening star. Then I realize that this sigil itself is a star, just not centered. Instead, it is pointed in a specific direction.

To cast power.

Power.

I've slipped into trance, and now the power of Inanna that I remember from two nights ago is awakening. It races like tiny fires through my veins. With power like this, I think I could short-circuit the egregore, maybe banish him from the world.

"I would be careful if I were you." The voice is deep and loud in my brain. My body jumps, my hands flying up to protect my face.

My heart is pounding, faster and faster. Pain grows inside my ribcage, like my chest is ready to explode.

Too much power.

The force is out of balance. I need to release it. The pain sharpens to an agony.

I crawl onto my hands and knees, place my forehead on the floor. Taking long deep breaths, I gradually manage to relax my body.

One sigil by itself won't be enough. That thought is now crushingly obvious. I will need them all. Otherwise, the power goes out of control.

Suddenly, I remember the voice that told me to be careful. Was that a warning from Frater Statera?

Or was it Gold Armor Guy, the magician I suspect is directing the egregore, warning me off his turf?

14. I'm talking about magic, *real* magic

22 days before

Friday at noon, I attend the memorial service for Alicia. About three hundred people are gathered in the main quadrangle at Claremont State. They stand on the sidewalks, on the shelves of the concrete planters, on the steps of the red brick buildings that enclose the area on three sides. The fourth side is open to a lawn that slopes down to the campus pond—where the waters lie still and murky under a blazing blue sky.

I'm perched at the edge of the crowd, in the shade of the law building colonnade. At the front of the quadrangle, the college chaplain stands on the steps of the administration building and leads a prayer. Our college president, Dr. Wilder, makes a short speech, expressing the grief of the community. He states his gratitude to the police, who as we all know, have arrested a suspect. He pleads with students to remain calm and respectful with each other and to maintain awareness of campus security. He finishes by inviting some of Alicia's teachers and friends to say a few words.

As the service goes on, I glance around at the crowd—students, faculty, staff members. Security guards and a few police officers stand at the edges. An unreal shock and sadness hang over everyone. I've been part of this school for less than two weeks, but I feel the emotions deep in my bones. I am part of this community.

But I am also different. Because I am not just a student here, I'm a true magician.

That makes me responsible for trying to solve this evil mess.

My self-absorbed reflections are disrupted when Ariel Henriquez is announced as the next speaker. He talks about Alicia as a founding member of the running club, how she always was kind and encouraging to everyone. His voice catches as he says how much she was loved and will be missed.

Sniffling, I watch Ariel hand over the mic to a short, stout guy with nerdy glasses who looks vaguely familiar. He introduces himself as Wendell Spriggs, and I remember him—Orientation Day, the guy from the LARPing group.

As soon as he mentions the Realm of Valor, people boo. Angry shouts roll through the crowd. President Wilder waves his arms for quiet, but the uproar grows louder. Wendell's voice cracks as he yells, claiming that his group is not to blame, they have nothing to do with hating people.

But the crowd's not buying it. People are screaming horrible things. Security guards move at the front of the steps. Wendell shouts back: "I'm sorry! It's not our fault." Finally, Dr. Wilder takes the microphone away from him and pleads in a loud voice for everyone to calm down.

The rage that swept over the crowd is horrible. *Unreasoning*. It came out of nowhere. And even as the roar subsides I feel the rage and hate washing back at me, stabbing into my heart.

Like the steel knife in my nightmare.

Part of my stunned brain is thinking, *it is the same*. The knife in the dream, the violence of the crowd's mood. On the mental plane, they're both just energy—the same hateful energy that killed Alicia.

I can't bear looking at it anymore. I jerk my head away and glance down the lawn to the pond. In the sky above the water, disembodied golden eyes are watching.

As the memorial service ends and the crowd disperses, I'm sitting on the steps of the law building, trying to calm myself. People walk past but I ignore them.

Until one of them says my name.

"Hello, Abby." Ariel peers down at me, a somber look on his face.

I blink at him. The horror is still with me, but settling. Aside from that, I feel frosty cold and numb.

He sits down next to me. "You doing okay?"

I almost laugh. I have no idea what to say. Then, along with the ice and the lingering fear, another feeling emerges.

Attraction.

I know. I'm crazy and weird to even *think* about feeling that at a time like this. But he is so nice and kind. And, yes, good-looking.

He's staring at me in a searching kind of way, trying to decide something. Then his face squeezes up and he says, "I'm glad I ran into you. I've been thinking about what happened the other day when you fell. How's the knee, by the way? All right?"

"Yeah, fine."

"Good. But, the other day, when you fell. Did you *see* anything strange?"

Only a monstrous white frog catching Alicia with his tongue and swallowing her. "What do you mean, Ariel?"

Again, he's struggling to choose words. "It's just that, when we picked you up, the first thing you did was ask Alicia if *she* was okay."

I have no idea how to handle this. "I-I don't know why I said that."

"Oh." He looks disappointed. "Listen, I don't have anything till 3:30. Would you like to grab some lunch?"

I'm a bit apprehensive about where this might lead.

But I *do* need to eat lunch.

Twenty minutes later, we walk into a Cuban restaurant in downtown Murdock. It has tall storefront windows and a black-and-white linoleum floor. The open kitchen stands behind a curved lunch counter with bolted-in stools. At this hour the place is crowded, noisy with clattering dishes, loud talking, and laughter. The warm air is fragrant with grilling meats and spices.

Ariel is apparently a regular. The guy behind the register gives a big smile and says something in Spanish as he waves us in. We grab a booth near the back. A waitress walks over and hands us menus. Her name, stitched on her uniform, is Carmella. She looks me over and then grins at Ariel suggestively.

I am feeling more and more confused.

The menu is all in Spanish, and I turn up my hands, baffled. Ariel smiles and suggests the chicken with rice and fried plantains. I just nod. After Carmella walks off, Ariel turns serious. He speaks in a quiet voice so no one else can hear.

"I don't know, Abby. After what happened to Alicia I kept flashing back to your asking her if she was okay. I just had this sense that there was something to it."

He stares at me with those piercing eyes, and I wonder if he knows something. And I wonder if I should trust him with any of it. If he was a spirit I met on the astral plane, I would just challenge him: *What is your name, spirit?* But that won't work here.

"Something, like what?" I ask.

He sighs, shows me his palms, fingers extended. "You'll probably think I'm crazy. If you do, at least know I am harmless in my craziness."

His look is so earnest, it melts my heart. "I trust you, Ariel." I hadn't meant to say that, but as soon as I do, I know it's true.

His look goes all tender. "Thank you, Abby. So, let me put it this way, are you ever prone to intuitions—or premonitions?"

Well, if I trust him, I trust him. "Yeah. Definitely."

"And when you fell on our run, did you maybe sense something—something about Alicia?"

Oh, boy. "Yes. I did. But if I told you, you would think that I'm the crazy one."

He laughs. "Okay. I will keep your crazy secrets if you'll keep mine."

Currents of energy flash between my head and my heart. This is getting too intimate. I shouldn't let it happen. But I *want* it to happen—to be able to share this madness with someone else. And his eyes are so gentle.

"All right," I tell him. "You go first."

"Fair enough." He pauses, smiling, looking down at his hands. His voice is quiet and serious. "Abby, I practice magic. Not stage magic, *real* magic. What is called, *Postmodern* Magic. I know how insane this sounds to most people. But believe me: it is real."

Oh. My. God. "Ariel, I am not most people."

"Yes. I believe that about you. I sense it very strongly. So, there is a group on campus that I study with. I've only been practicing a little over a year, but one of the things that magic does is amplify your psychic senses. And that is why, when you took your fall and asked if Alicia was okay ... I sensed that you had *seen* something and that something bad was going to happen."

He spreads his hands. "So that is my crazy secret. What's yours?"

As I'm trying to come up with an answer, our food arrives. We're both silent as Carmella sets down the plates. She asks Ariel in Spanish if we need anything else, and he smiles, shaking his head.

By the time she's gone, I've managed to frame my reply. I won't tell him about the Circle of Harmony. I've sworn an oath to keep that secret. Besides, there's plenty I can disclose that's more in answer to his question.

"You are right. I did see something when I fell. I am excessively prone to seeing things—things that are beyond normal. You might call them visions. I know how crazy this sounds, but when I fell on the path, I saw a giant frog, and I saw it eat Alicia."

Ariel's expression shows astonishment and horror, but also recognition. "You saw the *egregore*?"

"You know about the egregore?"

"Of course. It's all on the internet. So you—you know what it is?"

"Some. I've been reading about it."

"It started as a meme," Ariel says. "But I suspect there are people working magic to give it more power. That's one of the projects our group is looking into—to see if we can counteract its influence."

Whoa! I want to blurt out that I'm trying to work on that too. But again, I hesitate. How should I explain that?

We're both staring at our untouched food.

"Abby," he says, "I think that you not only have psychic ability but potentially a lot of power. Would you consider joining our magic study group?"

♒

I pick up my fork. Mustn't let the food grow cold. "Well, what would that involve? What do you do, exactly?"

That grin again. He picks up his sandwich and takes a big bite. He holds up an index finger, signaling me to wait while he chews. I shovel some chicken and rice into my mouth. It tastes delicious.

"So," Ariel says between mouthfuls. "Like I said, we study Postmodern Magic. There is a whole body of knowledge on the internet about it. But you have to be careful. Some of it is pretty strange. When you're dealing with magic, people make outrageous claims."

"Right. So how do you judge?" The Circle of Harmony tells us to judge by listening first to the heart, then analyzing with the mind, always guided by whether a statement or course of action is in harmony with the Five Principles.

"By experiment," Ariel says, his mouth full. He swallows and takes a sip of his Coke. "It's purely scientific. We start with the assumption that all beliefs should be questioned. Then, we test."

"How do you test?"

"Various ways. Basically, we formulate an intention, raise psychic energy, shape it to our intention, and cast it out into the Universe. Then we note and record the results. But I'm getting into the deep end of things now." He picks up his sandwich and takes another bite.

I watch him a moment, then busy myself with my lunch. My feelings are racing all over the place. I'm intrigued, apprehensive, blindly afraid. But also lured by this weird sense of comfort and longing. To find a group of people my age who do magic, who understand what I deal with. Maybe this is fate, the reason I ended up at Claremont State.

Take a breath, Abby. Don't go jumping off the dock. There is way too much I don't know here.

Ariel seems to read the tension in my shoulders. "I hope I didn't freak you out."

"No. Not at all. I can honestly say I'm intrigued."

"Good. Like I said, I got into the deep end there. We don't actually practice magic in our group, except for very basic energy work, to clear our minds and build up psychic power. We mostly do readings and then discuss what we've read."

Well, that sounds safe enough. I bite into a plantain and smile at the taste—scrumptious.

Ariel looks delighted. "Ever tasted plantains before?"

"Hmm." I shake my head. "Wonderful."

"So glad you like your lunch." He gestures around the café, as if he owns the place and is pleased I liked it.

"They seem to know you here."

"Oh yes. These are my people. Well, I am from Miami, but Cubans have a certain vibe. In sympathy with each other. You understand?"

"I can see it. That must be nice."

"So tell me about you. How long have you been having psychic visions?"

I'm not at all shy about telling him, revealing these parts of myself. We've established a rapport, and I sense it is something deep, heart to heart. I explain how I started having hallucinations during puberty, goblins and monsters from video games come to life. That I saw a therapist and went on meds, and that the creatures went away for a while. Then, my junior year in high school, things got really bad again. I don't tell him about discovering the Circle of Harmony last summer, and learning they were not hallucinations, but real. Instead, I say that I started doing meditation and "spiritual work," and that's given me a better handle on coping with it.

Maybe he senses my reluctance, but he doesn't press me for more details. "I knew when we met you were an unusual person. But I had no idea how unusual."

I give a small laugh. "I've learned to keep it under wraps."

He nods thoughtfully. "I get that. So, what do you think about coming to our study group?"

"Well, I am honestly very tempted. But I am also cautious. I'll need to think about it."

"I understand. I'll send you some links where you can read about Postmodern Magic. Then, if you have questions, you can text me or call me, okay?"

♒

When we've finished eating, Ariel insists on paying the check. I tell him that's not necessary, but he says it's been his pleasure. This makes me wonder if, along with our examination of our occult histories, this has also been, like a date. Is he attracted to me as much as I am to him?

I usually have pretty good radar for this, but with him it's hard to tell. Maybe it's a cultural difference, or maybe he's a more guarded person. *Or, maybe his magical training makes him harder to read.*

On the walk back to campus he asks me about growing up in New Jersey and how it compares to Florida. I explain how I lived in Harmony Springs until I was seven, and that's why I returned. I feel at home there. I even confess that I feel it's my spiritual home.

Ariel seems to understand that too. His grandparents and many of their neighbors in Miami came from Cuba. His parents were born here, but grew up with a feeling of exile, like Cuba was their lost spiritual home.

"Most people of my generation see it differently," he says. "We definitely consider ourselves Americans. And why shouldn't we? You know, there were Spaniards in Florida long before the Anglos came here."

"Sure, we learned that in history."

"Did you also learn that some Cubans are directly descended from the original settlers of St. Augustine?"

"No, I didn't know that."

He grins. "Sorry, I didn't mean to go into lecture mode."

"That's okay. Really."

We've stopped on the walkway outside the student center.

"I need to get to class," he says. "Will you be around later for running club."

"Not today. This has all been pretty emotional for me. I'm going to head home, but I'll be back on Tuesday."

He nods and reaches down to take my hand. Not in a handshake way, but in a *holding my hand* way.

"Thank you for having lunch with me, Abby. I really enjoyed it."

"Oh, me too." Right now, I am enjoying his holding my hand.

"I will send you those links. Let me know what questions you have."

"Right." Staring into his eyes, I smile and squeeze his hand.

"I hope you will join the study group," he says. "But whatever you decide on that, I hope we'll be friends. Good friends."

Walking toward my car, I reflect on everything that's happened this week. I could say my feelings are in chaos.

But that wouldn't begin to cover it.

The horror of what happened to Alicia, the terror that it could happen to me or any of us, the creepy, nasty presence of Ranae Virum haunting me, haunting the world. On top of all that, the dreadful weight of *responsibility*, that somehow I have to solve this horror.

All that's on one side.

On the other side, there's the power of Inanna—I only have to picture her in my mind to feel her presence, subtle and strong, like a promise. A promise that, whatever happens, I can handle this. There's my Grandma, who loves me unconditionally, and there's Violet and Kevin and Molly, all supporting me, trying to help in their different ways.

And now there's Ariel. Just thinking about him spreads a goofy smile over my face. Strong, soft-spoken Ariel with his warmth and gentleness. The way he held my hand ...

And he does magic. He and his friends are working on the same monster-challenge I am. Maybe we can solve it together. Maybe I won't have to feel so alone ...

Head down, staring at my feet on the sidewalk, I almost bump into someone.

We both look up, startled—two self-absorbed students who nearly crashed into each other.

I recognize him at once: Wendell, from the Realm of Valor.

"Sorry," he mutters and moves aside.

"No. My fault."

He looks so forlorn, and I think back with a shudder at how the crowd treated him. He hurries away, head bowed. But I call to him.

"Wendell. Hi, I'm Abby Renshaw. We met on orientation day."

He turns, squints at me. "Oh. Sure, sure. Hi."

He turns to go. I'm usually not so forward, but I feel compelled to talk with him.

"Listen. I saw how the crowd at the memorial treated you. I am so sorry."

His shoulders droop, and he shakes his head. "They wouldn't listen. I thought if I explained ..."

Maybe it's Inanna moving me. I step toward him. "I'll listen."

The look that comes over his face is so pitiable. "We're really not to blame. We're just a club, not a hate group. Yeah, some dudes post in the online forums about "arming for culture wars" and crap like that. But mostly they get flamed and called idiots. The Realm of Valor's not about that. We're just geeks who enjoy games and role-playing."

"I understand," I tell him. "I guess you got the blame hung on you—guilt by association."

"Exactly. Well, it's all over now. We're disbanding the chapter. We've gotten hateful messages this week, even death threats. My speaking at the memorial was a last effort to try to get people to understand ..." He blinks like he's suddenly realized he's even telling this to someone. "Thanks for listening."

He walks away, shoulders hunched.

Another victim.

15. Some things I need to study

So, now.

In addition to Business and Law I, the mystery of Frater Statera and his lost sigils, the mythology of the Goddess Inanna, and the identity of the gold-armored magician, I have a new subject to investigate.

Postmodern Magic.

Saturday and Sunday I spend hours online, using the wifi at Springs of Coffee and my phone as a hotspot in the back room of Grandma's shop. I peruse all the sites and forums that Ariel linked me up with. Of course, in the way of research, this leads me to many more sites, articles, and discussion groups.

The practice of Postmodern Magic is just as Ariel described: devise an intent, raise energy, cast the energy to actualize the intent. All of this happens in a relaxed and focused state of mind.

All magic occurs in the mind. That's a tenet of the Circle of Harmony, of course. And the basic blueprint for performing magic is much the same. In the Circle, we tend to use chants to raise energy. And we often encounter spirits. Postmodern Magic views spirits and entities as thought-forms, and there's a lot of debate as to whether they exist outside the mind of the magician—or the collective mind or "mass consciousness."

So there are definitely differences between the two schools of magic.

What seems like the biggest difference is the lack of any *guidance*. Postmodern Magic (PMM) offers nothing like the Five Principles—Love, Endurance, Balance, Amity, and Bliss—which are meant to form the basis of everything we do in the Circle of Harmony. PMM seems to have no doctrine at all, no moral code.

Anything and everything is okay to try.

I text Ariel and ask him about this: "How do you decide what's okay to try?"

Him: "You experiment and see what works."

Me: "I get that. But what about right and wrong? Is it okay to cast energy to hurt someone?"

Him: "Postmodern Magic is neutral on morality. Purely scientific."

Him again: "Of course, a good person would not use magic to hurt someone. Someone innocent. But the magic itself is amoral."

Him again: "The morality comes from yourself. Not imposed by the magic. Does that make sense?"

Me: "I guess so."

It makes sense. But it leaves an uneasy sensation in the pit of my stomach—a pressure that builds into a gnawing doubt.

I'd like to discuss this with Violet or Kevin, but I already know what they would say. True Magic has a purpose, to bring harmony into your spirit and into the world. The Five Principles are designed to keep you from straying from that path. It's all too easy and too tempting to follow power for its own sake.

This is all right there in the *Manifesto*, the first document an aspiring true magician ever sees. I re-read the copy that I have scanned on my tablet:

> And it was shown how the first letters of the Five Names of the Springs spell the name LEBAB, who is the True Spirit of the Springs. And it was further shown how the letters reversed spell BABEL, for the evil and confusion that inevitably comes to those who seek Occult knowledge without pure intent and strict adherence to the Principles.

But Ariel is a good person. I test that assumption—by listening with my heart and judging with my head—and he comes up pure every time. And I'm strongly drawn to a lot of what I'm reading about his kind of magic—and even more strongly drawn to working with him and his study group. I sense maybe they can give me a whole different angle on Ranae Virum, find some chinks in his armor.

Should I risk dipping my toe into Postmodern Magic? Or will that inevitably lead me to "evil and confusion?"

♒

20 days before

My gut fills up with this dilemma until it has to spill out. Sunday night, I bring it up with Grandma as we're drinking our bedtime tea. We're in the living room with the windows open. A cool breeze lifts the white curtains, moving them like lazy ghosts.

I take the plunge and explain it to her: my lunch with Ariel and Postmodern Magic, how that touched on all the other threads of mystery I'm trying to unravel. Grandma listens, eyes going wide at some points, nodding solemnly at others. Finally, she puts down her teacup.

"First, I'm really glad you're not blaming yourself any longer for what happened with your friend at the college."

"I know it's not my fault. But I still have to think about how I can stop this egregore thing. I mean, that's our duty as true magicians, to oppose evil, right?"

"Yes. But it's not all up to any one of us."

"Which brings me back to Ariel's Postmodern Magic group and whether I should consider working with them. If there's a team out there that can help me, it might make things a lot easier."

Grandma shows a little frown, but her head nods. "I see that. And I think you are right about what Violet would say. She's very strict about magical practices conforming with Circle principles. And of course, there's good reason for thinking that way. Power is power. Too much of it can be dangerous."

I stare down at my empty teacup. "I know."

Grandma sighs and pats my knee. "I can't tell you what to do, sweetie. I can only tell you what I think I would do. If it were me, and this boy Ariel appeared as solid and good as he does to you, I would give him a chance, try working with him."

I look at her with surprise. She holds up her index finger. "Going slowly. One step at a time, and testing everything with my heart and my mind along the way. You have good judgment, Abby. I think you need to trust it."

"Wow." *Up goes my self-esteem.* "Thank you for that. I really appreciate the way you treat me like an adult, Grandma ..."

She laughs and reaches to pour more tea. "Sweetie, you *are* an adult. With all you've dealt with and everything you've shown yourself capable of? And still a month short of 18. I can honestly say you're more adult now than I was at 30."

I give Grandma a hug and head up to bed. After a shower and brushing my teeth, I put on boxers and a t-shirt and turn down my bed. But before turning out the lights I sit down to meditate. Besides Violet, I have one other mentor I can ask for advice.

I go through the Ablution exercise, moving from fountain to fountain in my mind. When I've envisioned the waters of Bliss flowing out of my head and washing down over my body, I call on the ghost of Annie Renshaw.

In my vision, we're standing again at the Fountain of Balance, two basins of silver and blue, water flowing back and forth. Annie approaches, wearing a long skirt and light summer blouse, her black hair loose under a straw bonnet. There's a strange sadness in her smile.

"Hello, Fighting Eagle."

"Thank you for coming to me, Annie. You know why I called you?"

"Yes." She gazes at the tumbling water. "You must understand that my vision into your world is limited. I can mostly see around the Springs and those who come here—primarily through you. So what I see is influenced by your mind and feelings."

I guess I had sensed something of that in the past, but never heard her put it quite that way. "That makes sense, I suppose."

Annie's eyes are wide and unfocused. "I can see you are drawn to Ariel. From what I can tell, his spirit is pure. But I must warn you, based on my own experience. When Otis and Maisie and I did magic in our time, we thought we were adhering to the Principles of Harmony. And yet we raised the creature called Raspis, with results you well know."

Raspis was the Shadow Man who appeared again in Harmony Springs last summer. He too was a thought-form—an egregore if you want to use that term. He was created by Annie and her two friends when they were in their late teens, over a hundred years ago. Somehow, he got out of control. He caused Annie's death, drove Otis to despair, made Maisie his slave.

"It is so easy to make mistakes," Annie says, "to wander all innocently from the path of your good intent." She faces me, her expression wistful and full of past pain. "I know the threat you face is grave, and that it is a threat to your whole world. But I must advise you to caution."

"So, stay away from the Postmodern Magic?"

Smiling, she shakes her head. "No. I think you must explore every path that may help you thwart the evil you face. Just be careful that *you* are not seduced by evil."

This is scaring me. "But how can I know that? How can I be sure?"

"Dear friend, it pains me to say, but you cannot be sure. Of course, you must listen in your heart and analyze in your mind. But in the end, you can only follow your convictions as best you can. That is a challenge we all face on the path."

I nod. As I might have expected, it all comes back to me.

Annie shocks me by reaching for hand. The touch is as warm as life. "I give you my blessings, Fighting Eagle. And my earnest prayers for your protection."

16. Two illustrious gentlemen have come to town

19 days before

Next morning, after parking Veronica on Main Street near the antique shop, I pull out my phone. Two texts from Molly in the past 15 minutes.

Molly: "I think I'm on to something."

Molly five minutes later: "Come over as soon as you can!"

I text her back: "Where are you?"

Molly: "Violet's house."

What the heck is she doing there on a Monday morning? I start to ask, then change my mind and just reply: "On my way."

I drive the half-mile from downtown to Violet's neighborhood where the streets are shaded by giant live oaks. Pulling into the driveway, I see that Kevin's car is absent. It figures he has already gone to the bookstore. I also notice that the side door of the garage is open.

As I climb out of my car, Molly opens the front door on the porch. "Hey, Abby! I found something you *have* to see!"

I grab my backpack and head up the walkway. "You found something here?"

"Yeah. Come on in."

We step into the tiny living room. Kevin and Violet's house is usually cluttered—books, papers, nick nacks, magical implements. But today the front room is beyond all past definitions of clutter—

cartons and boxes, stacks of old papers, and folders everywhere. The window AC is cranking, and the air is a mixture of frosty and moldy with hints of incense.

"Is Violet here?"

"She's in her magic room, doing her morning rites." Molly speaks softly. She sits down cross-legged amid the clutter on the rug and gestures for me to do likewise.

I sit beside her and whisper: "What are you even doing here?"

"I've been coming here a lot. Researching, remember?'

"Yeah, but—"

"Violet has *a lot* more stuff than we saw that first day in the garage. We've been working through it a little at a time. You remember: we talked about writing a book."

What I remember is Molly asking, and Violet seeming not very receptive to the idea. "I didn't know she had agreed."

"Oh." Molly laughs. "I can be pretty persistent. I promised to not disclose any magical secrets, just write about the people—the Founders and the second and third generations. It's *so* fascinating. People came from all over to study here. And not just the U.S.: Europe, Canada, South America. Spiritualism was really popular."

She is leaning over, shuffling through papers and old volumes piled on the carpet. "Here we go." She shows me a little book covered in tattered leather. Worn gold lettering on the front says, "Diary."

"This is one of *the best,*" Molly whispers as if she's comparing ice-cream flavors. "It's the journal of Clarissa Petersen—one of six volumes that we have. She recorded *everything*. I wouldn't be surprised if she later became a journalist or something." She opens the diary to a page she's marked with a slip of paper.

"Here we go: 'February 14, 1919. Two illustrious gentlemen have arrived from the north to rejoin our community. Good friends, they are staying together at the Hayward house. Both were initiated into C of H in past years ..."

"C of H—Circle of Harmony, right?"

"Yeah. *Good friends* might be code for *gay couple*. I'm not sure." Molly continues reading: " 'One of these handsome sirs is Emmanuel Lock of Baltimore. His companion is the refined Kurt Friedrich Gentzen, born in Berlin Germany and, like his friend, a graduate of Harvard.' "

Molly lowers the book. "You've heard of Emmanuel Lock, right?"

"No."

"Lock *Tower*? Down in Lake Avalon? He built it!"

"Vaguely..." I recall something about a weird tower in a small town south of Orlando—an off-the-beaten-track tourist destination.

"It's a famous Bell Tower, built on a hill in the middle of the state. Anyway, you can read about it online." She resumes reading: " 'These gentles will certainly brighten the social scene with their elegance and charm, as well as sharing their varied metaphysical and scholarly pursuits.'—Now get this." Molly gestures with her free hand. " 'These interests are known to include Atlantis, Hollow Earth theories, and the occult study of ancient Egyptian and Mesopotamian deities.' Get it? Your Lion Tamer Lady!"

"Right. Inanna, Mesopotamian goddess."

"Wait. There's more." She scans through some lines, turns a page. "In addition to Spiritualist Congregation, Messieurs Lock and Gentzen are known to be attending two advanced study groups: Sanskrit Language, and Sigilization.' "

Molly sets down the book with a triumphant thud, and gives me a *Don't you get it?* look.

I think I get it. The one Sigil of Inanna we have is dated May 4, 1919. "So, in 1919, these two dudes who studied Mythology and would have known about Inanna, were here in Harmony Springs working on sigil magic. So one of them might be Frater Statera."

"Highly probable! They were both initiates, so they would have had magical names. And because they were visitors, not permanent residents, that matches up with our not finding any mention of

Frater Statera in the other records." She spreads her arms to encompass the messy room. "And believe me, I've looked!"

"That's really good work, Molly." I pick up the diary and scan the pages. Instinct tells me we are on to something. "So the next question is, if one of them is our sigil maker, which one? And how can we find the other sigils?"

"Right," Molly says, "and the way to go about that is to dig up more on Lock and Gentzen. There's bound to be plenty of info on Emmanuel Lock, he's pretty famous. You can do some of that research online. I'll keep picking away here and also check the library."

I'm looking again at the diary. "What do you suppose Hollow Earth Theory is?"

Molly laughs. "No idea. But I bet it will make it into my book."

♒

A door opens and Violet comes out, looking rumpled and otherworldly. She's wearing a shift of purple tie-dye. Her long white hair hangs loose, streaked with red and blue in anticipation of the Fourth of July holiday, which is coming up in a few days.

"Hello, Abby." She rubs the back of her neck. "I thought I heard you out here."

I stand up and give her a hug. "Hope we didn't disturb you."

"No. Not at all. It's lovely to have you two in the house. So much youthful energy!" She holds me at arm's length and examines me, gazing into my soul in a way she has. "You are still very charged up!"

"Yeah. I've been building my strength."

"Well, it shows!" Suddenly her smile vanishes, her mouth turning down. "I was so sorry to hear about your friend at the college."

My voice catches. "Thank you."

"I know from Kevin and Molly that the murder is related to the visions you were having. I wish I could have given you more help. I *have* tried looking into it. But ... Well, I just haven't been able to see much—except that it all feels very powerful and very obscure." Violet sighs. "The truth is, since Midsummer I've been on new medication for my blood pressure. I'm afraid it's making me a bit fuzzy in the head."

This worries me. I know Violet's health has been up and down the past year. I try to reassure her. "It's okay, really. I think I'm making progress. Also, I hear you and Molly are writing a book."

"Yes." She smiles, glancing around at the stacks of papers. "Molly's given me a much-needed kick in the pants. You know, Kevin and I are getting on in years, and there is so much knowledge that will be lost if we don't preserve it ... Can I fix you something to eat. Cup of tea? We've got some nice banana bread."

"No thanks. I had breakfast not long ago."

"Well, come into the kitchen if you have a few minutes. You can tell me what you've been up to."

Molly and I sit at the table while Violet fixes herself tea and toast. Molly's brought the diary along and explains what she's found out about our two illustrious gentlemen.

"Oh, yes. Emmanuel Lock," Violet says. "I remember that he joined the Circle at one point. Not sure I've ever heard of the other man."

"Kurt Friedrich Gentzen," Molly says. "Do you know anything about the Hollow Earth Theory?"

"Oh, that!" Violet chuckles. "There was this theory that believed the Earth was hollow and a whole lost civilization lived on the inside. Science fiction, really. Occultists had some pretty weird ideas back then."

Molly and I glance at each other and break out laughing.

"Unlike now," Molly says. "I mean, to most people, it's all weird, right?"

"True enough." Violet sets butter and jam down on the table.

"So we have some clues," I explain to Violet. "Our next step is to try to figure out if either Lock or Gentzen is Frater Statera. Because I've *got* to find those other sigils."

I tell her about my attempt to use the first sigil—how the power ran wild, and I realized I needed them all if I was going to use them safely.

"That makes sense, from what I know of sigil magic," Violet says. She's sat down with her plate of toast and teacup. Without touching it she bolts up again. "Let me try a reading. I've got a feeling, with the three of us here to focus, I might get something."

She goes into the other room and comes back with her deck. She pushes her food aside on the table and passes me the cards. "You shuffle Abby. Formulate a question and speak it out loud. We'll all concentrate on it."

"Okay." I consider as I shuffle. "Who is Frater Statera, and where can we find his other sigils of Inanna?"

After I cut the deck, Violet lays out a Celtic Cross. As the cards come up, I see some familiar faces.

Strength, the woman with the red lion, is at the Crown. The crossing card is my old friend the *Knight of Wands*. He represents Gold Armor Guy who, in my visions, I believe represents one or more occultists allied with the egregore. The *Knight of Wands* is on top of the *King of Pentacles*. Could he be Frater Statera, his energy blocked by Gold Armor Guy?

In the immediate past is the *Ten of Swords*, a figure dead of stab wounds. That makes me shiver. In the future position is the *Page of Swords*. I tilt back. His face reminds me of Ariel. Is he a danger?

The outcome card is the *Tower Struck by Lightning*. I flash back to my dream of Inanna on Midsummer Night.

"What do you see, Violet?"

Pondering, she picks up the crossing card. "These are the two men you read about—Emmanuel Lock and uh—"

"Kurt Friedrich Gentzen," Molly supplies.

"Yes. I believe one of them is this Frater Statera. But I'm not sure which ..." She points to *Strength* at the crown position. "A great power is helping you, but her energy seems to be thwarted at the moment."

Inanna. I need to find the sigils to free her power. "Yes. That rings true."

She points at the Hopes and Fears and External Influences positions—more swords—and then at the *Tower* card. "It looks like you will find the answer, but not without struggle and—I hate to say it—danger." She leans back, looking very tired. "This is a very challenging situation, I'm afraid."

Not like I don't know that already. I point to the card I think is Ariel. "How do you read this one."

"Immediate Future..." Violet says. "A dynamic person. I get the feeling he might help you."

Well, that makes me happy.

"So, to summarize," Molly puts in. "We do think Frater Statera is either Lock or Gentzen. But which is still a mystery."

Violet and I both nod our heads.

"So we need to know more about both of these guys. I can definitely dig into that. But I have another idea. Maybe we could call them up and ask them?"

I've had a similar thought, but hesitated to suggest it. Violet looks puzzled.

"Don't you get it?" Molly says. "They used to do this around here all the time. Hold a séance!"

Violet's expression of puzzlement twists into a frown. "Oh, I don't know, dear. I attended a séance or two when I was a youngster. But that was a long time ago. They *can* be effective. But it takes a lot of energy to do it correctly, and often they yield doubtful results."

After kicking the idea around, we agree to exhaust all the other possibilities first—researching the lives of Lock and Gentzen, asking for guidance during meditation, more readings. Molly's disappointed—none of those sound as thrilling as her séance idea—but she agrees to stick with the research in hopes of uncovering more clues.

Since Emmanuel Lock is the more famous dude, Molly assigns me to study him, while she tackles the mysterious Gentzen. So, that afternoon in the back room of the antique shop, I hunt up Mr. Lock on my tablet. Molly's right: there's a lot about him on the internet. He was born in 1893, to a wealthy family in Baltimore. He got his degree at Harvard and worked for a while in the family investment business. But his real interests are described as "eclectic"—art, ancient civilizations, physics, and the occult. He spent a lot of time touring Cathedrals in Europe and archeological sites in the Middle East.

In 1922, Lock inherited a huge fortune. He promptly dissolved the family business and retired to Florida. A year later, work began on his famous tower, which was finished in 1928. Pictures of the tower are amazing—pink marble, stained glass, bronze doors, and weird carvings. In a way, it reminds me of the tower on the Tarot card and in my visions, except instead of dark and threatening, this building is light and full of energy—like a living spirit. The interior is equally bizarre: high vaulted ceilings, tile floors, spiral staircases of black iron. It looks like a fantastical palace or some elaborate hotel in a steampunk story.

I find a picture of Lock himself, and it's disturbingly familiar. He doesn't exactly *look* like Gold Armor Guy from my visions, but I feel this eerie similarity. I've assumed all along it was a living magician summoning and directing the frog monsters. Might it instead be a ghost?

Lock lived in the tower after it was finished, and became something of a recluse. In his last years, he supposedly became obsessed with studying electricity and physics. One story says that he believed he could tap limitless energy if he could perfect his experiments with gravity. Reading this, I wonder if these experiments might have had something to do with sigil magic.

Because what I need is to find the missing sigils. Nothing I'm learning about Lock is helping.

So that night, alone in my room, I take a different tack.

Last week, I tried summoning the ghost of Frater Statera—and got nowhere. But if Emanuel Lock *was* the Frater, maybe knowing his earthly name will boost my power for summoning him. And if he was *not* Frater Statera, I might be able to contact his ghost and find out if he knows anything about the sigils of Inanna.

I arrange the ritual, setting up the candle, incense, water cup, and empty bowl. I fetch my wand and dagger from the top drawer of the night table. On my phone, I call up the picture of Emmanuel Lock and stare at his face for a while. Then I page back to *The Formula for Calling and Binding Spirits.*

After tracing the circle and pentagrams, I light the candle and incense, pour the libation. Raising the wand and dagger, I call the elementals. When their presence is established beyond the ring of energy, I take a deep breath.

"To this protected circle, I call you, spirit of Emmanuel Lock, who lived for a time in Florida and visited the places near these Springs. I call you here that you may talk with me and help me."

Staring into the blue fire, I chant in a low and solemn tone.

By the waters, bright and deep,
I call thee spirit, from thy sleep.
By this fire, clear and bright,
I call thee forth into the light.

As the chant goes on and on, the energy beyond the circle brightens and shudders. A figure made of bluish light appears. I sense a presence, but it is weak, struggling.

"Spirit of Emmanuel Lock, I call you here, that we may speak."

Words come, faint and distant, more thoughts in my mind than sounds. "Hear ... you ... cannot."

"You cannot come to the circle? Why?"

"... Bound. By another."

I could try the rest of the chant, bind him to my will. But I'm sure that would be wrong. This spirit is desperate. *Suffering*.

"Can you say how you are bound? ... Can you tell me if you were Frater Statera, who drew the sigils of Inanna?"

At those words, the ghost-form shivers and fades. Just before it's gone, I get a distinct impression—a hiss of pain.

The energy humming through the room dies down. The circle of blue fire evaporates.

I sit alone in the silence.

17. My second line of inquiry

18 days before

Which brings me back to my other line of inquiry—Postmodern Magic.

Tuesday I have class and—as luck or fate would have it—the PMM group meets on Tuesday afternoons at 3 p.m.

"The best time during summer session, given all of our schedules," Ariel explains to me in a text. "Plus it was when we could reserve the meeting room."

The meeting room, believe it or not, is a small windowless conference room on the first floor of the library. Not exactly your secret underground vault. When I get there at 2:50, I am instantly confused. The room schedule hanging beside the door says "3 p.m.: Jerome Sedgwick Mindfulness Group."

The room is empty. I wait outside, wondering if I've stupidly come to the wrong place. Then Ariel shows up.

"This is a test." He laughs. "Are you here for the Sedgwick group?"

To which I cleverly reply by frowning in confusion.

He laughs again and waves me inside. "Sedgwick Mindfulness is our cover," he explains in a secretive voice. "We picked the most innocuous name we could think of, to discourage curiosity seekers and trolls."

"I guess that makes sense." I'm also not sure how the library would feel about letting space to a society devoted to the occult.

Three other students show up. First is a tall woman named Isabel with wavy brown hair. She's dressed in high-heeled sandals, slitted jeans, red lipstick. She has a confident attitude and, along with Ariel, seems a sort of group leader. Next is a slim guy named Jerome—"Not the famous Jerome Sedgwick," he jokes. Finally, there's a girl named Leyla, with short, red-dyed hair and dark eyebrows. Her fashion is Goth—or as Goth as you can comfortably be in central Florida in summer: black tank top and skirt, black nail polish. She smiles at me but mostly has eyes for Ariel.

When we're all seated at the table, Ariel closes the door. "I am very pleased to have Abby Renshaw join us today," he says. "Abby's a first-year student and also in running club with me. She's here to see what the group is about. With that in mind, why don't we go around the table and talk about our specific interests and how we got started?"

Ariel goes first. He tells us that he's been interested in metaphysics since age thirteen when he started to question the religious beliefs he was raised with. He had a few strange experiences that led him to read up on different spiritual systems. He was drawn to Postmodern Magic because it was "free of doctrine and bullshit, a completely scientific search for truth."

Isabel, who speaks next, has a lot of experience. She grew up in Puerto Rico and learned *Santeria*, a traditional form of witchcraft, from her mother and grandmother. After her family moved to Florida, she got involved in a Wiccan coven with other teenagers she met online. Later, she took up Postmodern Magic. I gather she follows all these paths simultaneously, which I think would drive me crazy.

But isn't that exactly what I'm contemplating?

Jerome goes next. He tells how he was introduced to a men's occult group by an older boyfriend when he was seventeen. He's more interested in the practice of magic than just study for its own sake.

That brings up one of my questions. "So do you actually practice as a group?" I ask. "I mean, *here* in this room?"

"We do an energy circle at every meeting," Isabel answers. "It's very basic. We have done a couple of rituals, but nothing very complex. The group is new, and the synergy is still coming together. Of course, if you join us, that will alter the group energy again."

Leyla goes next. She is less experienced than the others. She says she's always felt she was a witch but never had any training. This is the first time she's been in a group.

Now they're all looking at me. I'm expected to talk about my history. As we've gone around the room my mind has been racing, trying to figure out what to say, how much to reveal, how much to leave out. Now that the moment's here, I'm frightened.

Stupid. Why wasn't I better prepared for this?

I mumble about having hallucinations when I was twelve, and gradually coming to believe that they were actually visions. I say that I've read online about different magical traditions. That much is true, and I don't want to lie. But I also don't want to confess about being an initiate in the Circle of Harmony or any of my recent experiences. It doesn't feel safe. I end awkwardly by saying, "I'm mainly here to listen and learn."

Isabel fixes me with a piercing stare. She can tell I'm holding back. Ariel's expression might be a little disappointed but is mostly sympathetic. The others seem nonchalant, like I've said about what they expected.

Next, each person talks about the magical work they've done since the last meeting. Jerome is working on increasing his prosperity. Isabel has done a spell to heal a friend's mother. She says it's too early to know the results. Leyla has only done some reading. This leads to a discussion of the book everyone in the group has been studying, something called the *Grimoire of Marius Black*. I gather it is a basic text in Postmodern Magic. Ariel suggests I look it up. It's available free in an online archive, and he texts me the link.

When it's his turn, Ariel brings up the egregore. He reminds the group about Alicia's murder and the link to Ranae Virum. I gather they discussed this last week, and Ariel announced his intention to investigate the link psychically.

"I probed the thought-form every night in a meditative state," he says. "I definitely sensed its presence around the college. Whether this is a lingering effect from the murder or whether the malevolent force is still present, I'm not sure."

"What do you see as a next step?" Isabel asks.

"I will keep probing. I've also begun composing a ritual to diffuse the entity's influence. I think that might make a good project for the group."

I find this idea both intriguing and scary. Jerome and Leyla seem open to trying it, but Isabel is frowning.

"I'm not sure the group is ready for something that advanced," she says. "It could be dangerous."

"Yes, I realize that," Ariel admits. For some reason, he looks directly at me. "I certainly wouldn't ask anyone to take it on without considering the risks. Anyway, a decision at this point would be premature. I need to investigate further and continue scripting the ritual. I will see how it goes and report back to the group next week."

"Sounds good," Isabel tells him.

Ariel nods and sits up straighter. "I'll just add this: I feel strongly drawn to attempt something along these lines. I believe this is the sort of thing magical power should be used for. So, when the time comes, if the group decides not to join me, I will probably go ahead on my own."

Before the meeting ends, we do an energy circle. With our eyes shut, we relax and breathe in unison. Isabel guides us through it, speaking in a steady voice, like someone who's done this many times.

We breathe in to the count of five, hold to the count of seven, and breathe out to the count of nine. After a few minutes of this, she instructs us to visualize a current of energy moving around us, a band of violet light flowing from brain to brain. As the current flows, people start humming, a low-pitched, gentle tone.

My body is vibrating. This is similar to group meditations I've experienced in the Circle of Harmony, but also different. There's no overriding sense of the Springs, no protection. The energy takes on jagged waves. I start to sense—or imagine—how the others are feeling.

Jerome is energetic but insecure. He's bright and sensitive, and his mind races a lot. Isabel, on the other hand, is calm and in control. She's confident and proud in her sense of leadership. Ariel is the same, but also a little uneasy. With a jolt, I perceive that he's concerned about me. He *really* wants me in the group. My rosy pleasure at that thought flickers away when I turn to Leyla. She's s taken a dislike to me. She's attracted to Ariel and jealous of what she senses of his feelings for me.

Great. I'm not here to compete for a boyfriend ... *Why am I even thinking about this?*

♒

After the meeting, Ariel walks with me over to the fitness center so we can change for running club. The air is steamy hot, the paths crowded with people hustling between classes. We walk at an easy pace, contemplating. Finally, he breaks the silence to ask what I thought of the group.

I've been wondering that too. "To be honest, I'm not sure. I mean, I like everyone, and I find the work you're doing interesting—I will definitely check out the Grimoire book ..."

"*But—?*"

I sigh. "The energy circle felt a little disturbing."

"Well, it takes some getting used to ..." He sounds disappointed.

"I'm not ruling it out. I just have to think about it."

"Sure."

Deeper disappointment. He *really* wants me in the group. He really *likes* me.

Then my mind switches back to the reason I showed up in the first place—the slimy evil that's infecting the campus and the rest of the world.

"I liked what you said about combating the egregore. I agree that is what magic power should be used for."

He stops and looks at me, his jaw tight. "Thank you for saying so."

Sometimes I'm impulsive, and this is one of those times. I take hold of his wrist and stare hard into his eyes. My voice is thick. "Whether or not I join the group—and whatever the group decides about your ritual—please don't do it alone. I'll help you."

Sometimes there's a fine line between impulsive and reckless.

18. We are creating a new order for your world

Text from Molly: "You coming to the park for 4th of July?"

I'm sitting in the campus parking lot, ready to drive home. I've had my run and my shower and I'm feeling pretty good. But Molly's question makes me frown.

Harmony Springs celebrates the Fourth of July with a big picnic in Founders Park. Pretty much the whole town parties all afternoon, culminating in fireworks over the river. But this year, Grandma's told me she's not feeling up to cooking and carrying stuff through the park. She's going to stay home and rest her sore foot. Violet and Kevin are also going to pass.

Reply to Molly: "Probably not. My grandma's staying home this year."

Molly: "You could eat with us."

That might be nice. Except I'd have to face her parents for the first time since that humiliating dinner when I fled from their house. And of course, I'd have to see Ray-Ray, which is not a pleasant thought ...

Molly again: "Picnic with the Quicks!"*<laughing emoji>*

Me: "You're kind. I'll think about it."

Molly: "Come ON! We can compare notes. I've got new info on Gentzen."

Well in that case ... And, really, I have to get over my shyness.

Me: "What time?"

≈

16 days before

Founders Park sits on the Harmony River about a mile downstream from the source of the springs. Asphalt paths wind through patches of giant live oaks and cypress, set among tennis and basketball courts, a baseball field, and wide sloping lawns.

I arrive a little after 3 p.m., dressed in cutoffs, tank top, running shoes. My hair's in a ponytail behind my Claremont State baseball cap. After parking Veronica on the street, I head up the path carrying a paper plate covered in foil. I was just going to stop and buy something to bring, but Grandma insisted on baking cookies as a gift to the Quicks.

I find Molly at the edge of the baseball field, where a line of booths is set up. She's helping Lewis and Benjamin at the Springs of Coffee stand, selling iced drinks and baked goods.

"I'll be done here in a few minutes," she tells me. "My family's up the hill."

She points up the trail where picnic tables overlook the river. I'm tempted to just hang out with her till she's off work, but decide that would look stupid. So I gather my nerve and march up past the tennis courts and a field where kids are throwing a football. I find Molly's parents at a picnic site under a tall slash pine. Chief Quick is cooking burgers and hot dogs on a portable grill, a spatula in one hand, a king-size can of beer in the other. Beatrice is laying out plates and cups on a plastic tablecloth. I'm relieved to see Ray-Ray is nowhere in sight.

"Abby. Hello!" Molly's mom greets me with a warm smile. "I'm so glad you could join us."

"Thanks for having me." I set the plate of cookies down. "After last time, and everything."

"Oh, don't be silly." She hugs me. "You're welcome with us any time."

I'm seated on the picnic table bench, sipping a cup of lemonade when Ray-Ray arrives, having climbed the path from the swimming hole. He's in wet trunks and flip-flops, a towel wrapped over his shoulders. Plainly, he is still working out with weights and looks fantastic. I try not to stare. He tells me how glad he is to see me and sits down across the table, popping open a can of soda.

Molly appears just as the burgers are coming off the grill. She helps her dad dish out the food and sits down beside me. We pass around the plates of meat, buns, salad, and bags of chips. Everyone makes small talk as we eat. They ask me how I like college, and I tell them a little about the Business and Law class. Happily, I do not experience any gruesome hallucinations or terrifying visions. More and more, I'm able to relax.

After we've eaten and helped clean up, Molly nudges me and tilts her head. We take a stroll up the path to the bluff over the river.

"So what about Gentzen?" I ask her.

"Oh, it's really strange! He lived for a while in this sort of commune in south Florida, over by Fort Myers. They really believed in the Hollow Earth thing, and actually funded expeditions to go and look for entrances at the North Pole and in caves in New Mexico. Later, he went back to Germany. In the 1930s, he did radio and wrote articles for the Nazi party—Yes, *that* Nazi party."

"Wow."

"I know. He disappears from the record after 1944. It's assumed he was killed in the bombing."

"Did you learn any more about the sigils?"

"Not much. Apparently, occult Nazis in the thirties did use sigil magic, but I haven't come across any actual pictures. Have you learned anything?"

"Not really." With a sigh, I tell her about my attempt to summon Lock's ghost and how it fell flat.

"Wow. So he's *bound* by something and you couldn't get him to talk."

"Right."

"We *really* need to try a séance."

"Maybe ..."

I tell her about my research on Lock's tower. Not surprisingly, Molly knows more about that than I do.

"Yeah, that place is pretty amazing. Unfortunately, the inside is closed to the public. They only open it for tours once or twice a year, and then only to patrons of the Foundation—which cost like a zillion bucks. Did you know he *lived* in the tower the last ten years of his life."

"I read something about that."

"Yeah. Spent all his time coming up with weird business schemes and experiments. No one understood much about what he was doing, and he was pretty secretive."

We've stopped at the high point of the path, looking down at the rolling blue water.

"Well, that's all pretty interesting," I tell her. "But it doesn't get us any closer to finding the lost sigils."

"I know. I'm telling you, girl: a séance is the way to go"

Actually, she may be right. More minds involved would mean more energy, and maybe more channels open for the spirit to come through.

Molly has her phone out and is swiping the screen. "I did find a picture of Gentzen, though. Here it is."

She holds up the screen. Glancing at it, my eyes go wide. A handsome Nordic man stares back at me, pale blond hair, high forehead, fierce eyes.

No doubt about it: Gold Armor Guy.

Molly reads my reaction. "Familiar?"

"Yeah. I've seen him in my dreams."

♒

At sunset, Molly goes back to the Springs of Coffee stand to help the guys close down. I say goodbye to her parents and head toward my car. On the path I meet Ray-Ray, coming from the basketball courts.

"Hey," he says. "You're not leaving."

"Yeah. Heading home." Exactly one year ago, I was at this same picnic, just getting to know him. Molly and I watched him play pickup basketball and cheered like crazy. The memory is bittersweet.

He stops before me on the path. "Aren't you even staying for the fireworks?"

"Nah. I'm gonna pass." I move to step around him.

"I've hardly had a chance to talk with you," he says.

Uh .... Where is this going? "Something you need to say?"

He looks uncomfortable. "It's just. Can we sit down for a minute?"

"Sure."

We step over to a bench. Across the open field, kids are already lighting sparklers. Ray-Ray stares at me, nervous and hesitant.

"It's just that, after what happened on campus, and even before that, what happened when you came to dinner a couple of weeks back. I guess I've been worrying about you. Are you doing okay?"

"Yes. It's been tough. But I'm a tough person. I'm okay."

I start to get up. He puts out a hand to stop me.

"I think about you a lot, you know? I care about you."

Great. "How's your girlfriend, Ray-Ray? Jen, right?"

He's sucks in a breath. "No! I mean, she's fine. This is not about that. I'm not trying to put a move on you. Can't we be friends?"

"We are friends, Ray-Ray." I stand up. "And I appreciate your concern, I really do." Now he looks hurt, and I don't want that. I take a breath and give him some honesty. "I care about you too. I don't blame you for anything. But right now, seeing you still hurts. I need time to get over it, okay?"

I don't wait for an answer, just walk.

But it's not Ray-Ray who's filling my thoughts as I drive through downtown and up the wooded roads to Bliss Spring.

It's the armored guy with the wand. Who I now believe is the ghost of Kurt Friedrich Gentzen. Who died eighty-some years ago, and was apparently a Nazi.

In my nightmares and visions, he's appeared several times—always in league with the creepy white frogs, summoning them, directing them. Their alliance now seems reasonable, since the egregore is a hero to crazy extremists, including present-day Nazis.

But is Gentzen the author of the sigils of Inanna?

Time to find out, if I can. I plan to use the same formula I used to call the ghost of Emmanuel Lock.

But this time, I'll include the part about binding the ghost to my will. I feel okay with that because it's pretty clear to me Gentzen is not one of the good guys. I'm going to want all the power I can raise to keep myself safe.

After saying goodnight to Grandma, I go up to my room. I take out my dagger and wand and gather the other tools. I begin with a banishing ceremony to cleanse the room of distractions and protect me from evil. Next, I draw the circle of blue fire in the air. Sitting down at the center, I light candle and incense and pour the libation. I call upon the elemental spirits of Fire, Air, and Earth, and ask for their aid and protection.

Calming my breath, I say in a low and strong voice. "I am Fighting Eagle, initiate of the Circle of Harmony. By the power of the Springs, I call you to this place, spirit of Kurt Friedrich Gentzen. You who spent time in Harmony Springs one hundred years ago, I summon you here now, to speak with me and share your knowledge."

This time I speak both verses of the chant.

By the waters, bright and deep,
I call thee spirit, from thy sleep.
By this fire, clear and bright,
I call thee forth into the light.

By stone and sand, by bank and hill,
I bind thee spirit to my will.
By the Earth on which we stand,
I bind thee spirit to my command.

The candlelight flutters; smoke from the incense rising in a spiral. I repeat the chant over and over.

For a long time, nothing happens. Is he reluctant or resistant? Passive-aggressive? Does he even hear me?

I stand up and lift the wand overhead. I have power, and I'm not afraid to use it. "I am Fighting Eagle, true magician of the Circle of Harmony. By the power of the Springs that flow in this place, by the great spirit Lebab who is the true spirit of the Springs, I command you, Kurt Friedrich Gentzen, appear to me now."

I point the wand sharply straight ahead. A whirl of flame and smoke erupts. In three seconds, it condenses into the form of a man. He's dressed in a tailored three-piece suit. He's a little taller and thinner than I expected. But the pale hair, square jaw, and fiery blue eyes are unmistakable.

Now that he's here, I confess I'm scared. "I am Fighting Eagle, initiate of the Circle of Harmony. Tell me your true name, spirit."

He grins, not worried at all. "I have been watching you. You really are a remarkable young woman."

"And you are Kurt Friedrich Gentzen."

"I *was* Kurt Friedrich Gentzen, in that other life."

He is beautiful in his ghostly way. There's something soothing in his presence. Almost reassuring ...

Focus, Abby. "Did you create the sigils of Inanna."

His smile turns mocking. "I *have* the sigils."

Not the answer I expected. And now, a spiral of golden smoke appears behind him. Another spirit coming through.

"Where can I find the sigils?"

His laugh is soft and creepy. "I might share them with you, at a later time. But that depends on you."

The cloud behind him flashes and condenses. Within the smoke and fire, I glimpse an inhuman face.

Ranae Virum.

"Does he frighten you?" Gentzen asks. "There is no reason that he should. As I have told you before, he is only a force, a power to be used."

"Used to destroy people? Drive them insane? Used to murder an innocent girl?"

"Oh. That was regrettable, I know. But you must understand that sometimes power, in unbalanced individuals, can run out of control. That was never my intention. It is counter to my mission. I seek to create strong young men *and* women, noble and pure. I have watched for a long time, ever since crossing over, waited for a new opportunity. I've noted the growing turmoil of your time—anger, disappointment, disaffection. Those feelings gave rise to the thought-form of the Gentleman Frog, and I have seized upon him, amplified his power ..."

As he speaks his image changes. Now he's dressed in the guise of the Knight of Wands, armor and yellow vest with salamanders biting their tails. He reaches his metal glove thorough the barrier of my circle. It is jeweled, beautiful.

"One with your talent could become a conduit for that power. It is capable of wondrous deeds. All you must do is put your education into *my* hands."

I hold the wand before me for protection. The beautiful glove draws back.

"What would this education involve?"

"Your true identity. Your heritage. The valor of your ancestors. Your race's rightful place of supremacy in the world." Behind his shoulder the white frog has come into focus, gaping, huge and hungry.

I clutch the wand tighter. "I don't think that's for me."

"There are others." Gentzen's eyes are faraway, contemplating his grand vision. "We are building an army, creating a new order for your world."

"Show me the sigils. Where can I find them?"

He laughs, and behind him, the egregore is laughing too.

"You cannot compel me. You have a certain power, true. But it is focused here, around these springs. Out in the greater world, it is diminished."

I hate to think it, but I know he's right. My magic is certainly strongest near the springs.

"Your magic is limited, but mine is building. Soon, we will overwhelm all who oppose our mission. You had best think over my offer." His head tilts toward the giant frog. "I will leave him with you, as a reminder."

With that, he raises his arms and disappears in a whoosh of glittering fog. Outside the circle, the egregore lingers, lipless mouth spread in an evil smile.

19. But please don't tell me not to worry

15 days before

I try over and over to banish the egregore, but each time he comes back. My snatches of sleep are erratic, waking each time to find him lurking in the corner of my room, watching me with his nasty frog-smile. I try the Ablution exercise to fill my aura with peace and protective energy. That helps some, but every time I glimpse Ranae Virum I feel his evil presence drawing off my energy.

Draining me.

When I stagger out of bed in the morning, my eyelids are heavy, eyes bleary and red. Grandma notices when I join her for breakfast.

"Abby, you don't look well. Are you feeling all right?"

I glance into the corner, where the egregore is hovering, having followed me into the kitchen. Folding my arms on the table, I let my forehead sink to my elbow.

"Not really, Grandma."

Over coffee, I tell her about my latest misadventure. Her face scrunches up with concern, and when she focuses on the corner where the egregore floats, she senses the entity and lets out a gasp.

"We've got to do something about this."

She goes upstairs and returns in a little while wearing her magic robe and carrying her dagger. Together, we do a banishing ritual, which causes the creature to fade away. We then focus on wrapping the house in a protective aura.

When we're finished, the egregore is gone, and the house feels safe. But Grandma looks exhausted.

"We've left you to deal with this alone for too long," she says. "I'm going to have a serious talk with Violet. There must be something more we can do."

♒

The good news is, I don't see the egregore in the house anymore.

The bad news is, while I'm driving Veronica to school he comes back. What Gentzen said is true—the farther I wander from the springs, the weaker my magic and the flimsier my protection.

Maybe I should have listened to Grandma and skipped class today.

But I refused. The Business and Law coursework is challenging, and I'm worried about falling behind. Besides, if I let this thing scare me out of living my life, what then?

I glimpse the frog through the top of the windshield, floating in the sky for an instant, then gone again. Later, driving down Highway 7, I whiz past him, looming at the side of the road like some gruesome hitchhiker. Later still, I spot his white shape from the corner of my eye, smiling in the passenger seat.

Each sighting makes me gasp. The anticipation is as bad as the actual visions, never knowing when he'll appear next. It reminds me so much of when I was twelve and plagued by hallucinations from online games. Just like then, I'm scared of losing my mind.

But, by the time I approach Murdock, I've adjusted some to the fear. The very constancy of it has dulled its effect. I have my wand and dagger in my backpack. I can banish the egregore over and over if I need to.

I've got a college course to pass, a run to do with the club, friends to meet up with. I have a life, and I'm not going to let some creepy Nazi ghost and his frog-faced monster scare me out of living it. The more I hold that thought, the less scary and real the frog seems. As I drive onto campus, I don't see him at all.

I park Veronica and pull out my phone. There's a text from Ariel, asking me if I can meet him for lunch or coffee. I answer that I can meet him right after my class.

♒

At noon the cafeteria in the student center is buzzing. Close-packed tables are crowded with people eating lunch. The room is a half-circle, with a curving wall of glass letting in the Florida light. Ariel's alone at a small table near the glass wall. He smiles and waves, but his face looks gaunt and shadowy in contrast to the brilliance outside.

I set down my tray and take a seat. He just has a cup of coffee.

"Glad you could join me," he says. "How's it going?"

I glance around and happily don't see any frog monsters. I'm tempted to tell him about that, but it's too long a story.

"Well, I've been better. What's up with you?"

Both of his hands clutch the cup. "I've come to a decision. Remember I talked in the group about doing a ritual to counteract the egregore?"

"How could I forget?"

"Right. So I did some serious scrying—You know about scrying?"

It's one of the Postmodern Magic techniques mentioned in the *Grimoire*—basically staring into space and looking for answers about something. There's a similar practice in the Circle of Harmony tradition.

"Yes, I've heard of it."

"Well, last night I had the most intense scrying experience of my life. I focused on the egregore and after a while, I could literally see him in the room with me."

I take a quick look around, making sure once again he's not in the room with us *now*.

Ariel misreads my meaning. "I know how crazy that sounds."

I laugh. I can't help it. "No. Not to me."

"Right. You saw it in a vision the day Alicia died. That's why I'm telling you, that and the fact that you said you wanted to help me. I haven't told anyone else in the group, except for Isabel. The thing is, from my scrying, I got the definite feeling that this is urgent. That the egregore's power is growing, and if we're going to do anything about it with magic, we need to act soon."

Gentzen told me his powers were building. *"Soon we will overwhelm all who oppose our mission ..."*

"Sunday night is the full moon," Ariel is saying, "when the feminine energies are strongest. Since the egregore feeds on twisted masculine energies, I figure he will be at his weakest. For that reason, I'm going to do my ceremony then, at the campus pond."

"Wow! Whoa. Can you even have a ceremony ready by then?"

"Yes, it's pretty simple. Words and gestures to raise protective energy around the campus—drawing that from the pond. Then summon the egregore with an invocation, then use the energy to drive him away." He lifts one shoulder in a shrug. "All magic is simply that: intention, raise power, direct it. It's all about the mental focus."

"Yeah, I get that. But ... You're going to do this at night by the pond? Aren't you afraid of being interrupted? What about campus security?"

"I plan to start around ten, when the moon is high. By then, the pond will be deserted. I've already cleared it with the security office. As a recognized student organization, the Sedgwick group is allowed to hold gatherings anywhere on campus, including at night. I told them it's a mindfulness meditation. They acted like I was crazy of course, but after a little smooth-talking, they checked with the dean and gave me permission."

Well, I guess that will work. Still, I'm uneasy. "What does Isabel think about this?"

Ariel sighs. "That I'm acting recklessly. She's doesn't see the same urgency I do. She said she would do some scrying and consider it. But I'm pretty sure I'm going to end up doing this on my own."

"No, you aren't. I said I would help you, and I will." *There I go being impulsive again.*

Ariel shakes his head. "I can't allow that, Abby. Isabel is correct in that it might turn out to be dangerous. That's why I haven't told Jerome or Leyla—they're just not experienced enough to try something like this without a lot of preparation. And you're the most inexperienced of us all."

Ha. You're wrong about that, Ariel. Of course, he's only going on what I've revealed to him.

"I didn't tell you all this because you offered to help," he says. "Although that was very brave and wonderful of you."

"Then why are you telling me?"

"Because—I don't want to frighten you, Abby. And I can certainly be wrong. But during my scrying, I had the sensation that the egregore is hovering around you in particular. I just wanted to give you a heads up, to be careful and do what you can to protect yourself. It-it might be a threat to you."

My laugh has an edge of hysteria. I stare down at my salad, which I still haven't touched. "Your scrying is right on target, Ariel." I really need to come clean with him about who I am and what I can do. I push the plate away.

"The egregore has been hanging around me for weeks now. I've seen him quite a bit. I'm actually not as inexperienced as I've led you to believe."

He stares at me intently. "I had a feeling you were holding back."

"Yeah, well ... What I'm going to tell you now must be in the strictest confidence. Promise?"

"Sure."

Sitting at the table, as the lunch crowd thins and the noises around us dwindle, I give Ariel a true but abridged version of my magical life story: the nightmare visions that brought me to Harmony Springs last summer, my haunting by the thought-form named Raspis, my discovery that magic is real, my initiation and training in a magical tradition that goes back to the nineteenth century. I don't mention the Circle of Harmony by name, and I tell him I can't explain anything about the tradition because it's secret. Then I go into my nightmares this summer, the frogs and the Goddess Inanna, my search for the missing sigils, and my attempts to contact the ghosts of Lock and Gentzen.

Ariel listens to it all with rapt attention, eyes widening and narrowing along the way.

"Holy shit," he murmurs. "I had the feeling you were something special—talented or gifted ... But you're not just a practitioner, you're an adept."

At least he doesn't think I'm lying. "Well, I wouldn't say that. I just do my best. What I've learned, I've learned from necessity."

"Yes, I get that. I know you haven't studied Postmodern Magic, but maybe you could take a look at the ritual I wrote—just to give me your thoughts. I'm still not asking you to do it with me."

"Oh, I'm doing it with you. You were right about the egregore threatening me—especially since last night. Maybe together we can drive the slimy beast away."

♒

"Hey, Grandma. How was your day?" I've just gotten home and found her in the living room reading a book.

"Fine, sweetie. But how are *you* doing?"

"Better, thanks. Listen, Sunday I'm going to spend the night in Murdock."

She sits up straighter, looking concerned. "You are? With whom?"

My first impulse was to tell her there would be a party, and it would end late, so I'd be staying with friends. I don't want her to worry, and I've gotten so accustomed to hiding my secret self from my mom, bending the truth here and there has become second nature.

But this is Grandma, and she knows all about true magic, and my struggles with the egregore. And I've already told her about Ariel and the Postmodern Magic group. So I sit down beside her on the couch and explain the plan.

Ariel and I will go to the campus pond a couple of hours after sunset, under the full moon. We'll raise protective energy from the water, and then use an incantation to summon the egregore. Once we've raised the bastard, we'll blast him with the cleansing energy of the pond and hopefully damage him—or at least drive him away from the campus.

When I finish, Grandma is not at all happy. "Abby, this sounds terribly risky. Are you sure it's something you should do?"

Well, I *was* very sure earlier today. But after reading through Ariel's ritual, I admit I have some doubts. The Postmodern Magic approach feels alien and bizarre. And now, seeing Grandma's reaction, I wonder if the whole idea is crazy.

On the other hand, Ranae Virum is still clamped on my psyche like a stinky, suffocating blanket. And Ariel and I both think his powers are growing.

"I know there's risk, Grandma. But this thing is haunting me. I glimpsed it on and off all day today. Right now, I'm keeping it away by will power, but I don't know how long I can keep that up."

Grandma winces, frightened for me. "There has to be a better way. I've talked with Violet again. She says she's working on the problem. But she hasn't been feeling well some of the time, and has to go slowly."

"I know. We mustn't let her risk her health. Besides, I suspect any protection she could cast would mostly be effective here in Harmony Springs. I can't hide here forever."

"I know that ..." Grandma thinks it over. "So after this ritual, you're likely to be exhausted, however it goes. You said you're going to stay overnight? Where? With Ariel?"

"Oh, that part's all arranged. Ariel lives with his aunt and uncle. They own a motel in Murdock, and they've offered me one of the rooms for the night. They're usually not full on Sundays, but even if they are, they said I could have the room, no charge."

"Have you met them? Have you seen the place?"

"Yes. I drove over there with Ariel, and he introduced me to the family. They're very nice." Although they *did* seem a little confused about my needing a room for the night. I'm clueless as to what they thought about that.

Thinking of Ariel reminds me of the other reason I have to face this ritual. If I don't, he's going to summon the egregore alone. He needs my help, and I won't let him down. Whether that's brave of me or just stupid, I don't know.

Grandma's shaking her head. "Abby, please don't do this. I have a really bad feeling about it."

I shift in my seat. My confidence is falling apart.

"I'm scared for you," she says. "And with your mother not here, I feel responsible. I know *she* would forbid you to do this."

"I'd never have told her about it," I answer, defensively. "I don't trust her with this stuff, the way I trust you."

We stare at each other for a long moment. I place my hand on hers. "Listen, Grandma. It's only one ritual, and I'll have a friend there with me. I've faced scarier things alone."

Her face remains rigid, lips clamped shut. Emotions struggle inside me. On one side is Grandma's psychic pull, her concern and fear, and love for me—adding to my own fears. On the other side is my concern for Ariel, and the duty I feel to fight the egregore.

In the end, it's Ariel, or duty, or pure obstinacy that wins.

"I have to do this, Grandma. Talking it out has only made me more sure. Please try not to worry."

"Oh, no." Grandma stands up, angry now. "I can't make you see reason. And I certainly can't prevent you from doing what you're going to do. But please don't tell me not to worry."

She storms out of the room and up the stairs.

Alone now, I hug a pillow to my stomach. I feel horrible for hurting her—and all the more terrified for myself.

But I'm also angry—and stubbornly determined.

♒

Text to Ariel: "I'm studying the ritual."

Ariel: "And ... ?"

Me: "I'm good on most of it. Still thrown by the barbaric terms of invocation."

There's a long string of words at the start, designed to loosen the mind from the normal state and help it enter the magical state. But to me, they read like nonsense syllables.

Me: "Can't figure out how to say them." I mean, how do you even pronounce, BALWYNNT NGGRATH TADLBTH?

Ariel: "Not to worry. You'll pick it up once we start chanting. Just follow my lead."

Ariel again: "Having second thoughts? It's okay if you want to bail."

Me: "No! I'll be there."

Ariel: "Great. What time?"

Me: "About 7. At the motel."

Ariel: "Can you make it 6? My aunt invites you to dinner."

20. Smothered in slime and burning cigarettes

13 days before

The Palm Court is one of those old Florida motels that you still see on the back roads and in the little towns—one story, with thirty rooms arranged around a parking lot and a big swimming pool in the middle.

Sunday at 5:45 p.m., I pull into a parking space in front of the motel office. I'm dressed in a skirt, blouse and sandals—appropriate, I hope, for dinner with Ariel's family. Later, I'll change into jeans and running shoes so we can drive over to campus and slay monsters.

As I climb out of my car, Ariel is there to meet me. He flashes a grin and gives me a peck on the cheek. "Hi, Abby. Are you ready for this?"

"Uh, which part of *this* are we talking about?"

He laughs. "Disposing of the egregore, of course. I promise dinner with my family won't be nearly so scary."

He directs me to park in front of Room 19, which will be mine for the night. He meets me there, holding a room key. I have an overnight bag and my backpack. He carries the bag up the sidewalk and opens the room for me.

The room is old-fashioned but nice, with two double beds, a TV and—thank goodness—wifi. The cleaning solution they use smells faintly of citrus. He leaves me to settle in and tells me to come down to the office when I'm ready.

After washing my face and putting on eye makeup, I stare into the bathroom mirror. I look older than I did just a month ago, mouth tight at the corners, worry-lines around the eyes. I won't be eighteen for another month, but sometimes I feel like eighty.

Of course, other times I feel like eleven.

I square my shoulders and take a deep breath. On the drive over, I've been thinking about the last time I was invited to dinner with the family of a guy I liked—at the Quick's house when the food turned to frogs and floating eyeballs.

Oh, well. A lot of stuff has happened since then, and I think it's made me stronger. I'm pretty sure if I start hallucinating, I'll be able to handle it better this time.

Small comfort, but it's all I got.

I have to admit, I'm nervous—and not just about the Postmodern Magic. I'm not sure what it means that the family invited me to dinner. Is this something Ariel has done with other friends? Is he interested in me not only as a magician but as a possible girlfriend? I can't seem to figure this out, and I don't want to jump to conclusions.

Still, I'll have this room to myself tonight ...

Just after six o'clock, I walk down the sidewalk to the office. Ariel's aunt Estefania comes out from behind the counter and takes both my hands. She's a slender woman with a high forehead and sharp eyes. Her smile is both friendly and appraising. She welcomes me to her home and leads me back to the family's apartment—leaving the doors open so they'll hear if anyone comes into the office looking for a room.

In the dining room, her two daughters are already at the table. Angela looks to be about nine or ten, and Natalia's maybe seven. They are cute little girls with thick, lustrous hair. When their mother introduces me, they stand up and formally shake my hand. But amusement shows on their faces. I'm wondering what Ariel has told everyone about me.

He marches in a moment later, along with his uncle Roberto. They carry steaming dishes that smell of meat, tomatoes, and onions. Ariel asks what I'd like to drink.

He comes back in a few moments with sparkling water for me and Cokes for the girls. Roberto opens a bottle of wine and pours some for himself and his wife. When everyone is seated, we bow our heads and Ariel's uncle says grace.

The family makes small talk as they pass around the plates. Mostly they speak English but occasionally throw in a phrase or two of Spanish. I took Spanish my first two years of high school, but that was a long time ago, and I only partly understand them. Ariel senses my confusion and reminds everyone to speak English.

Roberto, it turns out, is the cook in the family, and the food is delicious. I haven't had much today—too nervous. With the ritual coming up, I want to fortify myself but also be careful not to overeat.

Estefania asks me about my studies and how I like Claremont State. She has a Business degree from the University of Miami and used to work for a bank. I tell her about my mom's job in London. She asks about the "party" we're going to tonight, and I know I have to be careful. Ariel warned me that the family knows nothing about his magical studies—where spiritual matters are concerned, they're traditional and would not like it. He's told them we're going to a star-gazing party on campus, to look at the moon and stars. Several students are supposedly bringing telescopes.

"I just thought it sounded like fun," I tell Estefania. "Being that I'm new at the college and live so far away, I've been looking for ways to make friends." *Sounds reasonable, right?*

When I say this, they all cast their eyes at Ariel, who almost seems to blush.

"Well, I know you've made at least one friend," Roberto says. "This is the first time Ariel's asked us for a spare room."

Now everyone's staring at me. Natalia whispers something to Angela and they both burst out in giggles.

After dessert, which is a really sweet cake with *dulce de leche*, Ariel walks me to my room. It's dusk and the full moon is rising, huge and orange, through the pines behind the motel.

"Sorry if that was embarrassing for you," Ariel says. "They insisted on having dinner with you, and I didn't see a way to avoid it."

"Oh, it's no problem. They're really nice. The little girls are adorable."

He smiles, touched. "They are, aren't they? I'm so glad you didn't mind. Even though I'm almost twenty, my aunt and uncle think of themselves as my surrogate parents. And, you know, navigating magical activities around parents who know nothing about it can be—eh, *dicey* sometimes."

Reminds me of my mom. "I know that's true."

We've reached my door now, and I'm working the key. "Speaking of which, we should get started rehearsing, don't you think?" We had talked about going over the ritual a few times here at the motel before heading over to campus.

"Sure." Ariel suddenly looks hesitant. "That is if you're still sure you're up for it."

This surprises me. "Of course I am. I'll just feel better if we practice it together ... What? Why are you frowning?"

He answers in a soft, tense voice. "I don't know. The more I think about what we're doing, the more worried I am that I'm putting you into danger."

♒

The streets of Murdock are nearly deserted at 9:30 p.m. It's less than a mile to campus, and we drive over in Ariel's eight-year-old Subaru. It has bucket seats and I sit in the front, hugging my backpack.

Ariel pulls in at the "Home of the Bobcats" sign and drives up toward the quadrangle. We park in the lot across from the campus security office. I wait in the car while Ariel goes to check in at the desk and remind them about our "mindfulness meeting." The campus is eerily quiet, lit by the full moon and numerous lamps along the sidewalks and high over the parking lots. I've never seen it so empty.

Ariel returns and says we're all set. He takes his tablet and a lantern from the back seat, and then locks the car. Without speaking, we march across the parking lot and down the path that leads to the pond. The night is warm and muggy. A soft breeze ripples on the water, fluttering waves of moonlight. The pulse throbs in my ears.

We stop on the far side of the pond, a spot directly across from the quadrangle. This is the place Ariel has chosen for the ritual. Tall slash pines loom up behind us, and we stand midway between the nearest lamps that light the path. With a slither of terror, I remember this is the place where I saw the vision of Alicia being attacked. Her body was discovered in the woods not far away.

Ariel switches on the battery-powered lantern, and we both pull out our phones so we can read the ritual. I take a deep breath and look up to see if he's ready.

But his head is turned in the opposite direction. Someone is walking toward us, circling the pond. The walk looks familiar, and as she steps out of the shadows, I recognize her.

"Isabel!" Ariel says. "You decided to join us after all."

She nods. A quirk at the corner of her mouth says she still doesn't think it's such a good idea. "I decided I couldn't let you two go at this alone."

She's dressed in a long black skirt and a fringed orange shawl. When she opens her arms to hug Ariel, I spot a silver pentagram hanging in front of her blouse. She smiles at me and says hello, then holds up her phone.

"Are we ready?" she asks Ariel.

"Um, I made a few changes to the script." He taps and swipes on his screen. "Let me send you the latest."

I wait, staring at the water, while he messages Isabel with the new version of the ritual—whoosh, ping, tap. She opens the message, and they mumble together as she reads the attachment.

"Okay, I'm ready," she tells him. "*You* take the lead on the Barbaric names."

Ariel grins and glances at me. "Of course."

We stand side-by-side with Ariel in the center, backs straight, shoulders set. Ariel counts aloud as we take deep breaths: count four in, hold for seven, eight out. The energy wriggles up from my chest and slides into my brain. Then I feel it as a current, moving in a band through our hearts and circling in front of us.

The night seems to contract. I see only the dark pond, the reflections of moonlight, and the circling energy that is the same silvery color. Ariel's voice intones deep and smooth beside me.

BALWYNNT NGGRATH TADLBTH. BALWYNNT NGGRATH TOOSEM. CARRES NGGRATH BONUMINI.

He repeats the syllables again and again. Isabel's voice joins him, then I do likewise. The point is simply to match the sounds, let them resonate in your brain.

Hypnotic.

As I intone the words, I'm lifted out of my body. I stare down at the scene from a great height, the level of the treetops. Our three small shapes stand beside the pond, the water lapping near our feet. The circling band of energy grows, joining the reflections on the pond. From far away, I hear Ariel's voice.

"Now our minds are joined with the Mysterious Source of All. Its Power is ours, to wield and to use. By this Power that is ours, we raise protection from the land and the water. This pond at the center of our campus yields its energy to our intent. We raise the waters to protect us."

From high above, I watch the moonlit water seems to rise from the pond in a huge, slow wave, spreading over us, spreading over the whole campus.

"The waters protect us," Ariel intones.

I'm focused in my body again as Isabel and I repeat: "The waters protect us."

Ariel continues: "Now, safe in this protection, we summon an alien energy, the thought-form that has infected this place and caused death here. We call you forth, that we may destroy your power in this place. We call you forth to banish you. We call you forth by your name which we know. We call you forth, Ranae Virum. You cannot resist our call. You cannot resist our power. We summon you now."

Isabel and I take up the chant. "We summon you now. We summon you now."

New power rises in me, dark, irresistible, terrifying. We wave our phones like wands, striking the air.

I see the luminous mass of a giant white frog, rising at the center of the pond.

Ariel and Isabel suck in their breath. They can sense it if not actually see it.

"We banish you!" Ariel shouts. "Ranae Virum, we banish you."

But the egregore doesn't listen. It grows and expands. Like a shimmering cloud, it flows toward the spot where we stand on the bank. For a moment, I see the frog's gleaming eyes. Then the energy cloud blasts over us.

My whole body explodes with pain. I can't breathe. I open my mouth to scream but can't make a sound. There is only blinding light and agony.

Next thing I know, I'm on hands and knees, gasping, struggling to breathe. The air feels slimy in my lungs and smells toxic, poisonous. Ariel and Isabel have collapsed beside me, moaning, coughing. I draw in a painful breath and it chokes me.

Tiny white frogs are scuttling and hopping on the ground. One lands on Isabel's leg and she shrieks. Coughing, I struggle to my knees. The frogs are swarming us. Each time one touches me, it burns my skin like an ember spit from a fire. I shriek in pain and swipe them, but they keep jumping. Isabel is on the ground, whimpering, slapping and kicking at the frogs.

Ariel's gotten to his feet. With a growl, he flings out his arms. He shouts something in Spanish. The frogs react. They croak and leap, converging on him. He shudders and laughs, even as they burn him.

I realize he's called them on purpose, to get them away from myself and Isabel.

Taking advantage of the respite, I scramble to find my backpack. Grabbing my dagger, I raise it high and mentally summon the power of Harmony Springs. Visualizing the clear blue water, I send it down my arm and through the dagger-point. The water calms me. I'm able to walk around, tracing a circle of protection, drawing a pentagram at each quarter.

By the time I'm done, Isabel is on her feet, panting, watching me. Ariel has fallen over, writhing on the ground, coughing uncontrollably. The frogs have retreated, scrambling away into the night.

Isabel and I both rush to Ariel. Between fits of coughing, he slowly regains his breath. With our help, he stands, looks around. Everything is quiet and normal again.

Ariel looks at us both ruefully. "Well. I guess that one needs more work before we try it again."

His two fellow magicians just stare.

♒

Whatever fantasies I might have had about a romantic night with Ariel come to nothing. He is so weakened by the magic-gone-bad he can barely drive back to the motel—amid horrible fits of coughing.

By the time we get there, I'm coughing too. Ariel parks in the back of the lot and walks me to my door. He looks pale, and I'm worried he might have a fever.

"Will you be all right?" he asks.

"Yeah. You?"

"Sure." He touches my arm. "I'm grateful you were there, Abby. I think you saved us with that dagger move."

"I think you saved us first, when the frogs were all over us—Did you see them as frogs?"

"No. I just felt their energy. Like being smothered in slime and burning cigarettes. You actually saw frogs?"

"Yeah. But you called them off of Isabel and me and drew them to yourself. What was it you said in Spanish?"

"Oh." His laugh turns into another cough. "Not sure why, but I yelled, 'Spare these women. Face the man.' Silly macho stuff, I know."

That touches my heart and makes me smile. "Not silly. Brave."

We stare into each other's eyes for just a moment. Then he presses my arm. "Goodnight, Abby. Get some rest. We both need it."

Unfortunately, rest is not on the agenda. The room is unfamiliar, and I'm more traumatized by the ritual than I wanted to admit. I'm up half the night coughing and sneezing, the creepy frog vapors filling my lungs and pricking the back of my throat. When I do fall asleep, I'm haunted by frog nightmares, with Kurt Friedrich Gentzen strolling among the little beasts, sneering at me, warning me that I'd better reconsider my attitude.

21. What's a V-I-D? That's you, Abby.

12 days before

In the morning, Ariel's taken a turn for the worse.

His aunt Estefania comes to my door and tells me he's caught a bad cold and is lying in. "Runny nose, fever, terrible coughing. He wanted to see you, but I told him he's probably contagious and better not. Are you feeling sick?"

I grunt, clearing my throat. "I might have a touch of cold too."

She shakes her head, lips compressed. "Ariel's sorry he can't see you off, but I insisted he stay in bed. This is not like him, and I'm a little worried."

Me too. "Well, tell him not to worry about me. I'll talk to him when he's feeling better."

She asks if I'd like some breakfast before I go. I tell her just coffee. After packing up and putting my bags in Veronica, I deliver the room key to the office. Estefania invites me back to the family apartment and serves me a cup of coffee at the dining table. She sits down and watches me drink it.

"Are you sure you're all right to drive? You look a little dazed."

That's not surprising. Because I'm feeling dazed, and *more than a little.* But my defensive walls go up. "Oh, I always look this way in the morning."

♒

Ten minutes later, I'm pulling out of the Palm Court onto Highway 7. The air is cool and wet. As I drive through Murdock, dark clouds are blowing in from the north. I'm light-headed, sniffling, swallowing mucus, coughing. I probably should have tried to eat, but my stomach didn't want anything. I hope I won't get as sick as Ariel sounds.

But then, of course I won't. He's the one who absorbed the worst of the slimy frog attack—the dark energy of the egregore that we raised and then failed to dispel.

Postmodern Magic gone wrong.

With these thoughts, the frogs seep back into my vision. They blink and vanish on the windshield as raindrops start to fall. I switch on the wiper blades and try to ignore the little monsters. But even as I focus on the road, their evil faces penetrate my brain.

I shake my head to clear it. As I leave Murdock behind the rain shower stops. But the sky straight ahead is black, and forks of lightning slither to the ground. I wonder if I should pull over to wait it out, but I'm on a rural stretch now and there's no shoulder, only a drainage ditch.

With a blast of thunder the sky opens up, rain pouring so hard I can barely see the road. My headlights switch on, and the wipers are going full-speed. Still, the windshield is a sheet of sliding water. Headlights beam behind me, so I'm afraid to stop. I switch on the emergency blinkers and slow down to 30, then 25.

Panic rises inside me. Frantically, I peer at the roadside, searching for a place where I can turn off. I glance straight ahead and see a man.

He's walking down the middle of the road and I'm going to hit him.

With a cry, I twist the wheel, jam the brakes, and hear Veronica's tires skidding. As the car slides past, I glimpse the man's form like a rushing shadow—tall and elegant, wearing a three-piece black suit.

The ghost of Kurt Friedrich Gentzen.

The car bumps and jerks to a violent stop. My body snaps forward against the safety belt and I black out.

♒

Coughing brings me awake. I peer up through blurry eyes at the windshield, coated with water, flashing with reflected red light. The wiper blades are stuck as black diagonals.

Steady rain, and another noise ... tapping on the side window.

“Miss, we need you to open the door so we can get you out.”

I turn my head and grimace at a sharp ache in my shoulder. A man in a wet gray slicker is staring at me, motioning me to unlock the door.

A policeman ... I remember now. *Oh, God! I've wrecked my car.*

I clutch my head. No bumps. My shoulder hurts from jamming on the seat belt. The car is tilted forward and to the right. I find the handle and push open the door.

“How bad is it?” I ask the policeman.

He reaches to help me climb out. “You'll be all right, miss.”

“I know I'm all right! What about Veronica?”

The officer glances into the back seat, then frowns. “Who is Veronica, miss?”

“My car!” I stumble around to the front end, bent over, coughing.

The rain is falling slow and steady, and the whole world is gray. Veronica's right tire is blown, the bumper smashed. I can't tell if there's other damage.

“Oh, no. Veronica!” I hang my head, sobbing.

The officer puts his hands on my shoulder. “It will be all right. We've called for a tow truck. Right now, we need to get you out of the rain.”

He leads me to the edge of the muddy ditch. His partner is there and helps me climb out.

“Can you tell us your name, miss?”

“Yes. Abby—Abigail Renshaw.”

They ask to see my driver's license.

I point vaguely at Veronica. "In my backpack. Front seat."

The first officer goes and to get it. The other one helps me to the police car, an SUV with *Hobart County Sheriff* painted on the door above a golden badge. He puts me in the back and gets in beside me. He leans close and looks in my eyes. Then he asks if I can follow his index finger as he moves it back and forth in front of my face. He's checking me for something. I try to comply, but shifting my eyes makes me dizzy. Gold flashes appear, blowing into my brain like a blizzard.

... I'm coughing. I thought only a second had passed, but now suddenly the second officer is in the front seat. Rain drums on the roof.

"Are you all right, Abby?"

I nod amid the coughs.

"You blanked out for a minute. We've called the EMTs and they're on their way."

"Oh ... EMTs? Emergency medical—"

"Med Techs. They'll check you over to make sure you're all right."

Frontseat Officer hands me my backpack. "If you're feeling well enough, can you show me your driver's license, please?"

"Yes."

I fish out my wallet, open it, hand over the laminated license. Finding a packet of tissues, I pull one out and blow my nose.

"Do you remember how you lost control of the car?" Backseat Officer asks.

Oh, yeah. I remember. A hailstorm of tiny frogs and a handsome Nazi ghost. Better be careful what I say here. "It was raining really hard."

Frontseat Officer says: "New Jersey driver's license, and your car has New Jersey tags. Also, according to this, you are seventeen, which makes you a minor. How do you happen to be driving alone out here in Hobart County?"

"I live in Harmony Springs now, with my grandmother. I haven't had a chance to get my license or the tags changed. I'm a student at Claremont State." I show him my student ID.

He looks it over, makes a note.

Backseat Officer says: "While we're waiting for the EMTs, would you be willing to take a breathalyzer test? Just so we can eliminate DUI as a possible cause of the accident?"

I'm having trouble following this. Consciousness is currently a fragile thing. ... Waiting for the EMTs. Emergency Medical Technicians ...

"Sorry. What did you ask me again?"

"Would you be willing to take a breathalyzer test so we can eliminate DUI as a possible cause of the accident?"

"Oh. I don't drink. I mean, I haven't been ..."

"So you're willing to take the breathalyzer test?"

"Yes. No problem."

His partner hands him the breathalyzer, which is this square black device with a white tube on the top that you blow into. While he's instructing me on how to take the test, the radio in the front seat crackles.

"Car eleven. What is the status of your V-I-D?"

Frontseat Officer taps a button and answers. "Single driver. No visible injuries but appears dazed. EMTs en route. Subject has consented to field sobriety test."

"What's a V-I-D?" I ask Backseat Officer.

For the first time, he cracks a smile. "That's you, Abby. Vehicle in Ditch."

♒

By the time the ambulance arrives the rain has petered out. The EMTs, a tall man and a strongly-built woman, talk to the officers. They help me to step out of the SUV, then ask me a bunch of questions: What do I remember about the accident? Am I in pain and if so where? I'm alert enough to give them a vague story about going off the road. Except for my bruised shoulder and the stuffiness in my head, I feel okay.

While we're talking, the tow truck pulls up, amber lights flashing. I make the EMTs wait while I talk to the driver and fuss over Veronica. Where is he taking her? How bad is the damage? When will I have her back? Everyone is amused by my flurry of questions, but also sympathetic. Backseat Officer assures me that the towing service is reputable and works with the police regularly. My car will be towed to a garage in Murdock. They'll assess the damage and let me know about repairs. The driver takes down my registration and insurance information. He hands me a business card and tells me I can call that number later today or tomorrow.

"Superior Auto Repair, Murdock FL. Servicing all makes and models."

I put the card in my wallet. The woman EMT asks if it's okay to continue their evaluation now. I apologize. They test my eyesight, ask me to walk in a straight line. I seem to be passing all the tests. But when they tell me to shut my eyes and stand on one foot, black energy pulses in my brain, and I lose it.

In my vision, I'm back at the ritual last night, floating high over the treetops. I gaze down at the pond and three small figures overrun by a horde of leaping, blazing frogs.

Next thing I know, I'm flat on my back in a speeding car—No an ambulance.

The woman EMT is staring down at me. "How are you feeling now?"

"Stupid."

"You fainted. We're taking you to the Emergency Room to have you checked."

Great.

"Do you remember hitting your head when the car crashed?"

"No, I told you. Just my shoulder."

I'm not passing out because of head trauma. I'm passing out because I'm subject to Shamanic visions, and I'm presently overwhelmed by un-discharged energy from a Postmodern Magic ritual that blew up in my face.

Try explaining that to an EMT.

She pats my wrist. "You'll be okay."

♒

I'm discharged from the ER with a diagnosis of a bruised shoulder and a severe head cold. I've phoned Grandma from the hospital, and she's driven down from Harmony Springs to pick me up. Distress flicks over her face when she sees me, but she masks it immediately. She's all cheerfulness, sympathy, and reassurance as we check out of the hospital and drive home.

I'm really grateful she doesn't wail into me about what an idiot I am for driving through a thunderstorm when my head is already frazzled from dangerous magic. Or what an idiot she is for allowing me to get myself into this mess in the first place.

In other words, I'm really grateful she's not Mom.

At home, Grandma doses me with Nyquil and puts me to bed. I want to take a shower first; I'm all sweaty and gritty. But she's afraid I might get dizzy again and crack my head, so instead, she sponges me off in my bathroom, then dries me with a soft towel—just like she used to do when I was five and came in muddy from playing in the backyard.

I sleep for sixteen hours. When I finally get up at ten the next morning, my head is an aching sponge soaked in snot. I'm supposed to be in class today, but I'm way too sick to drive.

Also, no car.

And no internet or phone signal. I can't even text Ariel to see how he's doing. I can't get online to check into the student portal or send an email to my teacher. Not sure that's necessary, or if he'll even notice I'm not there. I remind myself this isn't high school.

I use the landline to call the garage in Murdock. They can replace the tire and hammer out the bumper so the car is drivable. To get the bumper replaced would mean towing it to a body shop, and that will take longer. After asking Grandma's advice, I opt for just fixing the bumper for now. I give them my credit card number for any charges not covered by the insurance. All of this has exhausted me, and I crawl back to bed.

The rest of that day and the next are a blur. I survive on cold medicine, tea, and toast. When I'm not sleeping I mostly lie in bed staring at the ceiling, my brain too foggy to think or make plans. I worry about Ariel and Isabel, if they are as sick as I am, or worse. I consider using the landline to call the Palm Court Motel, but decide against it.

Fortunately, I see no signs of Kurt Friedrich Gentzen or Ranae Virum, even in my dreams. I have no doubt that the protection around Harmony Springs is keeping them away.

Keeping me secure.

Passing the day in bed reminds me of childhood when I spent so many days here with Grandma, while Mom and Dad worked. All my five-year-old's feelings come back: peaceful, quiet, no worries or responsibilities. *Safe.*

But I'm not five anymore. I can't hide here forever.

Wednesday night, I'm recovered enough to be restless. I light a candle and perform the Daily Ablution. The water of the Springs rises up my spine, easing the aches. When I reach the Fountain of Amity, I meet Inanna.

She wears the image of the woman in the *Strength* card—tall and curly-haired, dressed in white and draped in flowers. She bends over the red lion, holding its mouth open. Her head tips up as I approach.

"Your strength may be tested many times. Know that your efforts are *not* wasted."

My voice comes out in a whine. "I don't even know what I'm doing."

"You are learning. And your connection with me *is* growing."

A tower appears in the distance, glowing like a fire against the night sky. Above it shines a star with eight points.

The voice of the goddess whispers: "Free my power."

22. I really don't need this stress right now

9 days before

Riding into town with Grandma the next morning, I hold my phone open. As soon as the cell tower signal kicks in, my messages download. Three texts from Molly, five from Ariel. I open his first. They started two days ago, asking if I'm okay, progressing in rising tones of alarm, the last one ten minutes ago.

I text him back. "I'm OK. Got a little sick. Also wrecked my car. Are you OK?"

He answers in a few seconds: "Oh no! Your car? What happened?"

I shouldn't have mentioned that. Stupid of me. "It's all right. How are you?"

Ariel. "Also sick. Acute bronchitis. No running club for a while <*sad face emoji*>."

Me: "I am so sorry. <*crying emoji*>"

Him: "Confined to bed. Getting better though."

Me: "I'll be at school tomorrow. Can I stop in and see you?"

Him: "<*smiley emoji*> That would be nice."

The Honda Odyssey slows and stops. We've reached downtown, parked in front of the shop. I open Molly's texts. She heard I was sick, expresses sympathy. Let's get together when I'm up to it. I message her back, arranging to meet her at Springs of Coffee at 2.

"You sure you're okay?" Molly sits down at our table in the corner. "You look pretty groggy."

"You should have seen me yesterday." I sniffle for emphasis. But I'm really not feeling that bad. The cold has dwindled from devastating plague to moderate annoyance.

"So what's been happening? You realize I haven't seen you in over a week?" She takes a bite of her tuna salad on croissant.

"I know. Things have been even crazier than usual."

"Frogs again?"

"Lots of frogs."

I gaze down at my turkey panini, finger a potato chip, put my thoughts in order. While Molly eats, I fill her in, starting with my all-too-successful attempt to conjure Kurt Friedrich Gentzen's ghost last week. Followed by his leaving the egregore as a nasty calling card. Followed by my agreeing to help Ariel's attempt to banish the egregore from campus. Followed by having dinner with his family at the Palm Court Motel. Followed by our disastrous magic ritual—resulting in our being asphyxiated by a swarm of burning astral frogs; resulting in my sleepless night and ending up a V-I-D.

Molly, familiar with police slang, goes bug-eyed. "Vehicle in Ditch! Don't tell me you crashed Veronica!"

"Well, you did ask what's been happening."

"Oh, my god! Abby, I am so sorry. Is it fixable?"

"Semi. They're hammering out the bumper. I'll have to see about getting bodywork done later." I pick up my sandwich, put it down again. My appetite has gone missing.

"Honestly, why am I even trying to deal with this stuff? Everything ends in disaster, and the disasters keep getting worse."

Molly's lips twitch, but she doesn't answer.

I stare down at my food. "The last two days have been so quiet and safe. I could just quit school and stay in Harmony Springs." I tilt my chin toward the counter where Lewis, one of the owners, is wiping a glass display case. “Do you think Lewis and Benjamin might give me a job?”

Molly huffs. “Come on, that’s not you.”

I’m thinking about what happened to Alicia, and how Ariel and Isabel and I almost choked on the burning vapors. “Are you sure?”

Molly slaps her hand on the table. “Yes! You’re fighting the monsters because you’re a true magician, and that’s what you’re called to do.”

Whoa. What makes her such an expert all of a sudden?

“What Gentzen’s ghost said about his forces growing? And what Ariel sensed about the frog meme growing stronger? I think they’re right. I’ve been keeping up with the online forums. There haven’t been any more murders, but there seem to be more and more people making outrageous threats. Some of the sites have been shut down, but new ones keep popping up. You know how the internet is.”

Molly’s words bring back all my desperation and fear.

“The evil is real,” she continues. “We all have to oppose it any way we can. Violet’s working on it too.”

“I know. How is she feeling, by the way?”

“Some days better than others. Kevin says she exhausts herself by taking on too much magic, and that’s how it looks to me too. Also, she’s disappointed in herself, because she hasn’t been able to do more about the egregore problem. She’ll be even more disappointed when she hears about your accident.”

“I’m surprised Kevin didn’t tell her. I know my grandma spilled it to him.”

Molly shrugs. “He didn’t mention it while I was there. Probably trying to shield Violet from more worry.”

“Yeah, that makes sense.” I pick up my sandwich and take a bite. If I’m going back to the battle, I’ll need my strength.

Molly watches me for a while. “So what’s our next move?”

“Ha. I wish I knew.” I tell her about my vision of Inanna last night, and how she reminded me that I need to free her power. “I guess that brings us back to the sigils. I don't suppose you've come across anything more about Lock and Gentzen?"

"Nah. That's a dead end. I mean, there's plenty about them both online, but nothing connected with sigil magic. And I've been through all of Kevin's and Violet's surviving papers from the Circle of Harmony. Nothing."

"Damn. Well, I've tried summoning them both, and you know how that went. Gentzen was threatening, and Lock was unable to talk."

"Yeah, *bound,*" Molly says. "I keep thinking a séance might work. But maybe that's just cause I want to see one."

I pick up a potato chip. "I don't know. We've tried everything else."

Molly shakes her head. "Violet doesn't seem to want to go there. I'm not sure why. They used to hold them all the time in the Founders' days."

Listening to her, I do have a feeling that a séance might get us somewhere. Of course, all I know about them is what I've seen in old black-and-white movies. Still, at this point, what have I got to lose? I've *got* to find those sigils.

So, these words come out of my mouth: "Maybe we could try it without her."

Molly brightens instantly. "Really?"

♒

I'm walking back along Main Street, past the storefronts and post office, under oak branches draped in Spanish moss. I'm remembering last summer, and how much I came to love this quiet little town.

My phone jangles me to alertness. Mom's ringtone. She's calling from England.

"Hi, Mom."

"Abby, are you okay?'

Uh-oh. What does she know? "Yeah, Mom. I'm fine."

"Then why is there a $90 bill from the Emergency Room on your credit card? And another one for towing service? Did you have an accident?"

"Just a small one." Grimacing, I stop on the sidewalk, lean my back on an oak, brace myself for the onslaught.

"What do you mean a little one? How little?"

I describe getting caught in a thunderstorm and ending up in the ditch. I mention that I had a bad cold that made me dizzy, and the EMTs insisted on transporting me to the hospital as a precaution.

"But I'm fine now. Why is there even a bill from the towing service? I thought they were going to file with the insurance."

"Because your policy has a *deductible*," Mom pronounces the word as though explaining 'dog' and 'cat' to a one-year-old. I guess I should have learned more about auto insurance.

"Are you sure you're okay?" Mom asks. "You're not still dizzy?"

"No. No. Grandma put me to bed for a couple of days. I'm fine now. Going back to school tomorrow."

"I never should have let you go to that school. Commuting 50 miles back and forth by yourself. It's ridiculous."

"42 miles."

"Don't split hairs with me, Abby. You know what I mean."

I stare up into the oak limbs, where the Spanish moss hangs so peacefully.

"What about the damage to your car?"

"Also not bad. They're replacing a tire and hammering out the bumper."

"No!" Mom says. "You need to get the bumper *replaced*. Otherwise, your car will lose its value. And at a Mazda dealership, not some rural body shop. The insurance will cover it."

"But that will take longer. I need my car to get to school."

"So you get a rental car. The insurance should cover that too."

"Can I even sign for a rental car? I'm not 18 yet."

On the other side of the Atlantic, Mom groans loudly. "Oh, that's right! I really don't need this stress right now. If you had just gone to a residential college like I wanted you to. With your grades and athletics, you might have gotten into Princeton or Cornell."

It is *very* peaceful Spanish moss. "I'll ask Grandma to sign for the rental car. I think she'll be okay with it."

"Yes, good. Please do that. Tell her I'll make sure she doesn't suffer financially—I mean, just in case there are *more* problems."

"There won't be. I promise. I'll be careful."

"Good. I'll look up the nearest Mazda dealership and arrange for them to pick up your car. You call this garage in Murdock and tell them to release it. You'll probably have to drop by there to sign something."

"Okay."

Mom exhales. "I'm sorry I blew up at you, Abby. It's just that I worry about you being down there by yourself, while I'm on the other side of the world."

"I know, Mom. It's okay. Try to get some rest."

Grandma's in the front of the antique shop, dusting the merchandise. She's bent over a case of glass figurines, meticulously cleaning each one. Not that I can see any dust, but she's a bit obsessive about keeping everything sparkly clean.

"How are you feeling, sweetie?" she asks as the door swings shut behind me.

"Okay. Let me help you with that."

Behind the counter, I drop off my backpack and find a dust cloth. When I get back, Grandma scrutinizes me from behind her glasses.

"You sure you feel like doing this?"

"Absolutely." I reach past her and pick up a little glass ballerina. "I'm much better today. And I haven't been pulling my weight around here."

My attempted humor falls flat. Grandma straightens up. "Abby, I told you not to worry about that. I'm perfectly capable of running this shop myself, and you have way too many other things you're dealing with."

I just smile, rubbing the little dancer.

"What's on your mind, Abby?" Grandma knows me way too well. I hadn't even realized I had an ulterior motive.

I put back the figurine. "I *do* want to help you, and I feel bad that I haven't been much help since I got back to Florida. But, now that you mention it, I do need to ask you something."

"Go on."

"I just talked with Mom. She knows all about the accident."

"Oh, I'm sorry. Did you tell her or did she suss it out on her own?"

I laugh. I think it's called a *rueful* laugh. "I told her—after she sussed it out on her own. Anyway, she was pretty upset, as you can imagine."

"Yes, I can."

"Instead of just repairing the bumper, she insisted we get it replaced. Which of course will take longer. And it means I'll need a rental car, which I can't officially sign for, being still seventeen. So she—I mean—I was wondering ..."

"If I would sign for the rental car?"

"Yeah. I hate to ask. You've been so good to me already—"

"Abby, it's not a problem." Grandma puts the glass cat she was dusting back into the case. "But are you sure you'll be comfortable driving a rental car back and forth to Murdock?"

Hadn't even thought of that. "Sure. I mean, we'll get a small one. I have to get to school."

"I know. I just wish there was another way." Grandma twists her lips in a frown. She shuts the case and heads to the back of the shop.

"Have I upset you?" I ask, walking behind her.

"No, sweetie. You haven't done anything wrong." She sits down on her stool behind the cash register. "I'm just sorry you're having such an awful time. I had a bad feeling about that ritual in Murdock, and I did try to warn you. But that's past now, and I'm over it. I'm just glad nothing worse came of it, and that you're feeling better. You are so precious to me, Abby."

I sniffle, and not from my sinus infection. "I know, Grandma."

She squeezes my hand. "I'm afraid for you. That's what's troubling me. That, and the fact that we haven't been able to help you. Violet keeps saying she's working on things. But I can tell she's baffled and worried too."

"Yeah, Molly's been talking with her. I keep coming back to the Goddess Inanna and needing to free her power. I feel that those missing sigils are the key."

Grandma shakes her head. "Violet, Kevin, and Molly have all searched for them. They might not even still exist."

"I know. Molly suggested we try a séance to contact the ghost of Frater Statera. I actually feel that might help. But she can't get Violet to agree."

Grandma's sets her jaw. "I don't understand why Violet's so against it. It's not like she's come up with any better ideas. Let's go talk to Kevin."

♒

Grandma sets off with a determined gait. I follow her through the wall opening and into Kevin's bookstore. There are no customers at the moment, summer being the slow season for Harmony Springs retail. Kevin is seated with his feet up on the counter, reading a Manga collection. As both a true magician and retired anthropology professor, he has many interests.

He raises his head as we approach. "Hi Kat, Abby. What's up?"

"We need to talk," Grandma tells him, leaning her elbows on the countertop.

Kevin stands up, so their faces are on the same level. "What's on your mind?"

Grandma summarizes all the problems I've had with the nasty visions and nightmares, culminating in my disastrous ritual on the campus last Sunday, then crashing Veronica the next day. Kevin is aware of all this, but he waits patiently for her to come to the point.

"I've asked Violet, and now I'm asking you," she says. "Isn't there something more the Circle can do to help Abby?"

"We *have* been working on it, Kat." Kevin shifts his glasses and rubs his forehead as he speaks. "Violet and I have both worked formulas to protect the town, and Abby in particular. But the forces we're dealing with are huge, and the power of the Circle has limits."

"I understand that," I tell him. "I realize I'm safer here in Harmony Springs."

Kevin nods. "The Circle can protect you best near the springs. Now, as to that ritual you did at the college, I assume that was *not* Circle of Harmony-based?"

"No," I admit, feeling a little guilty. "Postmodern Magic."

"Right," Kevin says. "I'm not here to lecture you, Abby. But the truth is, bringing other magical influences into the mix can be dangerous. That ritual probably eroded your protection."

I hadn't thought of that. "Why?"

"Because, Circle of Harmony magic has built-in safeguards, a framework that keeps the energy focused in accord with the Five Principles. Those Principles are not just spiritual precepts, they are markers on the path. When you keep strictly to that path, your actions are aligned with the same magical current as all other true magicians. That's a very powerful thing."

Kevin's words ring true to me, with the certainty of a powerful lesson. I've stupidly strayed from the path. But ...

"I see what you're saying, Kevin. Postmodern Magic has no frame at all. That sort of worried me from the beginning."

"Right," Kevin remarks. "You might say it's frameless by definition."

"I would never have attempted that ritual by myself. But my friend needed me. I just couldn't let him do it alone."

"I'm not judging you, Abby. In the final analysis, every true magician must choose their own actions." His glance wanders to Grandma's face, then back to mine. "You did what you needed to for your friend. And just like that, *you* are my friend and Violet's too. We'll do whatever we can to help you."

"Which brings us back to the reason for this talk," Grandma puts in. "Abby's looking for sigils from the early days of the Circle. She and Molly have tried everything to track them down ..."

"I know. Violet and I have hunted for them too."

"She's tried summoning the spirit of this Frater Statera on her own but hasn't gotten much. We're thinking a séance might add more force to the effort."

Kevin sighs and sits back on the metal stool. "Yes. Molly's brought that up to Violet a number of times. That young woman is determined, to say the least."

"Yes, she'll make a good reporter." Grandma smiles. "But the point is—"

"The point is," Kevin interrupts her, "again, a séance is not part of Circle of Harmony practice. I know the Founders held them all the time, but that was before the *Book of Lebab* was written down." Grandma starts to protest, and he holds up a hand. "I'm not saying séances are necessarily bad. But they are open-ended. Do either of you know much about them?"

Grandma purses her lips and gives her head a quick shake.

"Not much," I admit.

"Right. It's not just a formula to summon a spirit. Usually, all the participants join hands and focus on the intent. The collected minds do add significantly more power to the equation. One of the group acts as a medium—or sometimes the spirit chooses the medium. Either way, that person is literally *possessed*. And that can be a terrible strain. Given Violet's health issues lately, I'm reluctant to let her try this—because she would be the most qualified to take the lead and would most likely end up possessed by whatever entity comes through."

Grimly, Grandma and I mull this over.

"Maybe Abby and I can do it ourselves," Grandma says. "I don't want to put Violet at risk. But I'm feeling Abby is already at risk, and I'm willing to try anything to protect her."

Kevin peers at her, weighing his options. "Okay. I don't want you two trying this alone, and I don't want to lie to Violet either. I'll talk with her and let her decide if she wants to risk it. Mind you, I will try very hard to dissuade her. Regardless of what she decides, I'll do a séance with you."

23. Abby's temporary Focus

8 days before

The Ford Focus is actually a pretty decent car. Not nearly as sporty or stylish as Veronica, of course, but a solid, reliable ride.

Seriously? I'm just grateful to have wheels again. I picked up the "oxford white" Focus at the Budget Rent-a-Car office in Weaver, 17 miles from Harmony Springs. Grandma drove me down there at 8 a.m. and signed the rental agreement. I paid with Mom's credit card, thanked Grandma profusely, then headed down the road to Murdock.

My cold has subsided. No more running nose or dizziness, just an occasional cough hacking up from deep in my chest. I've been up since 5:30, meditating and performing extra magic for healing and to drench myself in protection.

Even so, I'm fearful. The farther I venture from the springs, the more vulnerable I become. As I speed down the rural stretch of Highway 7, I can feel the aura of power around me weakening, the malignant energy of Ranae Virum lurking beyond. I'm wearing a ring on a chain around my neck, my family heirloom from Thomas Renshaw, one of the Founders. As I drive, I touch the ring from time to time, invoking the magical current of the Circle of Harmony.

My first stop is Superior Auto Repair in downtown Murdock. I've already phoned them and arranged to come in and pay the bill. After it's paid, they'll tow Veronica to the Mazda dealership outside

Orlando, where Mom has set up the appointment for the bodywork. On Mom's strict advice, I remove my personal belongings and clean out the glove compartment, which I was too dazed to do on Monday. When I examine Veronica's crumpled bumper, I almost cry.

Collecting myself, I get back in the Focus and drive to campus, where I'm already late for *Business and Law I*. Having missed class on Tuesday, I'm frazzled as I dash across the parking lot and upstairs to the second floor of the business school. Mr. Ramirez has already started his lecture. He nods to me as I sheepishly creep to the back of the classroom.

At the break, I apologize to him and explain why I missed class on Tuesday. He's nice about it and spends his break time filling me in on what I missed. His kindness, and the soft tones of his voice, remind me of Ariel. I feel my eyes moistening.

I grab lunch at the cafeteria and pour over my textbook and class notes. By the time I finish the chicken rice soup and crackers, I'm confident that I've sufficiently caught up on my school work.

I won't stay for running club today, but before I head home, I want to drive over to check on Ariel. On the way, I pass a florist shop, and a crazy impulse makes me pull a U-turn. I buy him a bouquet in a glass vase—carnations and hydrangeas. I know it's a little weird, but I really want him to know I care.

Arriving at the Palm Court, I park in a spot near the office. When I carry the vase inside, Estefania is stationed at the counter. Her look conveys about seventeen different emotions in the space of two seconds.

"Hello. You brought him flowers." Two of the emotions are surprise and appreciation.

"Yeah. I hope that's okay."

"Of course. He told me you'd be coming by. I didn't see your car pull up." Emotion: puzzlement.

"I'm driving a rental today. Mine's in the shop."

"Oh." Two more emotions appear: worry and pain. "He's very sick, you know."

My heart sinks. "He texted he was getting better."

Her lips squeeze tight as she reaches for something under the counter. "Doctor says he could still be contagious. You need to wear this." She sets down a white nose mask, followed by a sanitizer in a foil packet. "Use this to clean your hands after. Ariel said you'd been sick too."

"Not as sick as him. Just a cold."

She stares at me suspiciously, like my mom when she knows I'm evading. "What were you two doing that night?"

That catches me off-guard. I fumble for an answer.

"You have to understand," she says. "With Ariel's parents in Miami, Roberto and I feel responsible. I know, he's almost a grown man, but he's still family. So, at the risk of sounding like a prying surrogate mother, I want to know."

She's a fierce woman, and I'm intimidated. "Well, what did he tell you?"

Estefania frowns and looks away. "That's what's worries me. The past six months he's gotten more and more secretive. I mean, he still does his work around here and seems to be keeping up with school. But he parted from his old girlfriend and spends a lot of time alone in his room. Sometimes, when he comes out, I get this weird feeling—almost like there are other people inside him. And now he's suddenly so sick ..."

She squints into my eyes, searching for a clue. "I don't believe you were out looking at the stars Sunday night. So what was it?"

Talk about being put on the spot. I don't want Ariel's aunt to hate me, but I certainly can't betray his confidence. She's waiting for an answer.

I straighten my shoulders. "Okay. I don't want to lie to you, but it's not something I can talk about. You'll have to ask him."

Her eyes flash with anger. "That's your answer?"

"Yes. I'm sorry."

She weighs it for a second, then turns away, dismissing me. "He's in room 22. The door's open. Make sure you wear the mask."

♒

Well, great. Now Ariel's whole family is going to hate me. But what else could I do?

I reflect on the question as I carry the heavy vase across the parking lot. By the time I reach room 22, I still have no answer.

My knock on the door results in a weak voice telling me to come in. When I step inside my stomach cringes. Ariel's sitting up on a narrow bed in the corner, hair uncombed, eyes glassy. In the daylight from the open door, his skin looks gray. The air smells sickly, stifling.

But it's worse than that. My perception flickers, and the room darkens with a sinister orange cast. White frogs are everywhere, huge fat ones hanging on the walls, small ones slithering on the floor and the bed, crawling over the sheet that covers Ariel.

"Abby?" His voice is a rasping whisper. "You okay?"

"I'll be right back."

I set the vase on the floor, turn and run out, shutting the door behind me. I rush across the parking lot to the Focus, flick the button to open the locks, pull my backpack from the front seat.

Returning to Ariel's room, I close the door and lock it. After switching on the overhead light, I pick up the vase and place it on a table. I snatch up the mask, which I'd also dropped on the floor. I shoot Ariel an encouraging smile, then fit the mask over my nose and mouth.

"How are you doing?" I ask, my voice muffled.

He watches me curiously as I look around, peering into the corners for evil spirits. I can still see them, but more faintly. The run outside has pumped up my blood. Physical exercise has the effect of grounding me in my body so that my awareness of the spirit realms tends to dim. Reaching into my backpack, I take out the wand and dagger.

Ariel's eyes widen with interest. "What are you doing?"

I walk to the middle of the room. "Just a little cleansing. You need it."

"That, I can believe." He gives a feeble laugh, which explodes into coughing. I can almost feel the pain in his chest.

With my magical tools in each hand, I throw my arms wide. I shut my eyes, visualize the Springs, and call on their power. I pace the edges of the room, tracing a circle with the wand. On each wall, I draw a pentagram of blue fire with the dagger. Returning to the center, I concentrate on the magical current of the Springs and call it into my body.

"I am Fighting Eagle, Initiate of the Circle of Harmony," I declare in my strongest voice. "By the power of the Springs of Harmony, in the name of the Great Spirit Lebab, I banish you, Ranae Virum, from this place and time. I know your true name and thus I compel you." I gesture and thrust with the dagger and wand, the power flowing out from me, stronger and stronger. "Ranae Virum, you cannot resist me. You must obey my command. Leave this place and this person in peace. *Leave now and never return*!"

I finish with my arms held high, shaking.

The room is silent as I look around—peaceful and empty. No malefic spirits that I can see. I nod my head with satisfaction.

From his bed, Ariel stares at me like I'm some rock star he can't believe he's met.

"How you feeling?" I ask as I put the magical tools away.

"Much better now that you're here." He coughs, but it sounds softer, less agonizing. "I can't believe you brought me flowers."

Behind my medical mask, I grin. "Too dorky?"

He smiles at the carnations and hydrangeas. "Not at all. It's the nicest thing any girl's ever done for me. Well ... except for that banishing magic you just did."

I flop into a chair near the bed. The power's draining out of me now, leaving me exhausted.

"So the egregore was here in the room?" Ariel murmurs. "I felt it all week. I thought it was delirium."

"No. It was here. Big time." I scan the edges of the room again. I can still dimly see my circle of blue fire. No frogs. "It's gone now. At least for the moment."

"Tell me about the Circle of Harmony," Ariel says.

"Oh, shit!" My hand flies to my mouth. It hadn't even occurred to me, but I've just done a Circle ritual in front of a non-initiate. That is totally forbidden.

"What's wrong?"

"I can't tell you. I can't tell you anything about the Circle."

"Oh." He nods, understanding. "Secret."

"Sorry."

"No. I get it ..."

We're quiet for a while, gazing at each other. A parade of strong emotions rumbles through me—relief that he looks better, grief over what we've both gone through, dread over what might come next. But also a kind of peace from just being with him. Peace and yearning. I wonder if I'm falling in love.

Which only sharpens my fear about the future.

24. A séance near a spring

7 days before

"It's a misconception that séances are only performed indoors," Violet explains. "From all accounts, the Founders had the best results outside, in broad daylight, and close to the springs."

Which is why we've gathered in Grandma's backyard, with the late afternoon sun slanting through the woods and the waters of Bliss Spring just beyond. The "we" in question being Violet, Kevin, and Grandma decked out in their magical robes, me in the white gown that serves as my magical garment, and Molly in civilian dress. The fact that Violet is treating this as a Circle of Harmony ritual and yet has allowed non-initiate Molly to attend might be surprising. Except, from what Molly's told me, Violet has gotten a lot looser about letting her in on Circle secrets in the weeks they've been working together on their book.

Which makes me feel better about my little slipup with Ariel yesterday.

As everyone who knows Violet would have predicted, she insisted on leading the séance. In fact, after Kevin discussed it with her, she did a complete 180 and got very enthusiastic about the idea, reading up on the topic in her collection of Circle writings. This is according to Molly, who was at their house yesterday afternoon when it all went down.

The air is warm and humid, the woods alive with the singing of birds and whirring of insects. Violet lights a white candle in a glass holder and places it on the ground. The five of us stand in a circle and join hands.

Violet leads us in a relaxation exercise, breathing in unison, visualizing the gentle movement of the spring. I'm holding Violet's hand on one side, Grandma's on the other. As my relaxation deepens, I imagine the water rising over the banks, flowing through us in a soothing stream.

Violet's voice comes from far away. "By the power of the Springs, our minds and hearts are joined. We are one in the spirit of harmony."

All of us repeat: "We are one in harmony."

"The spirit of harmony abides for all time," Violet continues. "And all who live and have lived abide in that spirit. All spirits are accessible. So now we call to this circle the spirit of one called Frater Statera. You were an initiate in our Circle, and so our bond is strong. Come to us now, Frater Statera, in the spirit of harmony. We have need of your wisdom. Now all please speak his name and call him here."

"Frater Statera, we call you," all of us say. "Come to us. Join us here."

With eyes shut, in low hypnotic tones, we repeat the call, over and over. There are pauses, times of listening in which all I perceive is the gentle current of the Spring circling through us from hand to hand. Then the call resumes, my own voice part of it, but sounding distant.

"Frater Statera, come to us. Join us here."

Call then listen. Call then listen. Nothing else happens. I'm beginning to think it's another failure. Then a different voice sounds.

"I answer."

My eyes pop open. Everyone stares. The words came from Molly. *But not in her voice*. The tone is hollow and strained.

"Frater Statera." Violet regains her composure. "We welcome you and thank you for joining us. We need your help. We stand in the century after your lifetime. We must reacquire sigils that you drew."

"The sigils of Inanna," I explain, and show Molly the drawing of the one sigil that we have. "The others that are like this."

"We devised many sigils," Molly intones. "My friend and I. But he betrayed me in the end ..."

The spirit's mind seems to wander. I'm afraid he may leave us at any moment and the chance will be lost.

"Can you tell us where the sigils can be found?" Grandma asks.

"Or can you draw them for us now?" I hold up the sketchpad and marker, which I've brought to the circle in case this might work.

Molly gazes at the blank paper in my hand. Her head slowly shakes. "I saw the evil that was coming. I wanted to awaken Inanna's spirit, to bless the whole world. But my friend was seduced by that same evil. He used other sigils to befuddle my mind. He corrupted our sacred work."

"The sigils of Inanna," I cry out desperately. "Can you show them to us?"

Molly's eyes narrow, and a thin smile crosses her face. "He thought he had stolen all of my work, but he did not realize. The sigils are in the tower. They will *always* be there."

"Do you mean the tower in Lake Avalon?" Kevin asks. "Lock Tower?"

Molly's smile widens. "Is that what you call it now? That would be appropriate. In that lifetime, my name was Emmanuel Lock."

"But what do you mean that the sigils are always in the tower?" I ask. They feel tantalizingly close but still out of reach.

Molly's mouth opens like she's laughing at a secret joke. "*Carved* on the inside!"

"Oh." That makes sense. From videos and photos, I know the interior of the tower is full of esoteric artwork.

I'm about to ask *exactly where* inside the tower they are carved, when Molly emits a loud groan. She shudders as the ghost of Emmanuel Lock leaves her body. Kevin thrusts out a hand to prevent her from falling.

Now we're all standing in the back yard, the sun dwindling behind the trees. Everyone is quiet, staring at Molly.

She blinks and looks around at us in confusion. "What? Did something happen?"

♒

"I can't believe it! I was the medium! Oh my god! Molly the medium. This could open a whole new career path for me."

We're gathered around the kitchen table, the tea kettle rattling on the electric stove as it nears the boiling point. We've changed out of our magical clothes, and Grandma's set out fruit and cookies and a loaf of banana bread that Violet brought over.

"But I don't get why I can't remember anything," Molly complains.

"Some mediums never recall the experience," Violet says. "That's actually quite common."

"Boggles my mind." Molly runs a hand through her kinky red hair. "Next time I'll have to record it."

Grandma and Kevin exchange a smile, and Violet chuckles as she slices the banana bread. "I don't know about recording it, dear. Might scare the spirits away, you know. But, yes, you did wonderfully well. We're all very proud of you."

"And grateful," I add.

Molly beams. "So I said—I mean, *he* said—that the sigils are carved *inside* Lock Tower?"

"Right."

"So Frater Statera *is* Emmanuel Lock after all."

"Right," I say again. "Now we need to figure out a way to search inside the tower. And that won't be easy." They only let people tour inside the tower a few times a year. Even then, it's only open to high-priced patrons.

"Might not be necessary," Kevin comments. "There must be thousands of photographs of the ornamentation in the tower. Many of them are bound to be online."

"That's certainly a place to start," I tell him. I've surveyed plenty of photos and videos of the tower on the internet. But now I know what I'm looking for ...

The kettle whistles, and Grandma gets up. "I toured inside of the tower when I was young," she says. "They used to offer guided tours to everyone who visited the park."

"That changed some years ago," Kevin replies. "The Foundation got very strict about allowing access, supposedly to protect the interior artwork."

"They must make exceptions." Grandma pours from kettle to teapot. "I remember a documentary on PBS, and spots on the local news about the carillon."

"That's it!" Molly cries. "We're journalists. I mean, we're *student* journalists. Abby's in college, and I've already applied for early admission to FSU. We cook up a plausible research project—They're bound to let us in."

By the time our little post-séance tea party ends, we have a plan of attack. Kevin and I will search online and scrutinize any images we find of the inside of Lock Tower. Molly meanwhile will send emails and make calls, starting with the park management and working her way up to the Foundation board of governors. She's also met a local TV reporter who might remember her and might be willing to help. As a retired professor at UF, Kevin offers to write follow-up emails sponsoring our "research."

I'm touched that they're all giving me such support. I feel loved, and protected by more than just the magic of Harmony Springs. For the first time since my car wreck, I have a semblance of control—like

I might come out of this nightmare summer with my mind and my life not destroyed.

♒

Of course, our plan of attack is not exactly a blitz.

Sunday and Monday pass with me and Kevin scouring the internet as well as some private online archives which Kevin, as a former University of Florida professor, manages to wrangle access to. We peer at grainy photos and original architectural drawings but discover no sigils. Meantime, Molly fills out web forms, sends emails and follow-up emails, and starts following *those* up with phone calls.

By Tuesday we've done lots of work, but I'm not sure if we've made any progress. Discouraged, I drive the Focus down to Claremont State and attend class. I consider staying for the Postmodern Magic meeting or running club, but decide against both. Ariel's still out sick—though his texts insist he's improving. Without the chance to see him, running around campus in the heat feels not at all appealing. As for the PMM group, I'm not sure if I'll ever go back. One magical tradition feels like all I can handle right now. And that ritual at the pond was not exactly a big selling point.

Instead, I hang out at the library and delve into my assigned reading. *Business and Law I* has slowly gotten more complicated, and I need to work hard to keep up. Torts and judicial proceedings are not exactly my friends. I have to make sure we're at least on speaking terms.

Wednesday, Grandma and I get up early. We drive to Weaver to drop off the Focus, then Grandma chauffeurs me all the way to Orlando to pick up Veronica. I told her I'd be okay taking a hired ride, but she insists, even though she has to leave the shop in Kevin's and Jenny Nesheim's hands for most of the day.

I am so happy to see Veronica whole again. Two new tires on the front, and the bumper looks brand new. It gives me a tremendous boost in confidence, like maybe everything will be all right. Mom's already arranged payment through the insurance company, so all I have to do is sign the paperwork and pick up the key.

I set the GPS for Harmony Springs and drive to the highway. Accelerating, I let out a whoop of delight. Veronica is back.

Seventeen miles down the road, my phone rings. The car speakers pick it up via Bluetooth, and the robot voice says: “Call from—Molly Quick.”

I tap the button on the steering wheel. “Hey, Molly!”

“Hey! Sent you texts.”

“Yeah. I had my phone off.” I kept it off while driving with Grandma and then at the dealership. When I turned it back on, I saw the texts but figured I’d answer them later.

“Where are you?” Molly asks.

“I picked up my car. I’m driving back from Orlando.”

“That’s funny.”

“Why?”

“Because we have to go to Orlando tomorrow. The head of Lock Tower Foundation has agreed to meet with us.”

25. Who's going to believe you?

3 days before

Molly and I sit in the outer office of Florida Insurance Partners LLC, on the 27th floor of a skyscraper in downtown Orlando. The receptionist, a young man named Jorge, took our names and invited us to sit on a flat sofa behind a glass coffee table. Lots of glass in this place, including the desktops, ornaments, and of course the floor-to-ceiling tinted windows. Through the windows, we see a sprawling view of looped highways and concrete stretching away to the horizon.

We're here to meet with William Lock Burkhart, president of this insurance company and also chairman of the board of governors of Lock Tower Foundation. A Google search disclosed that he is actually a distant relative of Emmanuel Lock, descended from Lock's younger sister. (Lock himself died childless.)

Our appointment was for 2 p.m. and it's now 2:35. Getting restless, Molly stands and stretches. Jorge looks over at us and twitches his mouth apologetically.

"Shouldn't be much longer."

Molly sits down, frowning. She is not the most patient person I know.

I have to marvel at her nerve and persistence. Getting brushed off by everyone she wrote to and called at the Lock Tower Foundation, she just worked her way up to the top. She admitted to being surprised when Burkhart agreed to speak with us in person this afternoon.

We're both dressed in slacks, button-down blouses, sandals. I consulted Molly on what to wear, and she immediately prescribed a look of "serious student merging into business attire." She brought her tablet for typing notes.

I stare out the window, watching cars and trucks flowing like tiny toys on the Interstate. So much is riding on this meeting. If the head of the Foundation doesn't give us permission to go inside the tower, I'm really out of ideas.

A chime sounds. Jorge presses a button and picks up his desk phone. "Yes, sir," he says, then looks at us. "Mr. Burkhart will see you now."

Butterflies crash around in my stomach. We stand and follow Jorge to a tall, polished wood door. He opens it for us, and I follow Molly inside. She struts across the room with the air of a businesswoman greeting a new client. I walk behind her and focus on keeping my shoulders from slumping.

"Mr. Burkhart. Thank you *so* much for agreeing to see us." Molly shakes his hand. "This is Abby Renshaw, my partner on the project."

Burkhart is tall and wide-shouldered, in a lightweight gray suit and silk tie. Handsome, around 60, with white-blond hair and a strong jaw. He smiles as we shake hands. But something in his touch, or his eyes, sets off an alarm in my nervous system.

We sit down in front of his desk. He leans back in his large leather chair. Out of the window behind him spreads a spectacular view of central Florida. "Now what can I do for you young ladies? Something about a research project?"

"Exactly," Molly says. "We're working together, documenting stories of certain Florida historic sites. Lock Tower is among them. I'll be using this for my Senior Honors Project, and Abby might eventually use it as part of her college work."

"Very interesting." Burkhart surveys us with a smile. I get the feeling he knows there's more to this. "What can I do to help you?"

"Well, we were hoping for permission to study the interior of Lock Tower. Just a few hours inside would make a world of difference to us."

His mouth turns down. He seems to be thinking it over. "That's very difficult, I'm afraid. As you must know, the interior contains priceless decorative arts, which are old and rather fragile. For this reason, the board must strictly limit access to the public."

"Oh, we understand all that." Molly is well-prepared for this line. "It's precisely because of the preciousness of the interior that we're doing this project. We're very interested in preserving all we can of Florida's artistic history ..."

While Molly speaks, I see the light around Burkhart fade. The color of his skin turns gray, then albino white. The alarm inside me shrieks.

Then something *really* weird happens. A tiny white frog materializes on Burkhart's desk. It crawls across the glass surface, until his hand reaches down and snatches it. Smiling at me, Burkhart pops the frog into his mouth and chews.

I jump to my feet, panicked. Beside me, Molly is still talking about our research project. But her voice has dwindled to a muttering drone. Her eyes are glassy, and I realized she's fallen into some sort of trance.

"Are you really so surprised?" Burkhart asks me.

Behind him, a luminous shape condenses and takes form. The ghost of Kurt Friedrich Gentzen. He's laughing at me, and Burkhart's laughing with him.

"Did you really believe I would agree to meet two teenage girls about a silly school project? Although, you *are* attractive girls—especially this one." He glances at Molly with a creepy, predatory expression.

"But no, *he* made me aware of your real purpose." He waves a finger at the ghost. "He's been watching you for some time, tracking your every move."

Through the shock and terror, I find my voice. "And you're just another of his pawns?"

Burkhart looks affronted. "Oh no. His *ally*. He and I both want the same thing—to preserve our country, to restore our people's rightful place. I've long been fascinated by my great uncle's occult work. I joined the Foundation expressly so I could have access to his papers. His library is stored in the tower. But of course, you know that. That's why you made this pitiful attempt to get inside."

Through it all the ghost is watching me, smiling smugly. Molly has stopped talking and stares vacantly.

Not sure where I find the courage, but I have to at least *act* defiant. "This won't stop me. I don't know how, but I'll banish your Nazi ghost and his frog monster too."

The ghost's smirk grows wider, and now he speaks. "You truly are remarkable, Abigail Renshaw. Such fire! What a shame if you destroy yourself by fighting me. My offer to join us still stands, you know."

Burkhart is moving around the desk. "This one is remarkable too," he says, indicating Molly. "Such a clever little liar."

He bends over, clutches her curly hair to tilt her head back. He kisses her on the mouth, while his free hand grabs her breast.

"Stop!" I yell and shove him as hard as I can.

Caught off-guard, he stumbles, then straightens with a mocking laugh. Molly is frozen, her face a grimace.

"You won't get away with that," I tell him.

He shrugs, walking back to his chair. "What will you do? Tell people I used magic to put your little friend into a trance so I could grope her? Who's going to believe you?"

He settles back in his chair, relaxing with hands behind his head. "Now get out of my office. Your request is denied."

♒

Molly's mind is still far away as I lead her out of the office. I clutch her arm, and she walks stiffly beside me, a dumb empty look on her face. Only when we've gone down the elevator and are crossing the high-ceilinged lobby does she suddenly snap out it.

"Wait, wait! What happened? How did we get here?"

"You don't want to know."

Sickening realization dawns on her face. "Did he *touch* me? Oh, my god. Abby, tell me!"

"Try to calm down. I'll tell you, I promise."

Back in the parking deck, sitting in the car, I tell her what happened. Molly, who's been panting with agitation, now turns furious.

"I'll kill him. No, I'll get my brother to beat him blind. No, I'll get my dad to ..." Her voice trails off. She looks small and wounded. "He's right, isn't he? Even without mentioning magic, no one will believe he sexually assaulted me in his office. He's a rich and powerful guy and ..."

She wipes at her mouth as if she's tasted poison. I shake my head, wanting to cry.

"It's the way the world is," Molly murmurs.

I've never known her to sound so defeated. I take hold of her hand.

"We can't let this stand," she says. "We have to figure out some way to break him. Him and his creepy ghost and all their monsters. You'll help. Right, Abby? You won't give up?"

"Never. I promise."

I can promise to never give up. But whether I can possibly win is another matter. Without any hope of getting into the tower, I have no idea how to acquire those sigils. And without the sigils, where can I begin to find the power to short-circuit Kurt Friedrich Gentzen and his egregore?

I'm out of ideas.

♒

1 day before

... But not out of frogs.

Next day, as I drive to school, I see them blinking on my windshield again, watching me with their beady little eyes. I grip the steering wheel tightly, staring hard at the road. When I finally get to campus, I pull out my wand and do a quick banishing inside the car.

I'm hoping to meet up with Ariel, either on campus today or back at the Palm Court Motel. At least we can compare notes about the egregore. Maybe he can help me come up with a new approach. Last I heard from him was Tuesday. He messaged to say he wouldn't make it to school, but that he was still getting better. My texts to him from Wednesday and Thursday have gone unanswered, so I'm starting to worry about him again.

I send him another text from the parking lot. If I haven't heard back by afternoon, I'll try calling.

After class, as I'm heading across campus to the student center, I run into Isabel. I haven't been to the PMM group again, and I haven't seen her since the night of our great debacle by the pond. She waves me aside, and we sit down together on the edge of a concrete planter, streams of students marching by.

"Have you heard about Ariel?" she says, in a way that makes me flinch.

"Not since Tuesday. I knew he was sick. Is it worse?"

"A lot worse." Her mouth goes thin. "I've not seen him since that night at the pond. But we've been keeping in touch by text. When he stopped answering his phone a few days ago, I got worried, so I finally called his aunt. He's in the hospital in intensive care. Pneumonia."

"Oh, my god!" My fingers cover my lips. "I thought he was getting better."

"So did I. So did he."

I thought the banishing I did in his room last week had helped, but I guess the effect wore off. A scary premonition rises in the back of my mind: Ariel's sickness will get worse, he might even die. Because of the egregore ...

Isabel shifts and crosses her legs in her long, flowered skirt. "Let me ask you something. You did some pretty serious work that night with your dagger. I've studied Santeria and Wicca and read about other traditions, but I've never seen anything quite like that. Can I ask where you learned it?"

"Oh ..." Again the dilemma of how much I should reveal. "Okay. I was initiated into a circle last year. The tradition is secret, so I can't say much about it."

"Interesting." She peers at me intently. "You probably noticed that Ariel took the brunt of the psychic attack that night. He did it to shield us."

"I know."

"Well." She straightens her skirt and stands. "I'm going to do what magic I can to heal him. You might want to do the same."

"Yeah. I will. Thanks for telling me."

When I stand up, she gives me a sad smile and a hug.

26. Hail to the Lady who lights the morning sky

What can I do to heal Ariel? What can I do to comfort Molly? What can I do to break the power of Kurt Friedrich Gentzen and his egregore and stop the evil they're spreading in the world?

All of the questions amount to the same thing.

And I have no answer.

Driving home, gloomy and hopeless, I review what I know. Circle of Harmony magic has helped, but it's limited. Postmodern Magic might be *unlimited*, but it's wide open, no safeguards.

If only there was a way to combine the two ...

That's when I think of the Goddess Inanna. From the first Tarot reading last month, from the ritual when I consecrated my wand, to my dream on Midsummer Night and then again in my vision last week—everything has pointed to her and the charge to awaken her power.

Her power is the key.

And then it hits me, something I read in all that material on Postmodern Magic that Ariel pointed me to. An egregore is a thought-form, a being that becomes independent because it draws on the mind force of multiple individuals. But there is something even stronger, because it has been known and venerated by many, many people for a long time: a *god-form*.

In the terms used by Postmodern Magic, Inanna is a god-form.

And there are rituals to invoke such a being.

♒

When I get back to Harmony Springs the shops are still open. I say hi to Grandma then hurry next door. Kevin is talking with a customer, so I browse the history and mythology sections. I look over the Encyclopedia of Mythology where I first found the image of Inanna, and then find another book, on ancient Near Eastern religions. The text is dense and scholarly, but the book contains translated fragments of actual rituals and hymns.

A little chill runs through me when I find a hymn to Inanna. The book feels like a gift from the goddess.

When Kevin's free, I take the book up to the counter. After telling me hello, he opens it and turns the pages.

"This looks serious."

"Yeah. I have serious work to do."

His forehead creases with worry. He knows we've come up empty on getting access to Lock Tower, so I'm sure he's got some inkling about what I'm going to try. I expect a dire warning about dabbling in non-Circle-of-Harmony magic.

So I'm surprised and grateful when he says: "Anything Violet or I can help with?"

"I don't think so, but thanks. I'll let you know how it goes."

I offer my credit card to pay for the book, but he holds up a palm. "This one's on the house."

♒

I spend the evening alone in my room, windows open so I can feel the breeze and hear the voices of the forest. I read the book of ancient religions, formulas from the Circle of Harmony, downloaded rituals of Postmodern Magic. I burn incense and call on Inanna. I meditate, visit the Fountains in trance, ask the blessing of Lebab. I copy verses in my squiggly handwriting, cross out words, write in my own. I'm attempting to construct a ritual that invokes the power of

Postmodern Magic but contains it in the frame of the Circle of Harmony.

I don't know if that's possible, but I'm going to try.

By eleven o'clock, I have a draft that I think is as good as I can make it. Now I have to practice.

After calming my body and mind, I begin to circle the room, moving in a slow-motion dance. I visualize myself performing the ritual, uttering the words. I practice over and over.

Eventually, I fall asleep, lying on top of the bed covers.

♒

If I have dreams, I don't remember them.

Suddenly I'm awake, sitting up straight. The clock on the nightstand reads 5:11.

It's time. I reach for my wand.

Cool air flows through the open windows. I can feel the night alive. Dressed in my nightclothes, I walk silently downstairs and out the back door.

Stars glitter overhead. In the east shines the faint glow of dawn. There, gleaming over the trees hangs the brightest star: Venus—the lamp of Inanna.

The grass is wet under my bare feet. A mosquito whines near my ear, and I feel another settle on my thigh. I wave the wand and order them away. Amazingly, they obey.

I stop at the edge of the mowed grass, where trees and sedges slope down to Bliss Spring. I hear the water swishing past. I point the wand in that direction.

"I am Fighting Eagle, true magician, initiate of the Circle of Harmony. I honor the Five Principles of Love, Endurance, Balance, Amity, and Bliss. I call now upon our Founders and all who have worked in the current of the true magic. I ask your blessings on this rite. I call upon Lebab, true spirit of the Springs. I ask your guidance and blessing on this rite."

High in the trees, an owl hoots.

I point my wand at the spiky, radiant light that is Venus.

Hail to the Lady who lights the morning sky!
Hail Inanna, blessed daughter of Heaven.
You who journey from the Great Above to the Great Below.
Lamp of Heaven, hear me.
Torch of Splendor, hear me.
I would be your priestess and wield your sacred power.
The need of our land is great for healing and for light.
Come into me, Inanna, first daughter of the gods!

I am circling now, wand held high, eyes fixed on Venus. I repeat the lines over and over, sometimes whispering, sometimes aloud. My head grows light. Despite the chill night air, I'm sweating.

My vision shimmers and shifts. I see myself in some ancient temple, surrounded by priestesses in sheer veils and gold jewelry, all of us dancing around a fire.

Hail to the Lady who lights the morning sky!
Come to us, Inanna, first daughter of the gods!

I'm back in my body again, still circling. The sky wheels overhead, making me dizzy. At the hub of the wheel is Venus, brightening, coming closer like a falling comet.

No. I'm moving closer to Venus, rising into the spinning sky.

Nothing remains but spinning starlight.

When I find myself back in the world again, I'm sprawled in the grass, flat on my back, arms stretched wide. I hear a breath, scramble up on my hands and knees.

Inanna stands before me, all gold and winged in her starry crown. A red lion lies curled at her feet.

"You have done well, my priestess."

Awed, I climb to my feet. I feel slow and stupefied. She's a goddess. I bow to her.

"My power is alive in you."

As she says this I feel it, radiant power in my arms and legs and down the center of my body. The same power I felt at Midsummer, but even stronger. The lion lifts its head and stares at me, responding to the power.

"This infusion of strength will last in you only for a limited time," Inanna tells me. "If you wish to free my spirit to dwell again in your world, you must go to the tower. My essence has been bound there, bound by magic."

Right. The tower. The sigils. "But how can I get inside?"

"Use my power, daughter. Do not allow yourself to be stopped."

♒

Parking near the cell phone tower, I tap in Molly's number. It's 7 a.m. on a Saturday, and Harmony Springs is just waking up. I took a shower, dressed in jeans, a t-shirt, sneakers, and a baseball cap. I grabbed coffee and cold cereal in the kitchen, and I left Grandma a note.

"Abby?" Molly answers sleepily. "You're up early."

"Can you get off work today?"

"Why?"

"I'm driving down to Lock Tower. Thought you might like to come along."

"Sure!" Molly's fully awake now. "Do you have a way to get inside?"

"I don't know. If not, I'm going to find one." Somehow, with the power of Inanna pulsing in my blood, this seems like a perfectly reasonable statement.

"All right!" Molly says. "Count me in."

"Get ready as soon as you can. I'll park at the corner."

Twenty minutes later, I look in the rearview and see Molly marching up the street from her house. I gulp in surprise. Ray-Ray is walking beside her. What does *he* want?

I climb out of the car as they come near.

"Hi, Abby" he smiles. "Mind if I come too?"

"He sniffed out where I was going," Molly explains. "And he pointed out that my parents might not like the two of us driving all that way alone. Rather than wake them up and have a scene, I agreed that he could come—or at least ask you."

"Why do you even want to?"

Ray-Ray shrugs. "I'm free today, and I thought I should keep an eye on my little sister—and her friend. Who is also *my* friend."

"I told him we have magical work to do," Molly says. "He promised to be supportive and not interfere."

He holds up his hands. "That's totally me. Supportive, non-interfering older brother and friend. I promise."

"Okay." I laugh. "Get in. And see that you keep that promise."

On reflection, I'm kind of glad to have him along. I hate to admit it, but I'll feel safer. Also, I didn't get much sleep, and it's about a two-hour drive to Lock Tower. Right now, the energy of Inanna has me buzzed like a quart of caffeine. But who knows how tired I'll be by the end of the day?

I might have to let him drive Veronica.

27. What are you doing up here?

So here we are, Molly and I, crossing the threshold into Lock Tower, stepping from the sunlight into cool, gloomy, sweet-smelling air ...

We stand in a narrow corridor that leads off in both directions. The walls are gray stone, with no carvings I can see. Molly turns and spreads her hands, asking me which way.

I point to the right and take the lead. From studying pictures, I know that most of the first floor is a huge lobby called the Heritage Room. We've entered through the back door into a service corridor. We pass storage closets, a small kitchen, a tall stained-glass window on the outside wall. No sign of the maintenance men who entered ahead of us.

So far, so good.

At the end of the hallway, we find an iron stairway leading up. To our left, a pointy-arched doorway opens onto the lobby.

I peek around the corner. In front of me is an old-style elevator in a black metal cage. Beyond that stands the Heritage Room, a soaring space of gray and pink marble with carvings around the colored-glass windows, painted tiles on the floor, and a vaulted ceiling three stories high.

The place is empty and quiet. We sneak inside to examine the decorations. From what Lock's ghost said, the sigils are *carved* somewhere on the inside of the tower. My gut tells me they wouldn't be in the lobby, but somewhere higher up. Still, the ceiling is so far away, with ornamentation all along the edges. Small circular sigils could easily be hidden there.

"Pictures," I whisper to Molly when we've reached the center of the floor. I point along the borders of the ceiling

She's brought her camera, with a telephoto lens. She fiddles with the settings and starts taking shots.

"Get everything you can," I tell her. "If you finish, go up to the next level."

I tilt my head to indicate the main stairway, built of black iron, which rises from the lobby. "I'll go up the service stairs."

Molly lowers the camera. "Are you sure we should separate?"

"Yeah, I'm sure. We might not have much time, and there are lots of places to look. If you're caught, you know what to do."

"Sure, I know the story." She grips my arm. "Good luck, girlfriend."

I hurry back to the arched doorway. In my backpack, I have a sketchpad and pens, my dagger and wand. My phone's in my jeans pocket, and I can use that to take pictures. But I think it would be better to draw the sigils—if I have time.

Just as I move past the elevator, a door opens on the far side of the lobby. At the top of the stairs, a man appears. He's wearing a maintenance uniform, carrying a bucket and mop. Molly sees him too and tries to duck out of sight. But her motion draws his eye.

"Hey," he calls. "What are you doing in here?"

Molly keeps shooting pictures.

"Hey! Girl! I'm talking to you."

"Oh, me?" Molly calls back, as the man starts down the steps. "I'm just taking pictures. Beautiful, isn't it?"

I want to bolt for the archway, but I'm afraid of drawing his attention. So I crouch behind the elevator and wait. He's coming to a landing, where he'll have to turn his back to me.

But he stops. "Do you have permission to be here?" His voice is loud and angry.

"Permission?" Molly asks, all innocence, and still deliberately snapping pics. "I don't understand."

He starts down again. As soon as he turns on the landing, I grab my chance and dash through the doorway. My heart is pounding, anticipating another shout. But instead he's haranguing Molly about permission to come inside the tower, so I know he's missed me.

I make for the service steps and climb as quietly as I can. The second and third levels are used for storage and a maintenance office. The second custodian who we saw coming into the tower is most likely up there.

As I approach the second-story landing, I see an open doorway. Keeping low, I crawl up the last steps and peer inside. The room is big, the whole width of the tower, lit by overhead fluorescents. Tables, shelves, and filing cabinets stand along the walls. I hear a noise and spot the custodian, hovering over a machine that looks like a vacuum cleaner or floor polisher. He starts to raise his head in my direction.

I duck back. When I don't hear him call, I take a chance and dash across the landing and up the stairs. I don't think he's seen me, and I try to move silently. But the stairs are metal and they rattle and creak. My heart's in my throat.

Rushing up two more landings, I find another door. Inside is a large room, the maintenance office. It's mostly empty, containing a few desks, tables and shelves. The lights are switched off, but this level has more stained glass. In the colored light, I scan the walls and ceilings. They look flat—no decorations of any kind.

Footsteps below make me freeze. The custodian is on the stairs. In a moment, I realize he's coming up. I panic and dash up the steps.

Four flights up, I stop. Through the grid of the metal staircase, I can see him below, climbing slowly. After pausing on the landing, he walks into the maintenance office and switches on the light. Either he didn't see me and is just going about his work, or he did and is looking for me.

The door in front of me is shut, and I pray it's not locked. I twist the handle and pull it open. I guess they don't see a need to lock the door, since only authorized persons ever come up here.

Except for me.

Like the floors below, this room takes up the whole width of the tower. But this one is way different. Past the elevator, I glimpse tile floors, Persian rugs, antique lamps and furniture. Bookshelves line the walls, stuffed with books and what look like bound portfolios. This level was part of Emmanuel Lock's living quarters and is now an archive.

My heart sinks. If the sigils are in here, finding them could take forever. The ceilings are twenty feet high and, without better light, I can't make out the decorations. Of course, they might also be carved around the windows or the marble fireplace. Since this was Lock's library, there might also be copies in some of these books.

Suppressing an urge to panic, I move quickly to the center of the room, set down my backpack, and pull out the wand and dagger. I pace around, drawing a circle in the air and tracing pentagrams. If Lock's ghost is really bound in the tower, I should be able to summon him. And his presence should be strong—hopefully strong enough that I can break through whatever resistance is binding him and get him to point me to the sigils.

I stand tall and breathe deeply, attempting to calm my mind.

In the silence, I hear footsteps, heavy on the stairs. *Someone is coming up and fast.*

Terrified, I snatch up my pack. My eyes dart around, looking for a place to hide. On the opposite side of the room is another door, which leads to the main staircase. I wonder if I should make a run for it.

"Hey! What are you doing up here?" The custodian stands in the doorway, a large bulky guy in a brown uniform.

"I - uh. I'm up here doing research on the tower..." I slip the magical tools into the backpack.

"Research?" He's walking toward me: heavy boots, thick beard, big shoulders. "Who gave you permission to come up here?"

"It's all right. I have permission, you can check with the Foundation office." This was the story Molly and I agreed to. Coming out of my mouth now it sounds hopelessly flimsy.

He's getting closer. Something about him terrifies me, and it's not just that I've been caught. Something about his face—it's wide and grim. Inhuman.

Like a frog.

My body lurches back. His eyes have turned gold. He reaches into his tool belt and pulls something out. It clicks, and a knife blade snaps out. His eyes blaze with madness.

On instinct, I bring up the backpack, swinging it by the strap. It smacks the arm holding the switchblade and pushes it aside.

I pivot and race for the door. His boots pound behind me. I gain on him and reach for the handle. But as I yank the door open he catches me and slams the door shut.

Gasping, I try to slip away, but his heavy arm blocks me. With his other hand, he grabs my throat and shoves me back. My skull cracks against the door.

Amid flashes of light I see his crazed, evil eyes. The knife in his hand whips up.

The thought screams in me that I'm about to die, stabbed to death like Alicia.

28. Certainly determined, but sadly overmatched

Inanna moves inside me. Her energy takes hold of my terror and changes it into power. Her voice issues from my throat, calm and deep and commanding.

"Stop. Step back."

I hold my hand in front of the man's face. He looks confused, startled—then afraid. He leans away, takes a faltering step backward.

My body straightens, and Inanna speaks to him. "It is all right. *You* are all right. I am the Goddess of the Land. I now release you from bondage."

With her words, I sense the power of the egregore loosening, slipping out of him. The knife drops and clatters on the floor.

"Be released. Be at peace, child of the Earth."

A look of abject sorrow rises on his face. He sinks to his knees with a sob.

Gently, I lay my hand on the top of his head. "Child of the Earth, be at rest. I now release your sadness and your pain."

He wails like a baby, sinks to the stone floor. He curls into a fetal position, hands covering his face as he weeps.

Snapping out of the trance, I cast my eyes around the tower. I still need to summon Lock's ghost. But I'm not sure how long Inanna's spell will last on the poor custodian. I'd best get away from him while I can.

I slip out the door and close it. The main staircase is narrow and zigzag, like the service stairs, but the wrought iron here is curly and decorative. I rush up four flights to the next level, where the stairs end.

The door is round on top, dark wood inlaid with ivory. It is covered in carvings, so I scan it quickly. No sigils. I push open the door and step inside.

This room, like the one below, has mosaic floors and lots of ornamentation. This was also once part of Emmanuel Lock's living quarters. Now it is used as a conference room. Not much furniture, but plenty of carvings on the walls and along the edges of the ceiling.

Round-arched windows of pale-colored glass provide plenty of light. I spend a minute examining the carvings. There are flowering vines and block-like figures of people and animals. Nothing that looks like sigils.

Stepping to the center, I set my pack down on the mahogany conference table. After pausing to listen for any sounds coming up the stairs, I repeat the tracing of the circle and pentagrams. Deliberately placing myself into trance, I summon the ghost.

"I am Fighting Eagle, initiate of the Circle of Harmony. I am also a priestess in the service of Inanna, charged with her power. To this place and time, in this tower that you built, in this room where you lived, I call you, spirit of Emmanuel Lock. In the name of Inanna, whose sigils you drew, I charge you to appear and reveal your knowledge."

Inanna's power, which felt gigantic in me these past few hours, now seems diminished. I drained a lot of energy driving the egregore out of the maintenance man downstairs.

I concentrate harder, repeating over and over: "Emmanuel Lock, I charge you to appear."

Shafts of light from the windows move across the floor. Where they meet, a bluish form spirals into being.

The wand tip points and circles in my hand. "Emmanuel Lock, I charge you to appear."

The blue light condenses. I glimpse a figure inside—a middle-aged man in a dark suit, with a mustache and heavy brows—Emmanuel Lock as I've seen him in pictures. Except he is wrapped in gold chains and his mouth is gagged.

"Emmanuel Lock, I charge you to free yourself and speak to me."

The ghost shifts, struggles. Muted groans come from him, but no words I can make out.

My voice is strong and commanding. "By the power of Inanna, I free you now and bid you speak!"

Then something unexpected happens.

The form of the ghost ripples and disappears. In its place, another figure unfolds.

Molly!

Whether it is an astral projection of Molly herself, or my own psychic energy manifesting as her, I have no clue. She looks exactly as she did at the séance when she channeled Lock's ghost.

And she is not chained or gagged.

"I bid you speak," I whisper.

"Thank you for coming to me," Molly/Emmanuel says. "Thank you for freeing me to speak."

"Where are the sigils of Inanna?" I ask, elated and desperate.

"Inanna ..." The voice is fond. "Wondrous goddess! She taught me her magic and her ways. Her spirit has power to bless the whole world."

Please, Mr. Lock, focus. "You had her sigils carved inside the tower. Where are they?"

Molly's expression bends into a smile. "At the top, of course. On the parapet, behind each bird."

From photos, I know there are statues of birds on the roof—marble herons 15-feet tall, positioned to look out over the land. In fact, I think there are eight of them.

One for each sigil.

I quickly trace a banishing pentagram. "I thank you, Emmanuel Lock. And I free you now to return whence you came." *And thanks, Molly.*

But Molly's head shakes, her voice full of sadness. "I cannot leave. My spirit is bound here by Gentzen's magic. But if you can employ the sigils, that might set me free."

"I will do my best. I promise."

♒

The image fades. I shake myself and grab my pack.

The two stairways and the elevator all end at this level. From this room, a spiral stair climbs up. Above me now is the just the belfry, five stories high and hung with the huge bronze bells that make up the carillon. Iron steps and a catwalk lead up to the parapet.

As I head for the stair I hear noise from below—footsteps coming up. I fear that the magic subduing the man with the knife has worn off. He's hunting me again. There's a lock on the round door to this room, but it needs a key. No help there.

I race up the spiral steps, praying to Inanna to lend me whatever power she can. Round and round I go, finally emerging through a square opening on the floor of the belfry. The space above me is enormous. Bronze bells of different sizes hang from steel beams. No glass windows, just openings in the walls to let the music out. These openings are covered with curving bronze grillwork, fashioned in the shapes of birds, branches, flowers, and vines. At the floor-level, pointy-arched doorways lead to small balconies 18 stories above the ground.

Ahead of me on the floor is a kind of enclosure. I know from videos this little room houses the carillon. It's like a huge organ with long wooden keys. The keys move wires connected to other wires which move tines inside the bells.

The door is open, and when I get there I stop.

A man sits at the instrument, moving his hands over the keyboard. But no bells are sounding.

The man stands up and looks at me—the ghost of Kurt Friedrich Gentzen. Unlike Lock's ghost, he looks solid and real, dressed in a tweed suit and wire-rimmed specs. He walks toward me. I have the impulse to run, but my legs refuse to move.

"Greetings, Abigail Renshaw. Or should I call you Fighting Eagle?" His smile sends a chill up my spine. "You certainly are a determined young woman. Even your encounter with my friend Burkhart did not dissuade you."

He slides through the door and stands in front of me, uncomfortably close, blocking the way to the parapet.

He's only a spirit, right? I can push right past him. But his energy tells me otherwise. I stand rooted to the spot, my hope draining.

Footsteps clatter behind me. I whirl to see the custodian rising from the spiral stair. The mad rage is back on his face. He's lost the knife but now holds a nasty-looking screwdriver.

"Stop, my son," the ghost of Gentzen orders him, holding up a hand. "Station yourself there and make sure she does not flee. I will deal with her in a *cleaner* way."

Obediently, the custodian stops, blocking the steps. As I turn back to Gentzen, I reach and pull out my wand. If he means to overcome me by mental power, I might have a chance.

Spotting the wand, he breaks into a grin. "Yes. A *very* determined young woman. And talented too, as you have demonstrated. But I practiced magic for more years than you have lived—and drew many sigils in this very place. I lived here with Lock when he first built the tower. Because of that work, on my death, my spirit was able to return here. I've waited many years for a time when the barriers between the realms would grow thin. Now the time has come, and my work again can flourish. I command the energy of Ranae Virum, drawn from the minds of thousands who give him power. So you see, you are sadly overmatched."

"Well, forgive me if I try anyway." I thrust the wand at his face and mentally call on Inanna.

He smiles and wraps the wand in his ghostly fingers. He wears rings of gold and rubies.

I try to speak, and fail. My knees have turned to water, my brain gone fuzzy. All I can see are his sparkly rings and his dazzling, frosty blue eyes.

"Yes." His voice slithers in my head. "Sadly overmatched."

My wand drops to the floor, the sound faint and distant. He prods my shoulder, turns me toward the opening in the outer wall, the balcony. Beyond the black-spiked rail lies open sky and hazy sunlit land, stretching away forever ...

Helpless, I walk toward the doorway. I fight his mental grip at every step. But my feet keep moving.

He's going to make me jump. Within the absolute terror of that thought, I'm furious. I call up the rage, try to transform it into power.

Still, I keep walking.

Inanna, I whisper. *Help me.*

"Your rage cannot defeat him, my priestess. For he draws on the rage of thousands. Turn instead to love."

Love? How can that help me?

I pass under the archway, into the blazing light.

"Call on those you love. Call on the love you have for them."

Those I love? My mom, Grandma? Violet and Kevin? They love me, but they're far away ... Molly, my best friend. She came here with me. I love her, and that power is strong.

But not strong enough.

I reach the rail. The spiked iron presses against my belly. Central Florida spreads below me out to the horizon, green and brown, dotted with blue lakes. How beautiful it looks under the summer sky. The air is hot and thick, so dense I could almost fly.

My body tilts forward and I look down. Below I see the park, the moat. Ray-Ray's down there somewhere. He came with me too.

"Ray-Ray!" I scream his name, a cry for help from deep in my soul.

My hands grip the rail, holding my balance. I remember his arms around me, last summer when we lay together under the stars. His strength and gentleness. The love I felt for him.

The love I still feel.

That emotion rises inside me, an energy like nothing else I've felt before or since. It condenses around me, and I feel Ray-Ray's presence, solid, holding me, keeping me from falling. Maybe it's Ray-Ray in an astral projection. Maybe it's just my feelings for him, pouring up from my heart, giving me strength.

Either way, I'm myself again.

And I'm brimming with power.

I whirl around. With all the beauty of Florida at my back, I face Gentzen. He looks perplexed, maybe a little frightened.

"Not happening," I tell him. "You Nazi creep."

I burst toward him, like a sprinter starting a race. Because he is only a ghost after all, I pass right through him. Inside, I glance at the custodian, standing at the top of the steps. He's no ghost, and he's still holding that screwdriver. But he doesn't come toward me, just stands glassy-eyed.

The power is swirling around me, the warmth of love transformed into something huge and strong. I scoop up my wand, point it at the custodian and then at Gentzen, discharging that force to freeze them in place.

"Stay!" I order them, "Stay where you are and don't follow me!"

Maybe it's my imagination, but as I rush toward the steps, I hear Ray-Ray's voice in my head. "Go ahead, Abby. I've got your back."

29. The Sigils of Inanna

My footsteps ring and echo on the metal—the black stairs and catwalks that rise into the belfry. The bells of the carillon hang from beams at many levels, some of the bells smaller than me, others enormous. On the brick walls are conduits—vents for the air conditioning that was added long after the tower was built. They lead up to a humongous exhaust fan at the roofline. Not exactly in keeping with the 1920s design, but I guess the top of the building is the logical place for the AC to vent. The roof is open space except for the fan and the struts that support it, and the parapet, a walkway twelve-feet wide along the edges.

As I reach the last stairway, the fan switches on. Hot air rushes up from below, and the roar of the motor drowns my footsteps.

Climbing to the top at last, I step onto the parapet. While the footprint of the tower is a rounded rectangle, the parapet is eight-sided. At each point stands a statue of a heron, 15-feet tall, solid and blocky. The sigils are supposed to be carved on their backs.

I'm five stories higher than the balcony where I stood a few minutes ago. But I've got no time to appreciate the spectacular view. I rush to the nearest statue. It stands with its back to me, looking out over the land. Stone wings are folded over the back, stone feathers forming ridges. In the blinding sunlight I peer up, searching for the sigil.

At first, I don't see it. Then, my eyes blinking, it comes into focus—a circle, like a medallion, carved at the top of the folded wings just below the heron's neck. Within the circle is an octagon, with thin lines linking certain of the points.

I take out my camera, snap a picture, then swipe to enlarge the view. Tiny letters are carved around the circle: *Inanna in the Underworld.*

I glance down into the belfry. The fan is still spinning, and there's no sign of any ghosts or killers coming after me. I take out the sketchbook and pen. On eight sheets, I've already drawn octagons. Now I trace the lines to complete the first sigil.

Quickly, I move to the next statue. This one faces southeast and the sigil is named *Eye of Inanna.* Again, I snap a picture, draw the lines, then move on.

As I work, I discern the pattern. Each sigil is matched to a direction of the compass. Those at the cardinal points are named for a position of Venus: *Inanna in the Underworld*, *Inanna of the Morning*, *Inanna of the Highest*, *Inanna of the Evening*. The other four are named for, and no doubt invoke, specific powers: *Eye of Inanna, Joy of Inanna, Voice of Inanna, Might of Inanna.*

In less than fifteen minutes I have collected them all: diagrams in my sketchbook, photos stored on my phone and uploaded to the Cloud. Having fought so hard to get here, I wanted to make sure I didn't lose the sigils.

When I've put away the phone and sketchbook, my shoulders slump with relief. I am elated and totally tired. I look around for the stairs.

The exhaust fan has stopped.

Above its blades floats the ghost of Kurt Friedrich Gentzen. Only now he appears in his guise as the Knight of Wands—gold armor, plumed helmet, long black wand with a crystal tip. Instead of a horse, he rides a white frog the size of an elephant: the egregore, rearing and swaying, mouth gaping open, scarlet tongue slithering out.

"You have not won!" Gentzen thrusts the wand at me. "You cannot win."

Taking a deep breath, I pull out my wand.

"You might have found the sigils of Inanna," Gentzen taunts me. "But I have others, many others. Sigils of gods and demons you've never heard of, whose powers you cannot imagine." He gestures toward his mount. "And I have *this* one, who lives even now in the minds of men. With their power, I will destroy you and Inanna!"

He's mad, shrieking. Which makes him all the more terrifying.

In the hot sunlight, trying to steady the wand, I trace the first sigil that comes to mind. A simple one, three lines like a bolt of lightning—the *Might of Inanna*.

In my spirit vision, I see it gleaming white in front of me. The air vibrates and ripples. Around the parapet, the eight sigils come alive, shining, pulsing like a heartbeat.

Gentzen is also drawing sigils. A stream of ruby light flows from Ranae Virum to the crystal tip of the ghost's wand. He moves the wand in violent sweeps and stabs. Sparkling disks fly from the tip.

They fly straight at me.

And disappear.

Inanna's power is stronger. In this place, where her sigils have waited carved in stone for a hundred years, her power is enormous.

Somewhere far below us, a thermostat clicks. The exhaust fan rattles and spins. Hot air roars up past Gentzen and the egregore. They float in place, unaffected by the wind.

Gentzen is furious, his wand still pumping out sigils. They continue to fly toward me. When they touch the barrier formed by the *Might of Inanna*, they burst like soap bubbles.

Gentzen's solid-looking ghost wavers and frays. "No! No!" He screams, his face turning down to Ranae Virum. "More power. You *must* give me more!"

Ranae Virum stares up at his rider with hatred. The frog can feel his power draining now, senses that the cause is lost, that he cannot defeat the goddess. The stream of red energy flowing up from him to Gentzen's wand flickers off.

Enraged, the ghost rises in the air and points the wand at the egregore.

The frog's mouth gapes open. The red tongue darts out, wraps up the ghost, and sucks him in.

Ranae Virum glares at me for a moment. Then his fat ugly form drops down into the blades of the exhaust fan. A silent explosion sends white sparks glittering into the sky, flying off in all directions, falling as they fade.

In my vision, the sky has turned to twilight, the faint blue glow of early evening. Stars glimmer faintly—except for one that shines brightly in the west. Venus, the lamp of Inanna, beaming her blessing onto the land.

The vision passes. It's day again, hot and muggy and deliciously *normal.* I shudder, standing alone on the roof of Lock Tower under the blazing sun.

♒

Numb, shaking inside, I make my way down the stairways and across the catwalks. I'm a little more than halfway down when a bell chimes. Then another tolls. The carillon comes alive, playing a melody. Inside the belfry, the sound is overpowering. I slip the pack onto my back so I can cover my ears. Still, the music of the bells vibrates through my bones.

When I reach the floor level, the man with the screwdriver is nowhere in sight. I approach the carillon room, wondering if I can sneak past whoever is playing. They have concerts each day at 10 and 3. I'm surprised that it's 3 p.m. already. Molly and I entered the tower around 11:30, and I didn't think that much time had passed.

But then, who can tell? I've been pretty busy.

I creep to the doorway and look inside. The man seated at the instrument is long-haired, dressed in an old-fashioned suit. He looks over at me and smiles behind his mustache: the ghost of Emmanuel Lock.

"Come in. Come," he tells me, his hands never leaving the keyboard. "I had to play my carillon one last time before I move on."

He smiles blissfully at the music as I step into the room. The bells ring out overhead, their tune vaguely familiar. I had a Music Appreciation elective senior year, and I think this might be Bach.

"Thank you for freeing me," Lock says. "I can't tell you how pleasant it feels after all this time." His expression turns grave. "It is a terrible thing, you know, to see so much evil pass in the world and be helpless to act."

"I can only imagine," I tell him. "Why did Gentzen keep you bound here?"

"We loved each other once. But he was seduced by a lust for power that grew deeper and darker in his soul. Holding me here was just one part of his betrayal. By keeping me bound, he was able to draw on my knowledge and skill, albeit against my will."

His hands pounce on the keys, producing a rising flourish of notes. "But I can see that you, Fighting Eagle, are a noble magician, with a pure and loving heart. And now you have the sigils of Inanna."

"Yes."

"May I give you some advice?"

"I can always use advice," I tell him honestly. Because I have no idea what happens next.

"Go and collect the other sigils, the ones taken from my tower by that foul man Burkhart. Study them all. There is great power to be gained by study and balanced practice. Your world, I fear, is in trouble."

"Yeah. I know that's true."

"So it was also in my day. We had a great war, which we hoped would result in progress. But the human race failed to learn. Humanity must realize that it is one, that the whole Universe is one. Violence and hatred directed at anyone bring harm to all. That is the lesson of Inanna. I perceive that your generation is called to learn that lesson, to sway the human heart. Will you rise to that challenge, Fighting Eagle?"

"I'll try," I answer, feeling so tired.

But I guess I'll have to do, at least till someone better comes along.

≈

The bells are still playing when I reach the bottom of the service steps. Outside, near the elevator, I hear voices. Standing in the shadows, I lean in just far enough to see past the archway.

Three men are standing there. One is my attacker, who looks bewildered. The other maintenance man, the one who cornered Molly on the ground floor, is arguing with a third man, a slim guy in a lightweight suit.

"There *was* an intruder, a high school girl taking pictures. But I caught her down here in the lobby and kicked her out." He turns to the other custodian. "Did you see anyone upstairs?"

The former servant of the Nazi ghost scratches his head. "I don't think so. I was all the way up in the belfry. I'm not sure how I got there."

"This is ridiculous," says the man in the suit. "*I'm* supposed to play the 3 o'clock show. I guarantee, whoever is playing the carillon now is *not* authorized to be up there."

"So what do you want from us?" The less-confused custodian asks.

"Well, I'm not going up there alone," says the carillon player. "Could be some maniac for all we know. You guys better come with me."

After some shrugging and grumbling, they agree. I slip back out of sight as they get into the elevator. I hear the door clang shut and the motor whine. Once the car is on its way up the tower, I dash for the back door.

Molly and Ray-Ray are standing outside the gate at the edge of the moat. They both grin when they see me. I hurry across the bridge and slip through the gate, past the *No Entry* sign.

Up in the tower, the carillon music has stopped.

"Are you okay?" Molly asks. "Did you find them?"

"Yeah, I got them. Let's get out of here."

We walk through the crowd of tourists, heading for the path that leads out of the park.

"Tell me everything," Molly says. "I want to hear all about it."

"I will, but later. I'm kind of tired." I was in the tower for a couple of hours, but it feels like a year. "What about you? Did you get in any trouble?"

"Nah, they just made me leave." Molly tilts her head toward her brother. "In spite of Ray-Ray's *dire* warnings."

He shrugs and shakes his head.

The asphalt path winds past cypress trees and flowering shrubs.

"It's weird," Molly says. "But at one point, I went into a kind of dream-state. It seemed I was up in the tower with you—you and Emmanuel Lock."

"You were," I say to her. "You channeled Lock for me. He was like on mute and unable to speak. I couldn't have found the sigils without you."

"Really?" Molly's face lights up. "That is *so* cool."

I look sideways up at Ray-Ray. Did *he* have any "dreams" of helping me in the tower? His expression is thoughtful but gives nothing away.

We exit through the visitor center and walk out to the parking lot. I am so happy to see Veronica: it feels like coming home. Pulling the key from my pocket, I press the remote button. The doors unlock with a beep. Ray-Ray's behind me and I hold out the key.

"Would you mind driving?"

He grins with surprise. "Drive your hot little car? Are you kidding? I'd love to."

"Great." I drop the key into his hand. "Molly, you can ride shotgun. I'm going to collapse in the back. I need a nap."

"Don't worry about a thing, Abby." Ray-Ray holds open the door and looks me in the eye. "I've got your back."

30. Well, now ... *That* was satisfying

Three days after

Tuesday after class, I drive over to the Palm Court Motel. I'm feeling great: no ill effects of my ordeal, no horrible visions. I haven't seen a single frog since Saturday afternoon on top of Lock Tower.

Plus, I'm feeling extra great because, on Sunday evening, I got a text from Ariel. He's been discharged from the hospital and is doing much better. He hopes to be back at school by the end of the week.

I didn't want to wait that long to see him.

I climb out of the car, picking up the bouquet of red carnations. I turn to see Estefania walking toward me from the motel office.

"Flowers again?" Her voice is teasing. "What is it with you and bouquets?"

"Too dorky?" I ask.

"No. Not at all. I think it's lovely."

"How is he?"

"Much better. And looking forward to seeing *you*. Go on."

With a grin, I head off toward his room.

I find him sitting up in bed, typing on his laptop. His face is thin and drawn, a bit hollow around the eyes, but his color is good. He's delighted to see me.

"Abby! Flowers again?"

"I know, I know. I can't help myself." I set them down on the table. "How are you feeling?"

"Much better. I can't believe how much better. And no longer contagious, the doctor assures me. I'm so happy you came to see me."

I sit on the side of the bed. He reaches over and takes my hand.

"I've thought about you a lot," he says. "Dreamed about you too. I, uh ... had the feeling you've been doing a lot of psychic work since the last time I saw you."

I have to laugh. "Yeah. You could say that."

He peers at me earnestly. "I also had the feeling—a very strong feeling that started late Saturday—that the egregore has been banished."

"Well. I don't know. My sense is he's been weakened at least."

"By what you did." It's a statement, not a question. "I want to hear all about it—I mean, as much as you can tell me."

"Well, it's a very long story."

"I've got plenty of time."

So, sitting beside him, holding his hand the whole time, I tell my tale. All of it. Well, I gloss over the parts about Ray-Ray. I'm not sure exactly why.

He listens intently, squeezing my hand at times, watching me with admiration, fondness, maybe something more.

"That is all so amazing," he says when I'm finished. "This Circle of Harmony magic. It sounds very potent, very disciplined."

"Yeah. That's fair to say."

"Do you think ... well. Are they taking any new initiates?"

"Oh wow. Yes, I don't see why not." I think Violet and Kevin would be delighted to bring another young person into the Circle. "I'll tell you what. I'll send you some documents, the introductory papers for new candidates. You can read them over and let me know what you think. If you're still interested after that, well ... I think something could be arranged."

"Fabulous." He leans back on the pillow, smiling. He's still gripping my hand. "There's one other thing I have to say if you'll allow me."

"Sure."

He pauses, gathering his resolve. "It might already be obvious, but I find you really attractive."

"Oh." I'm staring, lost in his brown eyes. "It might be equally obvious, but I've been attracted to you since the first time we met."

Some note in my voice makes him frown. "Is there a problem? Are you involved with someone else?"

"No!" I'm certainly not *involved* with Ray-Ray anymore. Even though I might still be *in love* with him—somewhere in my confused heart. But I have strong feelings for Ariel too ... "Listen. As you may have noticed, I'm kind of a weird person, to say the least. And I've got a lot going on in my head right now. Also, I've been hurt—emotionally, I mean."

"So you need to be careful."

"Exactly. Let's give it a little time, okay? Time for you to get better and for me to sort out my feelings?"

"Sure, I understand. Totally."

From a long time back, I am reminded of Violet's advice that I should love recklessly. I lift a shoulder and give a nervous laugh. "After that, well, I think something could be arranged."

♒

Five days after

Dressed in professional blouses and slacks, Molly and I march through the outer office of Florida Insurance Partners LLC.

"Can I help you?" Jorge calls from the receptionist's desk.

We brush right past him."We have a 1:30 appointment with Mr. Burkhart," I announce. "I'm sure he'll see us now."

We emailed Burkhart yesterday. The gist of the message was that we thought he might have noticed something missing since around

Saturday afternoon, and that we could explain it. We offered to meet with him today, provided he brought with him all the magical writings he had taken from Lock Tower. He wrote back almost immediately, accepting the offer.

I open the door to his office, and Molly and I march in. Burkhart jumps to his feet. His face is startled, worried. "It's all right," he tells Jorge, who has gotten up from his desk. "I'll see them now. Close the door, please."

The door shuts behind us as Molly and I step across the room. Burkhart is pale. Somehow he looks smaller than he did last week, diminished. He assumes a pose of self-confidence.

"Please sit down."

Stopping in front of his desk, I shake my head. "We won't be here that long. Did you bring the books from Lock's library?"

Sinking into his chair, he waves to indicate a nearby table. On top are three bound leather volumes and a large portfolio of drawings. Molly walks over to examine them.

"If they're not all there, I'll know it," I tell him. "And I'll force you to surrender the rest."

From his expression, I can read that he's brought them all.

"What is this about?" he demands.

"Just this." I've taken the wand out of my backpack. "I know you've been missing a certain ... *energy* the past few days. Lost contact with your invisible friend? No more little white frogs to snack on ... ?" As I speak I'm tracing a sigil in the air—*the Eye of Inanna.*

Burkhart watches me, worried but captured. "Yes," he mutters. "I don't know what happened."

"They're gone. That's what happened. I don't think you'll see them anymore." I draw a second figure beside the first, *Inanna of the Highest.*

"But how can that be?" Burkhart's voice is confused, frightened.

"Now this is what happens next. You're going to give us those books and drawings. Emmanuel Lock charged me to study them. After I've made copies, I'll return the originals to Lock Tower."

Burkhart tries to fight back. "But, I can just go to the tower and collect them again. Besides, how do you know I haven't made copies of my own?"

"That won't matter," I answer, staring at him hard. "You'll never be able to use them. From now on, whenever you try to read a magical text or draw a sigil, you'll lose track of what you're doing. Your mind will go blank."

I've completed the third sigil, *Might of Inanna*. Now I point the wand at Burkhart's forehead and dispatch their power into his brain.

He shudders, appalled, realizing that, no matter how outrageous it sounds, I have spoken the truth.

"You-You can't do this!"

"It's already done."

Molly steps beside me, Emmanuel Lock's documents wrapped in her arms, a pleased smile on her face.

Burkhart is almost in tears. "I won't let you get away with this!"

"What are you going to do?" Molly asks. "Say that Abby drew signs in the air to make you give us your magic books? Who's going to believe you?"

I put the wand away. We walk calmly out of his office.

"Thanks for the books, Mr. Burkhart," Molly calls in a chirpy voice as we're leaving.

When the elevator door shuts, she turns to me with a smile. "Well, now. *That* was satisfying."

♒

Seven days after

"We have a lot to be grateful for." Grandma raises her champagne glass.

Our little party's gathered around the table in her seldom-used dining room. Seldom-used china and crystal handed down from the Renshaw family are arranged on the linen tablecloth. Beside me is Molly, and across the table sit Kevin and Violet. We all lift our glasses, either champagne or sparkling water, and drink the toast.

"I am grateful for family and good friends." Grandma resumes her seat. "And especially that Abby has survived her awful battle and is feeling so much better. I am so proud of my granddaughter. And she's also a great cook."

I feel myself blushing. Grandma and I worked together on the dinner: salmon baked with maple syrup, rice with almonds, roasted veggies. Grandma baked homemade biscuits, and Violet brought a cherry pie for dessert.

As we dig in, amid the clatter of silverware and serving dishes, we each speak of what we're grateful for.

"To still be alive at my age," Violet laughs. "Alive and mostly healthy and surrounded by love. And, in particular, to have such bright and talented young people who are interested in my work and stimulate my brain." She tilts her glass toward me and Molly.

"I'll second all of that," Kevin says. "Especially about the young people. By the way, Abby, have you heard back from your friend Ariel about joining the Circle?"

"Yeah. He's texted me a few times. He's definitely interested."

"That is so wonderful!" Violet exclaims. "Another young initiate. The future of the Circle of Harmony will be in good hands."

I notice Grandma is eyeing Molly. There's an awkward pause as everyone remembers that Molly talked about initiating at one time but then withdrew. She looks around at everyone.

"Oh, I haven't ruled it out," she says. "I might still decide to initiate at some point. Especially now that I know I have such talent as a medium."

Everyone is smiling again.

"Of course, I have an awful lot going on," Molly adds. "Between work and getting ready for senior year. Not to mention the book I'm writing with Violet about the Founders, plus this new book Abby and I are thinking about, *Exploring Sigil Magic in Theory and Practice*. Honestly ..." She picks up her glass of sparkling water. "That's what I'm grateful for, along with my family and friends: Having so much interesting stuff to learn!"

We join her toast, then everyone looks at me.

I trace my finger on the rim of my glass, which, being crystal, makes a little ringing sound. "I'm just grateful for all of you. And for living in Harmony Springs. And for the fact that my life has quieted down this week, so I could get back to my schoolwork, so I can actually pass *Business and Law I*."

♒

After dessert, Violet and Molly sit over their coffee talking about their work in progress, while Kevin, Grandma, and I carry the dishes to the kitchen. Grandma's very careful about handling the old china and glassware. She shoos us away so she can do all the washing herself. Kevin wanders out to the back porch, and I follow him.

The yard is quiet in the early evening, the heat of the day slowly cooling. Kevin sits down in a metal chair. I slide onto the two-seat swing, which creaks under me. He looks at me with eyebrows lifted, like he's expecting me to say something.

"I've learned a lot this summer," I murmur. "But I'm not really sure about a lot of it."

"What, for instance?"

"The egregore for instance. I saw him devour Gentzen's ghost, and I sensed the ghost was banished, definitely gone from this world. Lock's ghost saying he'd been set free kind of confirmed that for me. But Ranae Virum, I'm not so sure about. I've got an alert set, and Molly's been monitoring some of the sites where the egregore's followers tend to hang out. We haven't seen the frog's image or his name mentioned all week. But I don't know ... What do you think?"

"I think he's a thought-form," Kevin replies. "And will continue to exist at some level as long as anyone thinks of him. I've been checking online too. The hate speech seems to be tamped down some, but it hasn't gone away. My guess is, even if this egregore disappears entirely, something else will rise up to take its place."

I stare into the gloom. "So the struggle goes on."

"Yeah, the struggle goes on. Which is why I'm going back to Gainesville on Monday. I'm joining a new committee with other retired professors, to help disadvantaged students get through school. Because that's something *I* learned this summer. No matter how old you are, it's never too late to do your duty."

I give him a smile. "I'm proud of you, Kevin."

"Not nearly as proud as I am of you, Abby. Just look at you: Started college, banished a Nazi ghost, learned about Postmodern Magic, *and* became a priestess of Inanna. Not bad for one girl, and the summer's not even over yet."

"Please. I think that's enough for one summer. I'm glad you and Violet aren't upset with me, about the Postmodern Magic thing."

"Well, we were worried at first, I have to admit. When you get older, you know, it's easy to get hide-bound in your beliefs. We've talked about it and decided that's another lesson for us. Everything that was right for our generation might not be for yours. The world keeps re-creating itself, and that includes the paths of magic. Besides, we both look at you and see absolutely no danger of you losing touch with the Five Principles."

"I appreciate that. I do my best." After a quiet space, I ask him. "What do you see about Inanna?"

"What about her?"

"Well, since I did that ritual to invoke her, she's become this energy inside me—a warmth and a presence. Her power ebbs and flows, but she's always in there somewhere. Where does that come from? How does the presence of an ancient goddess make sense in our world?"

"Good question." Kevin ponders it a while. "I can see maybe three ways. One, she's an element of your personal unconscious that you've activated by magic. Two, she's a figure of the collective unconscious that you've drawn into yourself by magic. Three, she's the spirit of a real ancient goddess who has always existed in the world, waiting for humankind to reawaken her."

"Good answers. Which is it, I wonder."

Kevin laughs. "My guess? All of the above."

♒

Later, when Grandma and I are reading in the living room with our feet up, we hear a car engine outside. We look at each other, puzzled. I go and peek out the front door.

"It's okay, Grandma. I know who it is."

Still, I am surprised to see Ray-Ray's old pickup truck park just off the road. I step onto the porch as he climbs out. Loping across the front yard, he waves to me. He's wearing flip-flops, shorts and a tank top. The half-moon is shining high over the trees.

I meet him at the bottom of the steps.

"Hi, Abby."

"Hi. What are you doing here? Molly left a while ago. Kevin and Violet drove her home."

"Yeah, I saw her come in. I actually wanted to talk with you." I've never seen Ray-Ray look shy. Except now he does.

"Okay ..." I sit down on the steps and gesture for him to the same.

Sitting beside me, he stares out toward the road. He hesitates, trying to find the right words. Finally, he says: "That day at Lock Tower? Molly wasn't the only one who had a hallucination, or a vision ..."

"Oh, yeah?"

"Yeah. It was weird. One minute I'm standing there by the moat, and the next I saw myself way high up, on one those balconies. You were there, and I was afraid you were about to jump. I know that's crazy. But I grabbed you and held you back. Then you went inside, and I saw two guys threatening you. I could see you were trying to get to the top of the tower, so I got between you and them and told you to go ahead, that I had your back."

"Right."

"What do you mean, 'Right'?"

"That's exactly how I saw it."

He stares at me, wild-eyed. "Really?"

"Yeah. You know, Ray-Ray, I'm a pretty strange girl, and a lot of strange stuff happens around me. If you didn't figure that out from last summer, I guess you've gotten another dose."

"Yeah. I know." He looks off toward the woods. "The thing is, all week I can't get this out of my mind. Up there on the balcony, when I thought you were about to die, I realized how much you mean to me. I'm sorry I screwed it up between us, that I hurt you."

I swallow. "Well, people change ..."

"No. I haven't changed. I know your life is strange. I think it kind of scared me, how weird things happen around you. But I still feel the same way I did last summer. I still want to be with you." He faces me, eyes sad. "I wanted to tell you I broke it off with Jen."

Whoa.

"Things hadn't been working between us for a while. I think she sensed my feelings for you."

My pulse is racing. Right here, in this moment, I am one hundred percent sure I am still in love with him. And yet ... "I don't know what to say."

"Is there someone else?"

Yes, there's Ariel. Is it possible to be in love with both of them at the same time? I've been advised to love recklessly. *But really?*

"There is someone else, sort of. But it's not only that. Like you said, my life is strange. I think it's always going to be strange. And I've got a lot to sort out right now."

"I get that. I want to be there for you."

"You hurt me really bad. I don't want to go through that again."

A wince of pain crinkles his face. He stands up. "I understand. I'm not asking you for anything. I just wanted you to know. And if I can do anything to help you, anytime, I'll be around."

My heart twisting inside me, I watch him walk to his truck. I flash back to our times together in the bed of that old pickup, lying under the stars on warm nights just like this one.

Feelings I've never known before or since.

We never know what lies ahead. I can't know what terrible things might happen in the world, what horrible evils I might have to face. I might succeed or fail, find peace and joy, or be driven insane or destroyed.

But right now, in this moment, I decide that if I fail or am destroyed, it will never be because I was afraid to love too much.

He's climbing into the truck when I call to him.

"Wait, Ray-Ray. Why don't we go for a ride?"

Author's Note

Abby's adventures are told in long stories and short. The ones written to date are:

- *Ghosts of Bliss Bayou* (novel)
- *Ghosts of Tamgrove Hall* (novella)
- *Ghosts of Lock Tower*
- *Ghosts of Prosper Key* (novella)

As you may have noticed, dear reader, this novel takes place in both real and fictional locales. Harmony Springs is fictional, although based on some actual places in central Florida. Murdock and Claremont State are also fictional.

Lock Tower is based on the real *Bok Tower* in Lake Wales, the true history of which can be found online. The man who built it, Edward W. Bok, had a fascinating life. However, Emmanuel Lock, his friend Kurt Friedrich Gentzen, and their ghosts are all completely fictional.

I'm very grateful to my beta readers: Marilyn Massa, John W. Kelly, Nadia Castro, Ben Kleven, Anita McDivitt Barrios, and Jennifer Saraí. Their input helped me tame a story, which at times felt as huge and unwieldy as an elephant-sized frog.

Special thanks to my sensitivity reader, Rosemi Mederos (http://americaseditor.com/) who corrected some silly mistakes and whose encouragement gave me the confidence to write about diverse characters.

And Thank You!

Thank you for reading *Ghosts of Lock Tower*. I sincerely hope you enjoyed it.

Please consider posting an honest rating and review on Amazon, as well as other sites. It doesn't have to be long, just what you thought of the story, and it would help me and Abby a lot.

I love hearing from readers. You can connect with me at

Web: triskelionbooks.com or jackmassa.com
Facebook: Facebook.com/AuthorJackMassa/
X/Twitter: @JackMassa2

www.ingramcontent.com/pod-product-compliance
Lightning Source LLC
Chambersburg PA
CBHW020755250626
47155CB00003B/1087

* 9 7 8 0 9 9 7 6 4 6 1 6 0 *